Published by Peachtree Teen
An imprint of PEACHTREE PUBLISHING COMPANY INC.
1700 Chattahoochee Avenue
Atlanta, Georgia 30318-2112
PeachtreeBooks.com

Text © 2024 by Jamie Pacton
Jacket illustration © 2024 by Andie Lugtu

Edited by Ashley Hearn
Design and composition by Lily Steele

Printed and bound in December 2023 at Lake Book Manufacturing,
Melrose Park, IL, USA.
10 9 8 7 6 5 4 3 2 1
First Edition
ISBN: 978-1-68263-492-9

Cataloging-in-Publication Data is available from the Library of Congress.

THE ABSINTHE UNDERGROUND

JAMIE PACTON

PEACHTREE
Teen

ALSO BY JAMIE PACTON

The Vermilion Emporium

Lucky Girl

The Life and (Medieval) Times of Kit Sweetly

To all the queer people throughout history who have loved each other quietly, fiercely, and—too often—secretly.
And to all the queer kids out there now, who deserve the happiest real-life stories, always

—J.P.

"After the first glass [of absinthe], you see things as you wish they were.
After the second you see them as they are not.
Finally, you see things as they really are,
and that is the most horrible thing in the world."

—attributed to Oscar Wilde

PART ONE

The Green Faerie

CHAPTER ONE
Sybil

The night was running away from them.

Sighing in frustration, Sybil Clarion abandoned her sketch pad and the sofa where she'd been sprawled for the last hour. Ten clangs shook the apartment Sybil shared with her best friend, Esme Rimbaud, sending most of their cats skittering under the closest couch, rattling teacups, knocking pictures off the walls, and making candle flames quiver. Even after a year, Sybil still wasn't used to living in a clock tower. But then, did one ever really get used to such things?

As the last peal sounded, Sybil paced in stockinged feet to the clockface. She stared past the ticking hands and into the night. Rain slicked the streets below, turning them into shadowy rivers. Sybil leaned her forehead against the cool pane, drumming her fingers against the glass. Her other hand clutched the bronze key she wore on a chain around her neck. The key was about the size of her longest finger, thin through the middle, with a crown of metal flowers and vines twisting together at the top. Eager to feel anything other than boredom, Sybil pushed her index finger into the seven teeth at the end of the key, letting them nip into her flesh.

Even with the rain and the late hour, the city was busy. Horse-drawn carriages and cabs clattered over the cobblestones, hurling arcs of dirty water that sent pedestrians scrambling. A bit farther down the block, three people came out of a brightly lit café. They huddled together under a single umbrella, laughing, cupping their cigarettes to keep them dry, and clearly having a marvelous time.

Sybil twisted the key through her restless fingers. Beyond her neighborhood, the gaslit signs of nightclubs and the glowing boulevards near the opera house painted the Vermilion and Lapis Districts in a soft light.

There was so much happening in Severon tonight! So many new rare posters going up, so many other gangs of poster thieves, beating her to them, and here Sybil was, stuck at home. Again. With no money to go out. And this month's rent due soon.

Sybil's stomach grumbled. Releasing her key necklace, she prowled from the window to the kitchen, looking for anything to snack on. Bread box, empty. Cabinet beside the sink, empty except for a tin of tea and a roach that skittered away as Sybil peered inside. Fruit bowl, empty except for one small tired-looking apple, but that would have to work. Sybil grabbed the apple and bit into it. Mealy, but at least chewing was something to do while she paced back to the window.

Tonight her impatience was almost as terrible as it'd been during those interminable nights in her father's country house, where she'd been stuffed into corsets and silk dresses and made to play the piano or listen to potential suitors drone on all evening. She'd run away to the city to escape this very boredom, and the weight of it sat heavy on her chest.

"Esme?" Sybil said through a bite of apple. She left the window and threaded her way to the kitchen table, where her best friend sat.

Since it was on the top floor of the clock tower, their entire apartment was one big room, not counting a tiny bathroom that mercifully had walls and a door. The apartment was crammed full—two threadbare sofas that served as their beds were pushed against one wall, a kitchen table and chairs sat in the middle of the room, dozens of half-empty paint tubes and not-quite-finished canvases that Sybil had forsaken rested against the walls, Esme's many books were lovingly organized on shelves, a dressing screen Sybil had painted with a forest scene took up one corner of the apartment, clothing was draped over lots of other thrifted furniture, and cats were everywhere.

Really. There were so many cats.

Esme was always finding them on the streets and bringing them home. Which, fine. One cat was lovely; two could be cozy; but seven was certainly too many.

Not that Sybil would say anything about it. After all, like the cats, Esme had taken Sybil in—it wasn't her place to whine about other strays living there.

Sybil moved past the biggest, meanest cat—Jean-Francois, a tabby with only half a left ear—and slumped into the rickety chair opposite Esme. It creaked beneath her, and Jean-Francois hissed, giving her a look of absolute disdain.

"Esme?" Sybil scowled back at the cat and then took another bite of the apple. "Hello?"

Esme didn't look up from the antique clock she was dissecting. In her lap dozed an enormous black cat—Jolie—who looked like a lump of the night itself. "Mmmm?"

Sybil couldn't keep a smile from her lips. Esme was so lovely and meticulous, it made Sybil's heart do funny things. Like the clock in front of Esme, Sybil longed to take her friend apart and figure her out. Maybe then she'd understand why being around Esme made Sybil feel so safe.

Esme's long black hair was pulled into a low bun with a pencil stuck through it. Her thick eyebrows drew together as she carefully lifted the clockface and removed a tarnished bronze gear. A triumphant noise escaped her lips as she did so. Springs, gears, screws, and other clock parts Esme had scavenged littered the table. Set between the parts was the cup of mint tea Esme had made for herself and then promptly forgotten. Beneath the tea was Esme's Plan for a Good Life list, which she always kept close, no matter what she was doing, as if she needed a reminder at all times of where she was headed.

Sybil had read the list many times before, but now she skimmed it again, her eyes roving over Esme's careful handwriting.

PLAN FOR A GOOD LIFE

- SAVE UP ENOUGH MONEY TO ATTEND SEVERON UNIVERSITY.
- GET JOB AT THE GREAT LIBRARY. KEEP THAT JOB FOR LIFE.
- BUY A SMALL COTTAGE BY THE SEA.
- RAISE CATS, DO RESEARCH, ADOPT ORPHANS?

That was it. All Esme wanted in life. Sybil couldn't imagine anything more boring, but who was she to judge? Granted, Esme had barely started item one, but there were lots of notes jotted under, around, and beside each step. Sybil figured these small plans within plans helped Esme feel more in control of the future, even while their lives teetered on the edge of destitution. Sybil hated to plan even an afternoon or a sketch, much less her entire life. She wanted to see things, do things, and be out in the world, experiencing it all.

Which was not happening by sitting around the apartment.

"We have to get out of here," Sybil said, finishing half the apple and putting the rest of it beside Esme's list.

"Why?" Esme said, still not looking up.

"I'm bored." Sybil twirled her key necklace again, snaking it through her fingers. "Let's go somewhere."

"Can't, sorry. I have to fix this clock."

"Why?"

"It's broken." Esme shrugged, as if that explained it all. She reached for her half of the apple and took a large bite without looking up from the clock.

Sybil glanced up at the three other clocks on the mantel, all of which kept different times and chimed randomly throughout the day, only very occasionally matching with the clock tower. Clearly they didn't need another clock, but there was no sense in trying to convince Esme.

"If we don't go now, it's going to be too late." Sybil dropped the key against her chest and twisted her long curly brown hair up into a high bun, securing it with one of Esme's pencils.

"Too late for what?"

"Everything! All of it! The whole entire evening." Reaching across the clock parts and Esme's list, Sybil grabbed a wine bottle she'd left on the table the night before. She shook it and smiled to hear the slosh of wine still at the bottom. After uncorking the bottle, Sybil tipped the alcohol into her mouth, finishing it in one long slug.

Familiar warmth filled Sybil as the wine hit her belly, settling her restless nerves for a moment.

Esme frowned, then turned her attention back to the clock. "What's there to miss?"

"Dancing, drinking, meeting other artists. Poster stealing. . . ."

Esme stopped poking at the clock and raised an eyebrow at Sybil. "I thought you weren't stealing anything tonight? Because of the rain?"

Sybil shrugged. She'd mentioned that earlier, when the sun was setting and Esme was fixing them sandwiches. But that had been hours ago, when all Sybil had wanted was a night at home with Esme. Now the minutes ticked away, crawling like roaches under her skin.

"Rain won't stop the other thieves." Sybil picked up Oliver, a tiny gray kitten Esme had found in a trash bin last week. He purred under Sybil's hand and she rubbed his tiny nose against her own. Yes, he was definitely her favorite of the many cats in the apartment.

Esme finished the apple, core and all, a habit Sybil still couldn't bring herself to replicate, no matter how poor they were, and reached out a hand to rip a leaf off the mint plant on the closest bookshelf. Esme's dedication to chewing mint was why there were so many mint plants growing in clay pots on nearly every surface of the apartment. Sybil had never given a thought to mint plants before meeting Esme, but now the scent was forever associated with her friend.

"I'm not going out with you tonight." Esme ran a hand over Jolie's head. The cat stretched on her lap and then hopped down, moving toward the couches.

"You promised."

Esme picked up a screwdriver and turned her attention back to the belly of the clock. "Wrong. I said I'd *consider* it, maybe. If it stopped raining. And I was done fixing this, which I'm not."

"You've been working for hours."

"And I plan on doing so for much longer."

"Ez. . . ."

"No."

"Please?"

"No."

"Do I have to beg?"

This got Esme's attention. A vaguely wicked smile curved her lips. "You can try."

That smile shot a bolt of adrenaline through Sybil.

This girl.

The things this girl does to me.

The things I would do for this girl.

Ignoring her racing heart, Sybil set Oliver down on her chair and dropped dramatically to one knee in front of Esme. "Please, oh, please, most charming and gracious Esme. Please come with me tonight." Sybil flung a hand across her forehead, like a forlorn heroine in the serialized novels Esme loved so much.

Esme arched an eyebrow, considering, and then shook her head. "Good try, but still no."

"Evil thing!" Sybil flung a balled-up piece of paper at Esme. "It'll be quick, and I need a lookout."

Esme batted the paper away, knocking it toward Oliver, who caught it eagerly between his paws. "It's still raining."

"It's already stopping. Come on." Sybil stood and paced back to the couch. She grabbed her boots and coat from where she'd flung them earlier.

Esme put her screwdriver down and took a long sip of her cold tea. She let out the weariest of sighs. "No. And, besides, I'd truly hoped you weren't doing *this* anymore, regardless of the weather."

This meant Sybil pulling on her thief's coat—the one with the deep pockets—and heading into the city long after most respectable people in Severon were in their beds. *This* also meant stealing things—specifically, the colorful posters that cropped up every Friday night all around town. Half marketing and half art, the posters sold commercial products like booze and clothing, or they advertised clubs and theaters. Since they were created by famous artists, they were also coveted by collectors. And collectors had pockets even deeper than those in Sybil's thief's coat.

"We *have* to steal a poster tonight because we need the money to round out my portion of rent," Sybil said. Their landlady had made it clear her patience was at an end. And Esme couldn't lose her beloved apartment just because Sybil couldn't keep a job.

Not that Sybil said any of that. She finished buttoning her coat and grinned at Esme. "Plus, there are supposed to be some really rare prints going up this week. Come on. *Please*. It'll be an adventure."

Sybil craved adventure in equal proportion to Esme's hatred of it. She knew this, but she still had to ask Esme to go with her. If only because she had no other friends in Severon.

"I'm not dressed for adventure." Esme gestured to her skimpy nightgown and loosely tied robe. "Besides, I'm having quite an adventure figuring out this clock." She picked up her screwdriver and began poking again at the contraption's insides.

Sybil rolled her eyes and tried not to stare at Esme's long bare legs. Esme wore the same thing every day—a gray working dress of which she had four identical copies—but she took off most of her clothing the minute she got home from her waitressing job, preferring to cook, read, snuggle cats, knit, and tinker with broken clocks in her pajamas. Not that Sybil had noticed or spent too many moments thinking about her gorgeous friend lounging around their place barely dressed.

For half a second, an image of running her hand up Esme's leg filled Sybil's mind. She immediately shoved it way down, locked it in a vault, and threw away the key. She wasn't going to lose her friend for the chance of a smile. Or a kiss. Or anything else. No matter what Sybil had done with other people in the past, she and Esme weren't like that together. Not at all.

Sybil picked up the pile of clothing Esme had discarded earlier. "Please, Ez. Get dressed and come with me. You don't want me to get caught, do you?"

Esme set her screwdriver down forcefully. "Of course I don't want you to get caught! But I don't want you to do *this* at all. I heard at the café that a bunch of other poster thieves were hauled off to prison last week. Do you want that to be you?"

"It won't be me. I'm too good, and you're going to be watching the street. We'll have the posters down before anyone even knows we're there, and they'll be sold by midnight."

"Won't they be ruined by the rain?"

"Not if we hurry."

Esme let out a weary breath. "Fine. But this has to be the last time, Syb. Promise me. It's too dangerous."

Sybil just shrugged.

Esme cast the dismantled clock one last longing glance and then stood and slipped out of her silk robe and nightgown. She was as shameless about her body as only a girl raised in a cabaret and then an orphanage where there was never any private place to change could be. Heat flooded Sybil's cheeks at the way the candlelight played over the planes of Esme's stomach and the hollows beneath her collarbones. As Esme pulled on her dress, Sybil hurried toward the other end of the apartment, where she kept her trunk and her thief's kit behind the dressing screen.

Hastily, Sybil stuffed a small knife, a glass bottle of water, a long piece of butcher's paper, and a ball of string into her pockets. Her hands shook as she did so, and she wrapped her fingers around her key necklace and exhaled sharply.

Why was she so jittery? Was it just the nerves that came before a job? Was it what Esme said about the other team getting caught? Or was it the fact Esme was half naked on the other side of the room? Whatever it was that made Sybil's hands shake, it had to stop. She needed steady, quick hands because she couldn't afford to get caught. Or to pay for a lawyer. And it wasn't like her family would—

"I'm ready," Esme called out, her delight in Sybil's embarrassment lacing her voice. "You can stop skulking like a prude."

"I'm not a prude!" Sybil took a deep breath and strode around the dressing screen. "Artists aren't prudes, and I've seen loads of naked models at the studio. Also, your buttons are crooked."

Esme looked down at her coat and swore. Shoving a screwdriver, a book, and her life-plan list into her pocket, she started to rebutton her jacket, but Sybil nudged her.

"We don't have time for exact buttons. Let's go." Sybil grabbed a bowler hat and smashed it over her curls.

"Wait." Esme's hand snagged on Sybil's elbow before she could open the front door.

Sybil turned around, catching sight of the two of them in a mirror hanging by the door. Esme was tall and lovely, but a lifetime of not enough food had carved her into sharp angles. A long scar— the product of some childhood injury—cut across the pale white skin of her left cheek, puckering it slightly.

Sybil smiled at her own reflection. She stood almost a head shorter than Esme, and her skin was also white, but freckles covered it. She had curly brown hair that never wanted to stay under a hat and green eyes that were "like a fern glen in springtime," her mother had always said. The Sybil in the mirror beside Esme was no longer a creature in conservative dresses or face paints, guarded and timid, as a proper young lady should be. Now, in her thief's coat and a bowler hat, she looked reckless, artistic, and a little wild. She loved it.

Esme frowned at their reflections, her sea-storm blue eyes darkening.

"What is it? What's the matter?"

"You didn't promise yet." Esme's fingers dug into Sybil's arm. Her nails were bitten all the way to the quick, but her grip was still intense, even through Sybil's coat.

"Promise what?"

"That this is the last time you'll steal posters."

Gently, Sybil uncurled Esme's fingers, rubbing at the spot where they'd been. A combination of pleasure and pain raced up her arm. It was still strange sometimes to be cared for like this. She'd never had a best friend, and it took some getting used to, even after a year.

"You worry too much, Ez."

"Promise me this is the last time, or I'm not going." Esme's voice held a frayed note, something that carried with it the tragic story of how she had lost her mother and her years at the orphanage after that loss. That hint of pain cracked Sybil's heart wide open and made her never want Esme to feel any hurt ever again.

"Fine, you old worrier." Sybil flung an arm around Esme's waist. "I promise this is the last time I steal posters. Does that reassure you?"

"Mostly not, but thank you for the promise."

Sybil squeezed Esme in a quick hug, inhaling her mint-and-metal smell before releasing her. "And now, really, let's go. I'm going to be furious if we miss out on the best posters because you've kept me here, lounging about like a rich woman and extracting promises."

Guilt spread through Sybil at the words, and she wished she could take them back. She knew exactly what it was like to lounge about like a rich woman.

Esme barked a laugh, oblivious since Sybil had never told her any details about her family or how different her upbringing had been from Esme's. "We're so far from wealthy, I almost considered eating a roach that crawled out of the cupboard this morning. Thank goodness I was able to bring home food from the café for dinner."

Sybil groaned. "Eating roaches truly is foul."

"I've eaten a roach before, you know," Esme said cheerfully. "When I was a child, before the orphanage, I had a cat—Leviathan—who would bring them to me as gifts. I was little and in a phase where I really wanted to be a cat too. One day, I thought I'd try a roach, to help with my cat nature, and let me tell you, they taste like—"

"Enough! Please, I beg you!" Sybil gave Esme a small affectionate swat on the arm.

Esme's guffaw filled the stairway as they descended to the street, and Sybil's heart soared, as it always did when she made her best friend laugh.

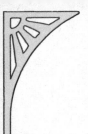

CHAPTER TWO
Esme

Stealing posters was almost as bad as leaving the house on rainy nights, but how else was Esme supposed to protect Sybil unless she went along?

Granted, she wasn't sure exactly what she was meant to protect Sybil from, but she'd slipped a screwdriver into her coat pocket, just in case. And she had her life-plan list in there too, of course, because that was always with her. And she'd also brought a small book—Madame Remington's latest edition of *How the World Works*—because it was always better to have a book than not have one. And she had two pencils, a small box with matches in it, a handful of screws, and a gull feather she kept meaning to fashion into a cat toy.

The screws rattled against the magnifying glass she'd also brought, making Esme clank a bit with each step. She sounded almost like one of the clockwork automatons she'd read about in the newspaper. Which was a delightful thought. A clockwork woman would get things done, quickly and efficiently, and her metal body would protect her from the outside world.

Yes, Esme liked that thought very much.

It was no longer drizzling, but the memory of rain misted around Esme's face as they walked down their street, hurrying past shops, bars, and a small square full of rowan trees some city planner had imported to Severon many years ago in an effort to beautify this neighborhood. Beside her, Sybil walked with eager steps, her short legs rushing toward an invisible destination that only she seemed to know.

Worry coiled through Esme's belly, and she chewed at her right pinkie nail, nibbling it down even further. Obviously, omens were nonsense, as was the idea that the weather could match a person's mood like it did in books, but on a night like this, when the fog coiled around their ankles and misty golden halos ringed every gaslight, it seemed just a little bit possible that something sinister was afoot.

"Where are we going?"

"We'll try near the market in Vermilion first," Sybil replied. "Always a good bet for a few new posters."

Esme perked up a bit and stopped chewing on her nails. Stealing in Vermilion was easier than in the other parts of town because there were fewer police officers and fewer people with things worth stealing. No one paraded about in diamonds in Vermilion, but there were still good posters to be had.

The seaside city of Severon was divided into four districts—the Orpiment sat in the middle of the city and contained the palace, university, and Great Library; that area was ringed by Lapis, a district where rich people went to be seen in the fancy restaurants, high-end boutiques, theaters, opera house, and museums; the Verdigris District sat on a bluff above the city, its name coming from the green-roofed mansions there; and then the Vermilion District, with its buildings roofed in cheap red clay tiles, spread through the rest of the city like a wine stain. Vermilion was full of factories, markets, tenements, churches, shops, nightclubs, and much more. Esme had lived in Vermilion her entire life, and that was where their current apartment was now. Living in a clock tower came with its own problems, but it was cheaper than Esme could get anywhere else for the amount of space, and besides, it was home.

Esme's foot landed in a puddle, sending a spike of cold water up her right calf. She swore loudly, making Sybil giggle.

"Don't laugh." Esme scowled.

"Don't step in every puddle we pass. You'll be much happier, I promise."

"I'd be happier if I were at home, reading a book."

"We'll be home soon enough, and then you can read and snuggle cats for the rest of the night. Now, come on, we're almost there."

Sybil pulled at Esme's arm, encouraging her to go faster. The touch sent Esme's heart racing, replacing her worry with something else entirely. Esme forced herself to take a steadying breath. This was ridiculous. She wasn't the type of girl to let people get close—that was how you got hurt—but here Sybil was, pulling on her arm, and Esme found herself following, as she always did. There was just something irresistible about Sybil's dimples, the way she laughed, and her eagerness for the world; it made desire coil in Esme, insistent and unfamiliar.

What would kissing Sybil feel like?

Esme had never kissed anyone, but she adored books where dashing heroines swept their beloveds off their feet, kissing them until they were dizzy and breathless. Somehow, over the past few months, Esme found herself wanting more with Sybil. Somehow, her ease with her best friend had turned into an aching need for lips and hands and whispered words after the lights went out.

She ignored it, of course.

Getting romantically entangled with Sybil was a surefire way to destroy the comfortable, perfect life they had. What if Sybil rejected her? Or, worse still, what if Sybil came to think of Esme as just one more passing fancy in a long line of entertainments?

Absolutely not an option.

Even if Esme couldn't do anything about her reckless feelings, she could protect Sybil during her reckless adventures. Which was why she stayed close as they cut through alleys and hurried past cafés and bars. Soon, they were deep in the Vermilion District, near a night market that was busy, even now.

"There!" Sybil said, pointing toward a poster on a quieter part of the street. On it, a black cat with piercing yellow eyes was printed against a red background, the title advertising a new café. The poster hung outside a clothing store, protected from the rain under an awning.

"Le Chat Noir. That one would look so good at home." Esme couldn't keep the excitement from her voice, and for the briefest moment, she wanted that poster for the apartment. It would hang over her couch, and she'd look up at it each morning. "Doesn't that cat look exactly like Jolie?"

"It does look like Jolie, and the poster would be perfect for home," Sybil agreed. "But it's by Toulouse, and it'll fetch us a lot of money."

Right, of course. They weren't here for home decorations. They were here to steal things that would help them cover the rent. Esme's tips had been slow lately, and who knew how much Sybil had saved. They were likely a long way from making rent, which was due in a few days.

"Home is perfect without it," Esme said. "I'll keep watch. You do your magic."

Sybil nodded, already taking out her thief's tools. The street wasn't entirely empty, and the market farther down was busy, but since the stores were closed at this time of night, most people on the street hurried past them without sparing a second glance.

Esme turned, scanning the sidewalk, as Sybil examined the black-cat poster. The trick to poster stealing, Esme knew from many nights like this with Sybil, was to get the poster down—as fast as possible—without damaging the art. Torn posters brought in less money. Every poster thief had their own methods, but Sybil preferred to slip a knife between the poster and the thick glue that pasted it to the wall, and then, using a quick, careful hand, pry the two apart. Sometimes it worked on the first try. Sometimes, Sybil had to use water to soften the glue enough to unstick the parts. When the poster was down, she'd wrap it in butcher's paper, and then they'd hurry away. All of which was often easier said than done.

As Sybil worked, Esme's thoughts turned again to the home she'd created since she'd been kicked out of the orphanage the minute she'd turned sixteen.

Home—especially with Sybil there—was Esme's favorite place. It had taken her a while, but she'd finally gotten it just so. Everything was in its perfect spot, and nothing needed to change, ever. At least not until Esme saved enough from her future job at the Great Library to buy a cottage by the sea, but that home would be much like the one they had now, just with more rooms. And maybe a bathtub. And a porch, where she could drink mint tea while overlooking the ocean.

Of course, Sybil's appearance in Esme's life was a great argument for the power of change, but that had been an addition, not a huge change.

Esme glanced over her shoulder, watching as Sybil's fingers flew over the space behind the poster, her knife slicing through the glue. Where had Sybil learned to steal like that?

Sybil never talked about her background, which was fine with Esme. If it was anything like Esme's own, she could imagine it well enough. The hints Sybil dropped whispered of a dead mother, a brother who was entirely consumed with his own pursuits, and a distant father. Esme filled in the rest, painting Sybil's life with her own misery—too many nights spent hungry, too much booze wafting off her mother's breath, too-thin sweaters in the winter and too-thin bowls of gruel throughout the year, other miserable children always needing something from her, and the deep, aching, desperate loneliness that came from being always surrounded by people, but never really having anyone see you.

That had always been the way for Esme, at least until she'd met Sybil.

"Esme?" Sybil called, interrupting her thoughts. She had the black-cat poster rolled up and tucked under her arm. The wall behind them was much barer than it had been a few seconds ago. Sybil smirked, making the dimples in her cheeks stand out. "I've got it, let's keep moving."

They hurried down the street, pausing here and there as Sybil assessed a new poster and how much it might bring in.

No, that one for umbrellas wouldn't work because—ironically— it was too wet from the rain, and besides, it was a little boring. Couldn't take that one with a woman in a yellow hat advertising kerosene lamps because it was faded by the sun, and besides, who cared about lamps? They were here for something really special! Yes, that one with the three dancers on it was perfect, but it had a huge tear down the left side, and what collector would pay for it now?

Esme's feet ached, and her littlest toes rubbed against the sides of her shoes, most certainly making blisters. Visions of iced buns and steaming cups of tea floated through her head when they finally paused in front of an apartment building deep in Vermilion. Down the block, people stood outside a bar, drinking, smoking, and talking loudly. Esme wrinkled her nose at the smell of spilled beer, urine, and horse dung. Beside Esme, Sybil tilted her head, studying a poster for a bicycle company. Painted in shades of blue, it featured a debonair frog in a top hat, riding a bicycle while floating above a city.

Sybil peered at the signature. "Another by Toulouse!" she crowed. "We're going to make so much money tonight!"

Sybil pulled out her knife, but before she could cut the poster down, a loud whistle split the night from somewhere above them. It was territorial and urgent—the sound of someone very much not okay with them being where they were.

Esme's stomach dropped as she looked up, trying to find the source of the sound. She couldn't see anyone, but that didn't mean anything. Another—even louder—whistle rang out.

"We should go." Esme gripped the screwdriver in her pocket.

Before Sybil could reply, three teens—two boys built like dockworkers and a fox-faced girl—strode toward them, bottles of beer still in hand.

Esme's fingers dug into the handle of the screwdriver.

"That's our poster," the girl said, drawing a knife out of her pocket. "You weren't thinking of taking our poster, were you?"

Sybil sneered. "Funny, I see Toulouse's name on it, not yours."

"It's ours." The tallest boy took a long sip of his beer. "Helene was just keeping watch, while we grabbed a drink." He nodded to the fire escape on the other side of the alley. A small hard-eyed girl perched on the metal balcony, glaring down at them.

"Still doesn't mean it belongs to you," Sybil insisted, an intense look on her face. It was the same look Jean-Francois, Esme's most ferocious cat, got sometimes. It said trouble was already here, and all you could do to avoid it was get out of the way.

"We can't fight all four of them," Esme whispered, threading her arm through Sybil's.

"We can try."

"You're terrible in a fight."

"We *need* that poster. Please let me fight them?"

Esme cast a quick look at the fox-faced girl, who glared back and slowly drew a finger along her own cheek as if she were slicing it.

Esme shuddered, the feel of a long-ago knife against her cheek blazing in her memory. "No. We can't win this. Plus, you'll lose this poster *and* the cat poster if you fight them."

Sybil shifted the rolled-up cat poster under her arm, chewing on her bottom lip. "Fine," she muttered at last. "They can have it. Though they don't deserve it."

Arm looped through Sybil's, Esme stepped away from the frog-on-a-bicycle poster. "It's all yours," she said to the other thieves.

"Good," the fox-faced girl said. "And stay out of this part of town. This is our neighborhood, and we don't allow others to take from us."

Sybil started to say something, but Esme pulled her away from the other thieves. One of them threw a bottle. It shattered off the brick wall to their right, dusting Esme's coat with glass, but she charged forward, not looking back. This was why she liked to stay home. There were no knife-wielding bullies there. No reminders of the cruelties of the orphanage. Just cats and knitting and clocks and Sybil.

"Are you okay?" Sybil asked after they'd gone a few blocks. Her voice was low and gentle.

"Yes." Esme shook glass slivers off her sleeve, walking fast enough that Sybil had to hurry to keep up with her.

Of course she was okay. She was always okay. That was what she did: be okay and keep moving forward.

It wasn't until they'd gotten through the market and were moving toward the Lapis District that Esme finally let go of the screwdriver she'd been clutching inside her coat pocket. Her heart had slowed down, but her nerves were still rattled.

"Do you think the one poster will be enough?" Exhaustion laced Esme's voice. She desperately wanted a cup of mint tea and dry socks.

Sybil cast Esme a sheepish look. "We need at least two in order to cover my part of rent. Sorry."

Sybil had recently been fired from her job at a famous artist's studio. Her work had been easy—she was just supposed to be sweeping up and doing other small tasks!—but as Esme knew from living with her, Sybil was terrible at sweeping or cleaning.

How was she so bad at sweeping? Wasn't that something you learned to do as a child? Esme certainly had. Besides, it was really less about Sybil's sweeping technique, and more about how with every job she had, Sybil got bored, stopped doing her work, and then was fired.

Why couldn't Sybil just make a plan and stick to it? That was how Esme got past every terrible thing life threw at her: with careful planning and by keeping her head down and not wanting things she couldn't have.

Things like kissing my best friend.

Esme blew out a long breath, ignoring her treacherous thoughts. "Okay, so we need more posters. Where are we headed?"

Sybil, despite her shorter legs and long skirts, was now several paces ahead. "We're wasting our time in Vermilion, and they usually have something glorious up in Lapis by this time on Friday night! Let's try Rue de Cerulean."

Rue de Cerulean was the main thoroughfare in the Lapis District. It ran past the opera house and several very expensive restaurants. Even at this time of night, it would be thronged with people.

"That's one of the busiest streets in the city!"

"Exactly! Which is why we'll have to be fast and why I need a lookout. And maybe a distraction."

Not a chance.

"Syb! You didn't say anything about me creating a distraction!"

Sybil stopped walking, a broad smile splitting her lovely round face. Amusement danced in her eyes. "Did I not? Sorry, must've forgotten. Come on. We have to get there before the opera lets out."

She laced her fingers through Esme's—the touch sent another thrill through Esme—and pulled her along, urging their steps faster. As they jogged through Lapis, Esme ignored how much her feet hurt and thought instead of how well Sybil's hand fit in her own and how the streetlight played off Sybil's freckles, mapping them in different constellations with each step.

Aching desire filled Esme again, and she had to bite her lip against words she couldn't take back.

As they neared the opera house, Sybil released Esme's hand and ran across the street without looking both ways. A horse-drawn cab nearly ran her over, and Esme threw out her arms to protect Sybil even though she was already safely on the other side.

"Watch where you're going!" Esme hollered after the cab. It clattered off, the driver making a rude gesture.

"ESME!" Irritation laced Sybil's voice. "Hurry up!"

"I'm coming." Esme dashed across the street. She glanced toward the wall between a café and a clothing store a few feet away. It was plastered with posters advertising everything from booze to books to club performers. "Are you going to steal one of those?" That would be easy enough. There were so many posters here, and this part of the street was a bit darker than the rest of the Rue de Cerulean.

Sybil shook her head. "What we want is over there."

Of course it was.

Esme followed the direction Sybil pointed, her gaze landing on a cylindrical column directly in front of the opera house. It stood between two streetlights, fully illuminated on both sides by the soft yellow glow of gaslights. Several horse-drawn cabs waited outside the opera house and a restaurant across the street was still open, with patrons dining at tables along the street.

Impossible. They could never steal this poster with all the people around.

Esme pinched the bridge of her nose and took a slow, calming breath. She tried to make her voice reasonable. "Sybil. Please. Stop and think about this. That column is in view of everyone. Exactly where we don't want to be."

But Sybil was already pulling her thief's kit out of her pockets and hurrying toward the poster she wanted.

Esme swore under her breath and followed.

Chapter Three
Sybil

Excitement *danced like champagne bubbles through Sybil's blood.* She hadn't had champagne since leaving her father's house—an estate in the country several hours from Severon—because she and Esme were far too poor for such things, but Sybil still remembered how a sip felt: light, fizzy, golden, and delicious.

The poster in front of her made her feel like she'd drunk too much champagne.

"Hello, beautiful," Sybil murmured, running a finger over the bottom corners of the poster. Its top corners hung far out of Sybil's reach, plastered on a column that was at least fifteen feet high. Protected from the weather by a green metal overhang, it covered many of the other posters on the column, as if it had been put up recently.

Visit The Absinthe Underground! it declared, advertising one of Severon's most exclusive and intriguing nightclubs. Neither

Sybil nor Esme had ever been to the Absinthe Underground, though they'd walked past it a few times, Sybil trying to get glimpses inside. Music, poets, laughter, artists, rich people, and smoke poured out of its doors, promising something exciting and mysterious. Sybil wanted to step inside the club so badly, it hurt. But she could never afford admission to a place like that.

"Are you sure this is a good idea?" Esme said, out of breath from running after Sybil. She nodded to the rolled-up poster under Sybil's arm. "We've already got the cat poster, and there are people everywhere. Maybe we've had enough trouble for tonight?"

"Absolutely not. The cat poster won't bring in enough for rent, and besides, this one will be easy to steal. Isn't it marvelous?"

Sybil couldn't tear her eyes away from the image on the poster: a beautiful, curvy dream of a woman with red curls piled atop her head. The woman wore an arsenic-green dress, which clung to her narrow waist and had a scooped-out bodice that left very little to the imagination. Pearls laced through her hair, and a wide diamond and emerald choker wrapped around her creamy-white throat. Her head was tilted back, her eyes closed, as if she were overcome by pleasure. A small secret smile played at the edges of her lips, and she held a fluted crystal glass full of green liquid. It was absinthe, of course, the wildly coveted, wickedly seductive drink Sybil longed to try. They called it the *green faerie* in the clubs, saying it enchanted you, making you see things that weren't there. The words *La Fae Verte* were written on the bottom of the poster, inviting and mysterious, just like the drink was supposed to be.

Sybil's fingers twisted the key around her neck to calm her racing heart.

What would it feel like to meet a woman like that? Or to *be* a woman like that? What would it feel like to have enough money *and* freedom to actually enter the Absinthe Underground and waste a night away, laughing with brilliant artists and poets? Who would Sybil have to become to join that glittering world? What would absinthe show her if she ever got to try it?

She wasn't sure, but getting this poster down somehow felt imperative. Like a crucial next step to experiencing more of everything in life. If she could get this poster down, maybe there could be more than just scrambling to pay the rent, looking for work, and spending nights at home with Esme and her cats.

"I'm really not sure you can do this." Esme put one hand on the column and glanced upward. Sybil could practically hear the gears of her mind calculating what it would take to cut the poster down.

"Of course I can. Stop worrying, and tell me what you think." She nudged Esme with her shoulder. "Isn't she magnificent?"

Esme glanced at the woman and then looked away quickly. "I suppose. If you're into that sort of thing."

Sybil noted the way Esme's cheeks pinked. They'd never talked about their romantic pasts, and Sybil often wondered if Esme had ever kissed anyone who wasn't a cat.

Not that it mattered.

A long silence stretched between them, broken only when Sybil cleared her throat. "No matter what you're into," she said rather roughly, "we can agree this poster will fetch a pretty price. It's stunning and truly unique—I've seen other Absinthe Underground posters, but never this one! It must be new this week, and look, it's by Mucha! We're going to make so much money! Here, hold these."

Sybil shoved the rolled-up cat poster, a glass bottle, and a ball of string into Esme's hands as she got out the other parts of her thief's kit.

Esme clutched the items to her chest as she stared up at the Absinthe poster. "Are positive you can do this? I'm taller than you, and I can't reach the top corners. . . ."

"I'll get it down, trust me. You worry about those people over there. Distract them." Sybil gestured toward the opera house, where a cluster of men in evening jackets and women in furs had appeared at the top of the steps, talking with one another.

"Sybil! I can't—"

"Please, Ez, just go! I'll be done in two minutes."

Stretching on her toes, Sybil reached up and slipped her knife between the lower right corner of the poster and the column. She pushed her tongue between her teeth as she concentrated.

"Make it one minute," Esme said, placing the bottle of water, the stolen cat poster, and the ball of string on a dry piece of ground at Sybil's feet. "And you owe me for this."

"I owe you big, now hurry!"

"I'm *going*! You hurry too!" And with that, Esme strode confidently toward the crowd.

Sybil watched over her shoulder as Esme flung out her arms and belted a bawdy song, like a street performer or someone in a cabaret. The crowd turned in the opposite direction from Sybil and the Absinthe poster, their eyes on Esme. Delight filled Sybil as she caught snatches of the song. In this moment, Esme was no longer a nail-biting, cat-loving shut-in who preferred clocks and mint tea to most people. As she sang to the opera patrons, Esme was poised, carefree, and looked like she'd been performing onstage her whole life.

This girl.

Esme met Sybil's gaze for a moment, shooting her a reproachful look. Right. Time was ticking away. Sybil had to get the Absinthe Underground poster down.

Turning back to the column, she sliced through the glue on the bottom corners of the poster with quick practiced motions. Despite her bold assurances, getting the upper parts unstuck would be trickier, especially since she was so short. With the knife extended, she stretched for the top edges of the poster, but she couldn't touch it, even on her tiptoes. What was she going to do? She glanced around, desperate for anything to climb. A newspaper box stood beside the poster column. She couldn't climb it in her dress, could she?

Of course she could.

In a quick unladylike move, one honed by a long-ago childhood spent chasing her brother through the woods, Sybil lifted her skirts and clambered onto the newspaper box. It was slick from the rain, but now, if she leaned over, she could almost reach the top of the Absinthe poster. Of course, the trick was to get the poster down in one piece and not fall or drop her knife.

Or not fall on her knife. That would certainly be worse.

She could do this. She had to. Steadying herself against the column with one hand, Sybil sliced away at the adhesive on the closest top corner of the poster. Her knife bit into the glue and stuck. She worked the blade deeper, wriggling it. The glue gave all at once, tension releasing as the edge of the poster curled away from the column. Sybil stumbled backward, nearly dropping her knife. She caught herself at the last moment, digging her fingers into the metal overhang. Her heart raced as she found her balance again.

Deep breath. One more corner to go.

To reach the last attached corner, Sybil leaned over the curled edge of the poster, stretching with her knife extended.

Almost there.

From the direction of the opera house, Esme's song finished, and a smattering of applause floated toward Sybil. A horse-drawn cab clattered over cobblestones on the street nearby. Sybil had seconds before someone came along and yelled at her to get down. Rising on her toes, she reached, extending her body, her fingers nearly at the corner of the poster. *One more inch.* Her shoes slipped on the wet newspaper box, making her stagger. Sybil swore and flung out a hand. She very nearly smashed into the curled poster, but her palm landed instead on the rough wood of the column.

Her heart galloped, and she took a long ragged inhale. Behind her, Esme started a new song.

Get moving. Now. Or you'll have to leave this poster here.

Drawing herself up to her full height, Sybil leaned on her tiptoes across the curled part of the poster, her knife aimed at the top left corner. As she did so, the key around her neck dangled in the space between her chest and the poster. Sybil strained, grasping at the edge of the column for balance. She lunged a little farther forward, and with that motion, her key brushed against the poster.

A jolt went through Sybil, fierce and sudden, like getting hit by a bolt of lightning. Her hand twitched at the shock. Her knife sliced across the top corner of the poster. In a blur, Sybil stumbled, dropped her knife, and then fell from the newspaper box, landing hard on her hands and left knee. The poster drifted down a moment later, rolling in on itself as it did so and resting on top of the still-wet newspaper box.

Sybil snatched up the poster. As she did so, her fingers brushed her key. It was still warm and humming vaguely.

What had caused it to shock her so suddenly?

She knew, of course. She just hadn't felt anything like it since her mother had died ten years ago.

Magic.

A jolt of magic had gone through her when the key touched the poster.

Grabbing her knife from the sidewalk, Sybil brushed street grime off her hands. She let out a ragged breath and dried the poster on her coat, her mind reeling.

Magic? Here? Now? On Rue de Cerulean? Entirely unlikely. Ridiculous. Impossible even.

Except it wasn't. Sybil knew that magic was real and very much possible.

How she knew that was thanks to her brother, Lucien. Five years older than Sybil, he had obsessively studied its history.

The thing about magic, he used to say, when he'd sneak out a book from their father's library and bring it to Sybil's room, *is that it's very tricky, and what people know about it has changed over the years, especially in Severon.*

He told Sybil how once, many centuries ago, artists had woven lace from strands of starlight and used that lace to sway politics and win wars. The knowledge of where that starlight came from was a secret lost for centuries, until about thirty years ago, when two teens from Severon discovered new starlight threads and learned how to weave the lace again. That had caused quite a stir, but eventually, the teens disappeared, and the city of Severon moved on. The last two rulers of the city had focused on science and industry, meaning magic had mostly been relegated to the realm of lore, old stories, and the history books. But Lucien believed there were still magical items in the world and that they—and perhaps the magical starlight—came from the world of Fae, a realm beyond their own—the realm Sybil's mother had also come from.

Sybil looked toward Esme, who was hurrying away from the crowd outside the opera house, her brows knit together in concern.

Sybil could never tell Esme about her mother.

"Sybil!" Esme grabbed her arm, pulling her out of her memories. She gripped Sybil's shoulders. "Are you hurt? You tumbled off that box. . . ."

Beyond Esme, the opera crowd was definitely looking at them, and farther down the street, a constable was drawing closer with each passing second. One of the opera patrons, a man in a tall top hat, waved the constable over.

Knee aching from her fall and mind full of questions, Sybil shook her head. "I'm fine." She rolled up the Absinthe poster and tucked it and the cat poster under her arm.

"Are you sure?" Esme's brow furrowed. "I saw you fall. We can get a cab?"

Sybil put all her weight on her injured leg, wincing a little, but then the pain lessened as she tried out a few steps. "No cabs. We definitely can't spend rent money on that."

"Maybe you shouldn't walk?" Esme fretted. She was studying each step Sybil took.

"I'm fine. Let's get out of here."

"Let me at least take one of the posters?"

Sybil handed her the cat poster, and Esme offered Sybil her arm. Together, they hurried off, Sybil limping a bit, before the constable could catch up with them.

✦

"Are you sure you're not badly hurt?" Esme asked, as they stopped outside a tall narrow townhouse on the edge of the Verdigris District. "You haven't said anything for the past six blocks."

"I'm fine," Sybil lied. Her knee ached, but mostly it was her heart that stung. Even now, ten years after losing her mother and a year after leaving home, grief snuck up on Sybil, rushing into the empty parts where her family's love used to live. Feeling the jolt of magic had brought back so many memories and unanswered questions, most of them about her mother's connection to magic and the Fae realm.

Her mother being from Fae was one of the great secrets of Sybil's life, one she planned to take to her grave. It was a secret she still had trouble believing herself, especially with so many months between her old life and her new one. But the fact remained: her mother had been a Fae creature living in their world who had married Sybil's father.

How Esme would've laughed if Sybil told her that truth. Esme liked clock problems, blueprints, and card catalogues. The existence of Fae fit nowhere within her tidy lists or ordered plans.

Sybil gripped the key around her neck—it was now cold and no longer humming with magic—and fought the urge to touch it again to the Absinthe poster. Her mother's face rose in her memory even as Esme started up the townhouse steps.

Sybil had known something was different about her mother from the time she was very small, but it had been Lucien who first told her the truth.

"You know those faerie stories Mother is always telling us?" he said to her one day, while they were hiding away in the fort he'd made for them in the woods on their estate. Sybil was seven, Lucien twelve. They were eating blackberries and watching squirrels race each other up trees. "Those stories are all true."

"They can't be!"

Lucien nodded, very serious. "They absolutely are. In them, Mother is telling us about her life before she met Father."

Sybil was surprised, of course, but some part of her—a deep part that seemed to understand things before the rest of her caught up—knew it was true. She peppered Lucien with questions, but only one seemed the most pressing.

"Does that mean we're half Fae as well?"

"What do you think?" Lucien took a leaf between his hands. He twisted it, and whispered: "Éclairer!"

To Sybil's delight, the leaf turned into a little green frog. It croaked sullenly.

"How did you do that?" She ran a finger over the frog's wet back.

"Magic," Lucien had said, grinning smugly.

Sybil found out later that the leaf-into-a-frog trick was just a street magician's trick, as was the magic word Lucien had uttered, but she'd also gone to her mother with questions. From many chats with her mother, Sybil learned Lucien was correct: all magic in the human realm was the result of items or creatures from the Fae world. Humans had starlight inside them, which could be used for magical creations like starlight lace, but they couldn't pull it out without a moonshadow creature, something that lived in the Fae world, to hunt it. Items crafted in Fae were especially powerful and could bring great power or trouble to the human world. Gems, jewelry, toys, and inventions from Fae—all these were stuffed with magic and incredibly rare. The few items that had made their way into the human world were coveted and guarded closely.

When Sybil asked her mother about being Fae, her mother showed Sybil one of the necklaces she'd brought with her from her world. It'd been made of twenty-five opals and glowed with trapped colors.

"Each of these stones has a rainbow inside," Sybil's mother said. "My father was one of the most popular jewelers in our realm, and though we weren't wealthy there, like the royal family is, he made this necklace for me."

Sybil's mother placed the necklace around Sybil's neck, and as her mother clasped it, a jolt of magic went through Sybil.

"Do all magical items make you feel like you've been hit by lightning?" Sybil asked.

Her mother laughed. "Perhaps."

There was so much more for Sybil to learn, and she ached to know more. How had her mother ended up in this world? Why had she stayed? But before Sybil could ask, her mother was thrown from her horse. On her deathbed, she gave both Lucien and Sybil the keys they wore around their necks, but she didn't tell them what to do with them. After his wife's death, Sybil's father was too distraught to help his children make sense of their grief or answer any of their questions. Lucien retreated deeper into his books and explorations, and Sybil grew up mostly alone. She'd never talked about her mother's origins, especially not in her new life in Severon, but part of her had yearned every day to feel that jolt of magic again.

And now she had. On a rainy evening in March, outside the Severon Opera House, while stealing a poster. Which didn't make any sense at all.

But maybe it didn't have to. After all, Sybil needed rent money, not magic. Maybe she should just forget it along with all the other unanswered questions from her old life.

Yes, that was what made the most sense to do. Not that she was in the habit of being sensible, but what choice did she have? It wasn't like her mother or brother were around to answer her questions.

Gripping the enormous rolled-up Absinthe Underground poster, Sybil hurried up the townhouse steps, following Esme. "Let's get these posters sold so we can head home."

"Best idea all night," Esme said, relief clear on her face. Still holding the stolen cat poster, she knocked on the townhouse door.

A maid answered and led them to a study on the second floor.

"Ahhhh, if it isn't my favorite poster thieves," Antoine Laurent said, as Sybil and Esme walked into the study. He gestured to the chairs in front of his desk. "Sit down, please."

Antoine was a middle-aged man with dark brown skin and a belly that strained at his buttons. He owned a high-end antiques and collectibles store a few blocks away, but he did most of his illegal business from home. Tonight he sat behind an enormous desk, smoking a cigar and peering through a magnifying glass at a pottery fragment. Framed art posters hung behind him. One of them—an ad for champagne featuring a woman sitting on the edge of the moon—Sybil had stolen a month ago, and the others she'd wanted to grab but didn't get to in time. Antoine's private collection of rare books, silver, ceramics, jewelry, ancient statues, and other antiques filled the study. A postcard-sized blue leather bag, decorated with intricately embroidered flowers and birds, sat on the shelf nearest to Sybil, and as she looked around, she wondered: Were any of these items magical? Would one of them send a jolt through her if she touched her key to them?

She wrapped a hand around the key, willing herself not to touch anything. Doing so would surely make Esme ask questions Sybil wasn't ready to answer.

Sybil shook her head. "We don't have time to linger, Antoine. But we do have some posters that will make your collection stand out above all others." She brandished the rolled-up Absinthe poster.

Antoine's eyes flashed eagerly. He rested his cigar in a crystal ashtray and got up from his chair, moving toward a long book-covered table on the other side of the study.

"Show me what you've brought." He set some papers and a pile of books on a chair.

Sybil moved forward, her heart in her throat. If Antoine liked these posters, then they were set for at least two months of rent. But if he didn't—if he objected to the small tear at the top of the Absinthe one—then Sybil didn't have another plan. She needed this to work.

Slowly, for the extra drama Antoine liked, Sybil and Esme unrolled both posters simultaneously. His eyes passed over the cat one with a gruff nod, and then he drew in a breath as the woman in the Absinthe Underground poster was revealed.

"She's magnificent, don't you think?" Sybil kept her hand over the rip at the top of the poster.

"She is indeed," said a smoky feminine voice from behind them. It carried an edge, sharp and threatening. "But you really shouldn't have that poster, now, should you, girls?"

CHAPTER FOUR
Esme

*E*sme *spun as an elegant young woman sauntered into Antoine's* study. She wore a dark purple dress that nipped in at her waist, and an enormous purple silk hat sat on top of her red curls.

Something about her was instantly familiar, and Esme glanced between the woman in Antoine's study and the poster on the table. Remarkably, the woman from the poster was standing in front of them, almost as if she'd walked off the paper and into the room.

Esme felt the blood drain from her face. "It's her."

Beside her, Sybil swore and twisted the key she always wore around her neck through her fingers. "What's *she* doing here?"

Esme nibbled her pinkie nail, studying the woman. Although she looked to be only a few years older than them, something about her was so very different. Maybe it was her expensive clothing or her confidence, but she didn't just move through the study; it was more like she made the space move around her. Clearly, this woman commanded every room she walked into.

"Maeve, darling!" Antoine exclaimed happily as the woman walked toward the table where the posters were laid out. "What a surprise!"

The woman—Maeve—let out a musical little laugh, and her gaze slid from Esme to Sybil and then back to the poster.

"She's so lovely," Sybil whispered.

Esme huffed out a breath. Yes, the woman was objectively stunning, but Sybil didn't need to stare like that. Esme had the strongest urge to pull Sybil from the room and flee into the night. Instead, she brushed her fingers over the items in her left coat pocket— the screwdriver, her life-plan list, the seagull feather—all familiar, comforting, useless at this moment. Forcing herself to stop fidgeting, Esme tried to smile. It felt more like a grimace, and she dropped the expression as Maeve walked toward them.

"Oh, Antoine," Maeve said. "I was just in the neighborhood. I thought I'd see what my favorite collector was up to." Her accent was lilting, but her eyes narrowed as she looked between Sybil and Esme.

Antoine let off a booming laugh. "Well, excellent timing. As you can see, we're examining your portrait." He gestured to the poster on the table. "I must say this likeness is really one of your best."

Esme stiffened as Maeve stepped up to the table, her skirts brushing against Esme's hand. Maeve's perfume—oranges, spice, and something Esme couldn't place—washed over her.

"Yes, well, you know we could give you a copy of this print at any time. You don't have to buy stolen ones." At the word *stolen,*

Maeve's voice turned sharper, all music and lilt gone. She turned to Esme and Sybil. "We do *punish* thieves in this city, you know."

Dread snaked through Esme. She grabbed Sybil's arm. "Come on, let's get out of here."

They would find another way to get rent money. Didn't matter what it was. Esme would work double shifts for the foreseeable future if she had to. She was well and truly done with this evening and all the trouble it had brought.

Sybil shook off Esme's touch, her starry-eyed expression replaced by ferocity as she glared at Maeve. "We're in the middle of a transaction with Antoine. I don't see how this is any of your business!"

Maeve arched an eyebrow. "It's quite literally my business."

Esme tugged harder on Sybil's arm. "Sybil. Please, let's just leave."

Sybil shook off Esme's grip. "No!"

"Yes! We're caught. We have to go!"

"We can't just walk away." Sybil's voice held a frantic note. She fidgeted with the key around her neck and turned to Antoine. "How much do you think these posters are worth? We'll take anything. Please!"

Maeve's eyes landed on Sybil's key, and she inhaled sharply. Confusion crossed her face, as her brow furrowed, then it was replaced by something hungry, predatory. It was a series of looks that made Esme's skin crawl.

Another wave of fierce protectiveness went through her, and she looped her arm through Sybil's insistently. "We're leaving. Now."

"Where did you get that key?" Maeve said, her voice shaking slightly. "Did you steal it too?"

Sybil crossed her arms over her chest. "That's definitely none of your business."

"Don't antagonize her," Esme pleaded in a whisper. "What if she calls the police?"

"We're not leaving without our rent money!" Sybil shot back. She touched the key protectively, defiant as she turned to Maeve. "I didn't steal this key."

"If you didn't steal it, where's it from?" Maeve persisted. "I'm just curious. . . ."

Antoine nodded. "I've always wondered that too. Tell us where it's from, won't you. For collector's curiosity purposes."

Sybil let out a long sigh and uncrossed her arms. "My mother gave it to me, if you must know." Her voice slammed shut over the words, as if they were a closed book she wished had never been taken off the shelf.

Which, of course, made Esme all the more curious. Perhaps it was the future librarian in her, or maybe it was that she too had wondered about the key, with its ornate filigree top, but she'd always been too afraid to ask.

"Your mother?" Maeve's eyebrows shot up at Sybil's words.

"Is that a problem?" Sybil muttered.

"No." Maeve tapped her finger against her own cheek. "It's just . . . interesting. . . ." She gave Sybil an appraising look.

Esme felt suddenly like she'd missed an entire unspoken conversation. "Please don't call the police on us," she said, because it made more sense than whatever was happening now.

Antoine gave a genial laugh and held up his hands. "Let's not even speak of the police. Maeve, darling, why don't you stop scaring these children and introduce yourself?"

Esme felt Sybil bristle beside her, but Esme was used to rich people infantilizing her. It'd been happening her whole life, and she knew the best thing to do was smile and get out of there as soon as possible.

Maeve studied them for a few moments longer and then gave a small laugh.

"Right, yes." She smoothed a hand over her skirts and smiled at Esme and Sybil. "My apologies. Let's try this again, shall we? Hello, darling girls. I see you've met my artistic representation"—here she nodded at the poster—"but I'm pleased to make your acquaintance in the real world. I'm Maeve—muse, model, and owner of the Absinthe Underground."

Esme's dread ratcheted up to full-on fear. To calm her racing heart, she nibbled at the remaining fragments of her thumbnail. They were so caught; even if Maeve was being charming now, it wouldn't last. Not only had they stolen the poster with Maeve's image on it, they'd also taken away valuable advertising for the club she owned. If Maeve decided to call the police, no matter how much Antoine wanted the poster or encouraged her not to involve the law, Esme and Sybil were in trouble.

"We're so sorry." Esme forced herself to stop biting her nails and hold Maeve's gaze. "We didn't mean to steal your image. Well, no, that's not true. We did mean to take it, but we didn't know you'd be here. Or that we'd be taking business from your club. Or that it would even matter. It's just, you see, Sybil knew Antoine likes the best posters, and we—"

Esme interrupted her own speech by taking a huge gulp of air.

"It's fine." Maeve rested a hand gently on Esme's shoulder.

"I— What?" Esme stared at Maeve's hand. The coolness of her touch seeped in, reminding Esme of standing in a patch of shade on a hot summer day.

"I said, it's fine."

"But haven't we lost you valuable advertising space?" Sybil said.

Maeve laughed at that, her musical lilt back. "Not at all. I suppose I was just surprised to see the poster, and so I overreacted. If nothing else, Antoine will display it to an exclusive number of people who will tell their friends about it. Eventually, more and more people will want to see it, perhaps Antoine will make prints, and then in a few weeks, it'll be of legendary status and something people will remember a hundred years from now. In the meantime, everyone will be talking about the Absinthe Underground, and more of them will come to the club."

"That's exactly correct," Antoine chimed in. "They'll be lining up outside your door!"

"They already do that, darling."

"Well, in that case, you're welcome," Sybil blurted, unable to keep a relieved, smug grin off her face.

Esme nearly burst out laughing, Sybil's giddy relief infecting her like too much wine.

Maeve cocked an eyebrow at Sybil. "Oh, I do like you. Spirited."

"This one is trouble," Antoine confirmed. "Now, let me just go get you girls some money."

"No money!" Maeve said, her fingers still gripping Esme's shoulder. Esme stiffened under the touch. "At least not for the Absinthe poster. I'm fair, but I'm not senseless. If word gets out you paid them handsomely for one of our posters, there'll be none left in the city. Besides, I have something else in mind for these two."

Fear shredded Esme's insides. What could Maeve possibly want from them? Esme shifted her feet, trying to get Maeve to release her shoulder.

"Fair enough, fair enough," Antoine said. "I'll just get you money for the cat poster then." He walked toward a carved wooden box on the bookshelf. It sat beside an embroidered blue leather bag that looked out of place among all the other fancy items in the study.

As he moved away, Maeve took a step closer, her grip tightening on Esme's shoulder. Across from Esme, Sybil's mouth was a thin line, as if she wanted to say something about Maeve not letting them sell the Absinthe poster, but Esme shook her head slightly. They were so close to getting out of here and going home. Whatever Maeve asked of them, they just needed to listen and go.

Maeve leaned in toward the girls and whispered, "Have either of you ever been to the Absinthe Underground?"

Oh no.

Esme turned to Sybil, sharing a quick glance. Sybil's eyes were saucers, her smile barely restrained. Unfortunately, there was nowhere else in the city Sybil wanted to visit more. Exhaustion threatened to overwhelm Esme at the thought of a nightclub.

"We haven't," Esme said, keeping her voice as neutral as possible. "We're not the type of people who go to places like that."

"But we want to be!" Sybil's voice was breathless. "We just can't afford the entry fee." She gripped the key around her neck tightly.

Maeve blinked prettily for a moment, as if she were trying to acquaint herself with the idea someone might not be able to afford the few coins it took to enter the Absinthe Underground. "Well, all that changes tonight. How would you both like to come to the club this evening, as my guests? I have a job for you. Something that your skill set is perfect for."

"What is it?" Esme dug her ragged nails into her palm. Was it too much to hope that Maeve wanted a clock fixed or a sweater knit?

"I need some thieves," Maeve said.

Of course she did.

"To steal what?" Sybil asked.

Maeve held one finger to her lips, glancing at Antoine. She lowered her voice. "It's best we discuss it at the club. Trust me, I'll make it worth your while. If successful, you'll be given more money than you can possibly spend." She looked pointedly between them.

Esme felt how poor they were—as they stood beside Maeve's finery in their threadbare secondhand coats and drab dresses—in that stare. "How much money exactly?"

"A lot. Enough to buy a townhouse grander than Antoine's and never work again if you'd like."

Sybil inhaled sharply, but Esme hesitated. Her blistered toes ached. The bottom of her dress was soaked with street filth and rainwater, and she wanted nothing more than to curl up on her couch and sleep. Not go to a club or take on another job, especially one that might involve stealing, no matter how much money Maeve might offer.

"Yes!" Sybil said eagerly, before Esme could speak. "Yes, we'll come to the club. Thank you for inviting us."

"Thank you for saying yes," Maeve said, finally removing her hand from Esme's shoulder. "I think you'll both be quite enchanted by the Absinthe Underground."

Maeve pulled a small green-and-silver card from her handbag. "Give this to the man at the door, and tell him you're my guests.

He'll let you in, and you'll drink for free. But it's only good for one night. If you don't show up tonight, you won't be able to enter the club or do the job for me."

She put the card in Esme's hand, closing her fingers around it. Then she tapped a finger quickly against the key around Sybil's neck. An expression of surprise lit up Sybil's face, as if the touch had jolted her awake somehow, but it was there and gone before Esme could think too much about it.

✦

The rest of their business with Antoine concluded quickly—he bought the cat poster, but for a very small sum. Pockets barely full of enough money for groceries, much less rent, Esme and Sybil followed Antoine's maid back to the front door. The green card in Esme's hand felt almost like a living thing, something that could bite if not handled correctly. Sybil kept glancing at it, her gaze hungry and curious. Esme fought the urge to rip it in half or throw it in a puddle.

Once the door closed behind them, Sybil whooped. "Maeve was glorious! Can you believe we met her? And that she invited us to the Absinthe Underground?" Sybil snatched the green card out of Esme's palm and studied it.

Esme stood very still, unable to shake her worry or exhaustion. "It's strange, though, isn't it?" Something wasn't right here. Esme tried to put the pieces of the puzzle together like they were a clock, but she couldn't make sense of it because so many parts were missing.

"Strange?" Sybil echoed, still studying the card.

"Yes, don't you think it's odd that the person on the poster we stole happened to show up where we were selling it?"

Sybil frowned. "Yes, it's odd, but it's also exciting! I told you we'd find adventure tonight! Let's go!"

"Where?"

"To the Absinthe Underground." Sybil looked at Esme like she'd forgotten her own name or that she needed to eat to stay alive.

"We don't have to go, you know."

Please. For the love of all good things, let's just go home. And sleep. Or read. Or knit something.

Sybil's cheeks were flushed, and her breathing was a bit ragged. She looked like someone who'd just been offered the world on a platter. "Of course we have to go! We've got a calling card that gets us through the door! We're Maeve's guests, which probably means we can drink for free and meet all sorts of interesting people! Plus, Maeve has work for us! And she's going to pay us a lot of money. How can we pass it up?"

Esme's cats, her tea, her clocks, her books, her couch called, but the look on Sybil's face made her pause.

"Don't you want to maybe get a bottle of wine to split at home?" Esme rarely drank, and Sybil drank too much, but it seemed like a good time to make an exception.

Sybil shook her head. "Please, Ez! We can do that any old day. Tonight we have an invitation to the most exclusive club in town. We can't pass it up!"

Esme let out a long breath. She rattled the screws in her pocket, sifting them through her hands, and held on to her life-plan list. Going to a club like the Absinthe Underground was nowhere on her list, but Sybil wanted it so badly. And Esme didn't want to disappoint her. Besides, how much harm could it do? "Fine then. We can go to the Absinthe Underground. Do you at least want to stop at home and put on fresh clothes?"

At least that way Esme could hug one of her cats, and maybe Sybil would change her mind once they got back to the clock tower. Plus, both their coats were damp with rain, and the way Maeve had looked at them sat in Esme's memory. She'd felt like she was twelve again, going to school with kids who didn't live in an orphanage and didn't have holes in their stockings or too-small shoes.

Sybil shook her head. "Who cares what we're wearing! I don't want to miss another minute of this night. Let's go!"

Sybil leaned her head against Esme's shoulder, resting there for a moment. Esme exhaled, fighting to release her worry. Sybil was her home. Wherever she was, that was where Esme wanted to be. Plus, maybe Sybil was right. Maybe it was going to be an incredible night, and then tomorrow everything would go back to the cozy, perfect normal Esme had so come to love.

"Lead the way," Esme said, letting go of her life-plan list and forcing all her worry, dread, fear, and exhaustion to the back of her mind. Adventure—that great, troublesome beast—awaited. Might as well make the best of it. And maybe she could get a cup of tea at the Absinthe Underground. That wasn't too much to hope for, was it?

CHAPTER FIVE
Sybil

A mess of feelings swirled in Sybil, jumbled like colors mixed on a paint palette, as she and Esme stood outside the Absinthe Underground.

Adrenaline whipped through her, the product of all the unexpected encounters, from being bothered by those other poster thieves to meeting Maeve. Excitement about what might happen tonight also filled her, as did anticipation and a giddy sense of potential. It felt like she was on the edge of a great change, and her only options were falling or soaring into something very grand and new.

Shadowing all those feelings, though, was the biggest one: curiosity.

Despite her passing desire outside Antoine's house to dismiss her questions, Sybil *needed* to know more about the jolt of magic she'd felt when the key touched the poster and then again when Maeve touched the key. She needed to know why Maeve was so interested in the key. She also needed to know what the job Maeve had for them was and why she needed Sybil and Esme to do it. Did it have something to do with magic? How was that even possible?

Sybil glanced at Esme, who was now chewing her left pointer fingernail down to the quick. Esme's brow furrowed as she stared at the line of people curved around the block outside the club. Sybil was surprised to see a screwdriver gripped in Esme's right hand. Where had that come from?

A sharp current of worry for Esme cut through Sybil's other feelings. Accompanying the worry was also the nagging sense that Sybil was being a bad friend for dragging Esme along on tonight's adventures. What if going to the Absinthe brought up some terrible memory from Esme's past, something awful from the time when her mother was alive and working in a cabaret? Should Sybil mention that? Why couldn't they just go home? That would make Esme happy. But Sybil couldn't bring herself to walk away from the Absinthe Underground and all the questions she might get answered tonight.

"Are we really doing this?" Esme asked, shoving the screwdriver into her pocket. She fiddled with a button on her coat.

"We really are." Sybil glanced at the club, exhaling slowly, as if that could make her calm down. She fought the urge to ask Esme about the screwdriver and instead focused on the details of the Absinthe Underground, taking them in with her artist's eye.

Although she'd walked past the club many times, Sybil hadn't grasped how enormous it was. Built into a sprawling ancient mansion—one that even her father would've found of acceptable size—it took up an entire block. The front door was twice as tall as Sybil and carved with flowers and faces. Green stones shaped like vines framed the door, ornate lanterns with green-glass panels hung on either side of the entrance, and a sign above the threshold declared the name of the club.

A muscular man stood outside, letting people in and keeping people out. In the time Sybil and Esme watched the entrance, he'd ejected three teenage boys who'd tried to sneak in.

Sybil squeezed Esme's elbow. "This is going to be an amazing evening. Thank you for coming with me."

Esme stopped fidgeting and straightened her shoulders. She let out a long breath. "Of course. I wouldn't let you do this alone. Plus, I must admit I *have* been curious about this building for a long time. When I was a child, it was owned by an old dowager, but no one ever saw her. I read somewhere that she had clocks from all over the world, and perhaps those are still inside . . ."

Sybil beamed at Esme. "Only you would come to the most glittering nightclub in Severon and be looking at the clocks."

"Clocks are quite exciting! I mean, did you know there's one in the Great Library that's been keeping exact time—to the second!—for the past two hundred years?"

"Perhaps we'll go see that someday, as a special treat when we're bored with dancing, drinking, and meeting artists and poets."

"I assure you the clock will still be more exciting," Esme said, unable to stop a smile from breaking through. "Not that I expect you to appreciate the way gears work together or the precision needed to fix them. Though I find they're really best considered when I'm wearing significantly less clothing. . . ."

A vision of Esme in her silk nightgown and robe filled Sybil's head, sending a whole new mess of feelings through her. She opened and closed her mouth to speak, but then Esme winked at her.

Winked! Sybil nearly fell over.

Was Esme . . . flirting with her?

It sounded like it, but surely that couldn't be right? Esme was just being factual. Sybil cleared her throat and pulled Maeve's card from her pocket. "I'll do the talking," she said, rather more roughly than intended. "Let's go."

Sybil stepped forward, putting a lifetime of lessons in posture, etiquette, and ladylike comportment into the movement. She would look like she belonged in this club, even if her clothes said otherwise.

"Excuse me?" She wedged her way into the front of the line, pulling Esme along with her.

The bouncer by the door didn't even look at Esme and Sybil, though two girls behind them in line cast them furious looks.

"You can't just cut," one of the girls snarled. She wore a feathered hat and a bodice-plunging gown.

"They're not even dressed for the Absinthe," the other said, sneering. She adjusted her glittering shawl and turned away.

The bouncer scowled at Sybil and Esme. "Back of the line's around the block."

"But I have this card?" Sybil flashed the green slip of paper Maeve had given them.

Understanding lit the bouncer's face. He even smiled a little, which made his forehead wrinkle like a bulldog's. "Well, why didn't you say you were Maeve's guests? Come on in."

Then, to the protests of many other people waiting in line, he gestured Sybil and Esme through the open door.

Sybil gasped when she stepped inside the Absinthe Underground's foyer. An enormous crystal chandelier hung from the ceiling, and the walls were made of light-green marble. A low haze of blue smoke hung in the air, and music, clinking glasses, laughter, and riotous conversations filtered into the space. A pair of brass doors waited at the end of the room, promising entry into another world.

It wasn't that Sybil had never been in a grand house full of luxurious items—she'd been in those since before she could walk—but it was something else entirely to be in an old mansion repurposed into a space meant for dancing, drinking, and many more enchanting things. The air practically vibrated with a sense of dazzling darkness, just waiting to devour those who stepped inside. Sybil adored it.

She clutched Esme's hand and did a little dance. "We did it! We're really here!"

Esme looked around and shrugged. "There are far fewer clocks than I was hoping for, but it's nice enough, I suppose."

Sybil snorted at that and spun in a slow circle. Towering plants filled the marble-floored foyer, making the space feel lush. On the right wall was an enormous painted mural depicting a lithe red-headed faerie with gauzy green wings, wearing a revealing dress the color of absinthe and an emerald-and-diamond choker. She had a coy smile and mischievous tilt to her head, as if she were daring patrons to spend the night with her. Her crystal goblet of absinthe was filled to the brim and raised in a toast. Beneath her image, huge letters declared:

THE GREEN FAERIE WELCOMES YOU
TO THE ABSINTHE UNDERGROUND.

"That looks like Maeve," Esme observed, her voice flat.

The faerie was most definitely patterned off Maeve, and her pose was much the same as the one on the poster Sybil had stolen not long ago.

Sybil looked around, taking in the rest of the lobby. It was elegant and overly grand like the ballrooms she'd grown up in, and a pang went through her. Maybe she had missed this level of splendor, just a little bit.

"What do we do now?" Esme asked.

Sybil nodded toward a coat check booth beside the brass doors. A woman with short black hair and golden-brown skin sat at the counter, smoking a cigarette and reading a book. "Let's ask her."

"Hello, lovelies!" the woman said enthusiastically as they reached the booth.

Her name tag read *Lilah*, and Sybil's face flushed as Lilah's eyes passed over her dusty patched jacket.

"First time at the Absinthe Underground?" Lilah set her cigarette into a crystal ashtray.

"How could you tell?" Esme asked, her voice edged.

"Just a guess. Here's how it works. You pay me admission here, check your coats if you'd like, and then you can go on through to where the magic happens."

Sybil placed the green card on the counter. "We have this. From Maeve?"

"Ahhhhh!" Lilah's smile fully materialized. "Well, that changes things entirely now, doesn't it?"

She stood and gestured for the girls' coats. Esme glanced at Sybil.

"What about the rent money in our pockets?" Esme hissed. "Someone might steal it if we leave our coats here."

Sybil shrugged. "It'll be fine, I'm sure. Give her your coat."

They handed over their coats—both of which looked quite shabby next to all the furs and wraps on the hangers behind Lilah.

Lilah picked up her cigarette again. "Now, of course, you can stay dressed as you are—we have a few patrons who opt for the run-down look—more of a starving artist costume, really, that some of the wealthy folks like to put on—but since Maeve gave you her card, you're also able to access her dressing room. You can pick anything you'd like and wear it tonight, just for the full Absinthe Underground experience."

"I think we're fine—" Esme started.

"We'll do it!" Sybil interrupted. "Why not have the full experience, Ez? This is our one chance to come to this club. Might as well look like we belong here."

Plus, if they were in Maeve's dressing room, perhaps they could learn more about her and why she'd invited them in the first place.

"Excellent!" Lilah declared. "Maeve's room is up the main staircase and down the hall on the right. Last door at the end. You can't miss it. Have a good night, ladies." She beamed at them and then returned to her book.

Excitement twisted through Sybil as she and Esme pushed through the bronze doors and into the main room of the club. They were really doing this! They were going to spend the evening at the Absinthe Underground!

The noise hit Sybil first. What had been a whisper outside, and then a dull roar in the coat check area, was now a full-on thrum of music, laughter, and the murmurings of a hundred different conversations. The entire first floor of the mansion was a vast open space, and it buzzed with life. Long low couches, all of them upholstered in absinthe-green velvet, ringed the room. People of all genders and races lounged on the couches, in all sorts of pairings, talking with one another, kissing, drinking, smoking, and arguing. On one side of the room was a dance floor, and on the other was a long marble bar with a wall of mirrors behind it.

Several harried-looking bartenders worked behind the bar, pouring liquid over sugar cubes, lighting the sugar cubes on fire, and then serving green-hued glasses of liquor to patrons. A handful of gaming tables for cards and billiards filled the back of the room, and on a mezzanine, a band with guitars, violins, and drums played a wild song that sent Sybil's heart racing. Groups of dancers in silver-and-green costumes and black stockings performed on a raised stage, each kick and wiggle a bit more scandalous than the last. Servers wearing matching black tuxedos moved through the crowd, handing out drinks, offering cigarettes, and flirting with the customers.

From the ceiling, interspersed among crystal chandeliers, dangled lithe scantily dressed contortionists who twisted their bodies around silver rings, defying gravity and thrilling the crowd. There was a mural painted on one wall with the same mischievous, beautiful green faerie holding a glass of absinthe.

In the center of the club, with a view of it all, was an enormous opera box, at least three times larger than the royal box Sybil had seen once on an outing to the Severon Opera with her family. Dark green velvet curtains framed the box, and a waist-level railing separated it from the club. Couches and chairs filled the space, and Sybil glimpsed Maeve in the box, talking with a pair of women in stylish dresses.

Esme's eyes were wide as she looked around, her voice almost reverential. "This is so much nicer than the cabaret I grew up in."

Sybil wrenched her attention away from Maeve and the box she held court in. "What do you mean?"

"La Lune was nothing like this. Maybe it was different in its prime, but by the time my mother worked there, it was as shabby as a fourth-hand coat. This is magnificent."

Sybil wanted to ask more, but she just squeezed Esme's hand. "I think we go up there." She pointed to the staircase that curved upward on one side of the club. It was on the opposite side of the room from Maeve's opera box.

After showing the bouncer at the foot of the stairs Maeve's card, they were allowed to ascend.

"Maeve's is the last door at the end of the hall," he called out. "You can't miss it."

Sybil's heart thundered as they moved along the second-floor hallway. It was lit by flickering gas lamps, and the walls were made of that same green marble that lined the foyer. Every few feet hung round portraits of the mischievous green-winged faerie they'd seen in the lobby. Richly woven carpets covered the floor, and beautiful performers in elaborate costumes, servers with trays laden with drinks, and other patrons filled the hall.

As they walked toward Maeve's dressing room, they squeezed past a sweating middle-aged man holding a bouquet of flowers and waiting outside a showgirl's door He bowed in as the door swung open. Laughter drifted out from behind another closed door. A door labeled OFFICE was open a crack, the sound of raised voices and arguing filling the hall. Sybil and Esme hurried past that one quickly.

Maeve's door was painted gold, and a small sign hung from it that said THE GREEN FAERIE in elaborate script. Drawn beside the words was a bottle of absinthe with a green faerie on the label.

"They've really leaned into the theme," Esme muttered beside Sybil.

"And not a clock in sight."

Esme burst into laughter, and Sybil grinned too, dizzy with the air of the club and the promise of things to come.

Sybil knocked on Maeve's door, but there was no answer. They waited a few seconds, knocked again. A woman wearing a low-cut dress and a feathered headdress glanced over at them from the doorway of the closest dressing room.

"Whatcha doing back here, loves?" she called out.

"Maeve gave us her card." Sybil held it up. "We saw her out there, in her box, but Lilah told us to come upstairs?"

The woman looked back at them and shrugged. "Just go on in then. If you've got her card, you can choose your outfits and head back down into the club. Maeve is dealing with business right now, but I'm sure you'll bump into her eventually."

The woman turned away, and Sybil and Esme shared a glance.

Sybil put a hand on the doorknob. "Shall we see what's in here then?"

"After you." Esme made an elaborate bow, imitating the man with the bouquet.

Laughing, Sybil turned the knob and pushed on the door. She gasped as it swung open.

It was marvelous. Beyond anything Sybil had ever seen. Or imagined.

Clearly, Maeve's dressing room used to be a bedroom because there was a large raised platform in the middle with a dressing table and mirror on it. Gas lamps lit the room, casting a warm glow across the racks of lovely spangly dresses. Beneath a tall window—through which the night and the rain-washed streets of Severon were visible—stood a rack of men's clothing in all colors, styles, and textures. Two sofas upholstered in pale green velvet with golden accents sat in front a fireplace carved to look like an open maw. Hanging above the fireplace was a portrait of Maeve wearing a green dress and the choker she'd worn in the poster, a glass of absinthe in her hand.

"Wow," Sybil said on the end of an exhale.

"Wow," Esme echoed.

Sybil had been around dressing rooms and amazing clothes most of her life, but her mother's bedroom and closet had been half the size of Maeve's. The richest women in Severon probably didn't have wardrobes like this to choose from.

Slowly, Sybil ran her hands over some of the dresses on the closest rack. She hadn't missed wearing expensive clothing until this moment, and these dresses were nothing like the boring ones she'd been forced to don after her mother died. She could definitely see her new self—her adventurous, artistic, drink-life-to-the-dregs self—in these sorts of clothes. Sighing happily, Sybil pulled a blue gown, something the color of the winter sky at twilight, off the rack.

"Ez, this was made for you. Look, it's the exact shade of your eyes."

She held it out, and Esme took the gown. Pressing the dress up to her body, Esme turned to the mirror.

Sybil's heart kicked as Esme ran her fingers along the neckline.

"It's lovely," Esme said, her voice soft. "But let's keep looking."

Their fingers flew over the clothes on each rack, and they pulled off silver dresses, green ones, bright gold ones that shimmered with tiny beads. . . .

Ah. There it was. What Sybil had been looking for somehow, though she hadn't known it.

She pulled a gauzy dress made of deep-green material the shade of pine trees from the rack. Minuscule silver stars decorated it, and the neckline plunged to her belly. It was scandalous, daring, and the kind of dress no decent girl would wear. Perfect. Slipping out of her old dress, Sybil pulled the green one over her head and studied her reflection.

In it she was lovelier all at once. More interesting. A little bit otherworldly, like she was truly half Fae as her mother had promised. Her hand flew to the key around her neck, and she gripped it, hoping to feel that jolt of magic again.

"You look incredible," Esme murmured. Her eyes widened as they took in Sybil's appearance.

The look sent Sybil's heart galloping, and she forgot all about the key or her mother. "More interesting than gears and clockfaces?"

Esme made a small strangled sound and just nodded.

Sybil didn't quite know what to say to that, so she turned back to the dresses. "Your turn. What are you wearing tonight?"

"That one," Esme said, pointing to a black dress fringed with purple feathers.

"Excellent choice."

Esme slipped off her dress. This time, Sybil didn't look away as Esme stepped into the black dress.

"Do my buttons?" Esme asked, turning her bare back to Sybil.

Sybil was going to faint. She placed a trembling hand on Esme's lower back and wrestled the first button into place. The mint-and-metal smell of Esme went to Sybil's head, pushing all other thoughts from her mind. She longed to rest her cheek against the smooth space between Esme's shoulder blades or run her fingers down the trail of pebbles that formed Esme's spine. The closest gas lamp flickered, making shadows dance along Esme's skin. Sybil kept buttoning the dress, slowly covering Esme's back in black silk. Before she closed the last buttons, Sybil noticed a tiny pair of moles on Esme's left shoulder that she'd never seen before. Just knowing they were there felt breathtakingly intimate.

Sybil finished the last button but let her hands linger on Esme's shoulders, turning her gently toward the closest mirror.

"You're so lovely," Sybil whispered.

"*We're* so lovely." Esme slipped her arm around Sybil's waist. "We don't even look like ourselves." Her eyes met Sybil's in the mirror, burning with something curious and dangerous.

This girl.

Sybil exhaled, ready to finally, finally plunge across the space and—

And then the door to the dressing room flew open.

Both Sybil and Esme turned, letting go of each other, the moment between them broken, as Maeve swanned into the room.

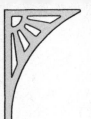

CHAPTER SIX
Esme

Esme's *index finger pushed into her bottom lip, pressing it hard.*
For one long, agonizing moment, as Sybil had held Esme's
gaze, wearing that damned green dress, her dimples deepening as a
smile curled at her lips, her breath a touch ragged, Esme had hoped
Sybil was going to kiss her. She'd almost pulled Sybil toward her and
tangled her hands into Sybil's hair, just to hurry things along.

But thanks to Maeve, the chance was gone.

Would you have stopped yourself if Sybil had asked you to kiss her?

Yes? No? Esme wasn't sure. There was too much to lose, that
much she knew. Sybil went through lovers like Esme went through
cups of tea. Well, perhaps not like that, but she'd had several dalli-
ances in the past year, people she never mentioned again after
a night or two. Sybil was probably swept up in the excitement of
tonight, and she wasn't the kind of girl to commit to anything. Esme
wouldn't destroy their friendship because she thought Sybil might

want to kiss her. Even if that was what Esme wanted more than anything.

Pushing all these impossible, complicated thoughts aside, Esme focused on Maeve, who had collapsed onto one of the couches in front of the fireplace. She beckoned the girls over with one hand while the other held a crystal bottle full of green liquid.

"I'm so glad you both made it," Maeve said, her speech just the slightest bit inflected by the drink. "Let me see what you've found to wear." She gestured for Sybil to spin around, and an actual giggle left Sybil's lips as she did.

Esme had never heard Sybil laugh like that, and it made her insides twist. Perhaps Sybil did belong in a world like the one at the Absinthe Underground.

Maeve gestured for Esme to step forward, which she did, rather stiffly.

"Exquisite." Maeve nodded. "Both of you. You'll be perfect for this job." She took three fluted crystal glasses from a tray on the table and filled them with green liquid.

"What's the job?" Sybil asked, sitting on the sofa next to Maeve's.

Esme sat beside her, having to adjust the outrageous feather train of her dress to fit, and started chewing on one of her nails. She missed her jacket, with its pockets full of things to fiddle with. She missed her life-plan list, which she'd forgotten to grab as Lilah took their coats. Sybil squeezed her knee reassuringly.

Esme took a steady calming breath and stopped biting her nails.

"First, a drink," Maeve said. "This is absinthe, our club's specialty, of course. Normally, we pour it in a glass, then drip water over a sugar cube to dilute and sweeten it, but who has time for such things? It's delicious this way too, I promise." The green drink shimmered in the glass, gleaming almost like emeralds made liquid.

Sybil took hers eagerly, but Esme hesitated. She'd heard so many things about absinthe and what it made one feel or see. Most of them were things Esme wanted nothing to do with.

"I don't really drink," Esme said, her hands clasped in her lap.

Maeve shot Esme a smile. "It'll make everything I tell you much easier to swallow."

Sybil drank enthusiastically, making a face at the taste. Right, Esme was here to follow Sybil on this reckless adventure, wherever it led.

Esme took a cautious sip. A sharp tang of licorice coated her tongue, followed by the burn of alcohol as it hit her throat. It was surprising but not altogether unpleasant. Esme took another sip, letting the alcohol seep into all her tired, sore, lonely places.

Maybe this wasn't so bad after all.

Maeve raised her own glass toward them. "Finish those, and then I'll tell you everything."

Esme glanced at Sybil, who gave her an encouraging nod. Oh, alright. She tipped the glass of absinthe back and drank deeply. Sybil did the same. The drink hit Esme harder this time, making her head spin.

Maeve filled their glasses again and gave them an appraising look. "Now, lovelies, if you want to do this job for me, there are three seemingly impossible things you must accept as facts."

Esme glanced over at Sybil, who had put her glass down and was holding the key around her neck in both hands. Esme fought the urge to lean into Sybil for whatever was to come next.

Be brave. That's the only way you can protect her.

Maeve continued. "They will be shocking, perhaps, as it's always surprising to learn there's more to the world than you might think, but I hope the absinthe in your bellies makes the truth go down a little easier."

Sybil nodded eagerly. "Just tell us. We're ready."

Esme wasn't sure she was ready, but she nodded as well.

Maeve leaned closer, and the light from the gas lamp on the table caught in her eyes, as if it were imprisoned there. She was still beautiful, but in a sharp, deadly way, like deep winter or the silver gleam of a knife. Unable to help herself, Esme shuddered.

"First," Maeve said, "you must accept that your world is not the only one. Fae is real and a realm entire beyond this one. You've been told about it in faerie stories, but what you must understand is that everything in those stories is mostly true."

How was that possible? Esme wanted to laugh, but the serious look on Maeve's face told her not to make a sound.

Esme took another sip of absinthe, reeling as she thought about all the Fae stories she'd read over the years. They were tales of pixies, brownies, High Fae, and mischievous faeries. Of course, she'd dismissed them as fiction, even if she'd always wanted them to be real. But here Maeve was, telling her they were true. How was that possible?

Maeve pressed on. "The second thing you must accept is that *I* am a Fae creature who has come into this world."

That was absurd, of course. Esme opened her mouth to laugh, but then she paused, watching the way Maeve's hands held her own glass of absinthe. Esme knew how things like clocks were assembled, and now that she was looking closely, she could see all the ways Maeve didn't quite seem to fit together. There was something off about her, almost like looking at the image on a stained glass window. Esme was aware all at once that the entire picture she was seeing of Maeve was composed of many fragmented little parts.

Ridiculous, of course. But so was Maeve claiming she was Fae. She had to be joking. Esme took another small sip of her drink.

Beside her, Sybil scoffed. "How do you expect us to believe you?"

"I'll show you," Maeve said. "Drink more and prepare yourself."

Esme raised an eyebrow at Sybil, who was twisting the key around her neck with such ferocity, Esme was certain the chain would snap. Maeve made an impatient noise, and Esme took another long sip of absinthe. The drink numbed her tongue, and the boozy shadows in her mind became clouds, gathering on the horizon.

"Ready?" Maeve asked.

"Ready," Esme and Sybil said at the same time. Esme slipped her right hand into Sybil's left.

"Try not to scream." In one quick movement, Maeve removed a comb from her hair. Her red curls tumbled down, framing her face. She placed the comb on the table, and then she ran a hand over her face. As she did so, her beautiful, pristine image dropped, her flesh shifting somehow.

Esme's mouth fell open in astonishment as Maeve's face elongated. All at once, Maeve's cheekbones became more pronounced. Her eyes widened, and the insides changed to solid purple with no hint of white at the edges. Her long red hair shortened, and her skin tone transformed to the palest malachite. Her now-green fingers stretched into twigs, with bloodred nails at the end. A delicate pair of small wings sprouted from her dress, bursting through the satin as if they'd been held down for too long. She met Esme's gaze, ethereal, dangerous, entirely not of this world, despite her dress and the way she perched on the sofa.

Esme made a tiny terrified sound. It was one thing to forgo her life-plan list for a wild night of drinking, dancing, and adventure, but it was another entirely to be faced with the possibility of Fae sitting right in front of them. Sybil gripped Esme's hand.

"Steady, Ez," Sybil whispered. "Change back, please, Maeve."

"Oh, fine," Maeve ground out, her voice creaking like the wind through leafless trees. She ran a hand back over her face, reverting instantly to the beautiful—human—red-haired woman she'd been.

Terror coiled in Esme, barely restrained. "Who—or what?—are you?" Esme feared if she spoke too loudly, the world might crack around her.

"A green faerie," Maeve said, twisting the comb back into her hair. "From the Moonshadow Kingdom in the Western Realm of Fae. It's a mountain kingdom ruled by Queen Mab and her terrible daughters."

Esme lifted her glass of absinthe with shaking hands, taking a long sip, as if drinking more would make it all make sense.

"You're an actual green faerie?" Sybil deadpanned. "How terrifically clever."

Esme glanced over, surprised by Sybil's calm tone. She seemed far less shaken by Maeve's transformation than Esme was. But then, perhaps Sybil just saw this as another stage in the great adventure that was her life. What was so clever, though?

A moment passed, and Esme finally put it together. "*La Fae Verte*. The green faerie, of course. That's you, as your true self, on all your posters and the walls of the Absinthe Underground. So smart."

"It's a version of my true self and my glamoured one, yes." Maeve shrugged. "Sometimes the truth is right in front of you, but people want so badly to believe it's a lie, they don't look any closer."

"How did you get here?" Sybil blurted, her voice laced with a sharp curiosity. It was a good question, but Sybil made it sound like an urgent one. A necessary one. Of everything Esme wanted to ask Maeve, this was low on the list. Sybil released Esme's hand and went back to twisting the key around her neck.

"It's a long story," Maeve said. "But that's the third hard truth you must accept if you want to do this job for me: there are people in this world who have keys that can open doors between our worlds. I met someone who had a key—just like yours, Sybil—and he opened a door between our worlds."

"Lucien?" Sybil whispered.

Who was Lucien?

Esme looked between Sybil and Maeve as they shared a knowing glance. She felt suddenly, completely left out and unimportant. She took another sip of her absinthe, which dulled the feeling, just a bit.

"Lucien's her brother," Maeve filled in helpfully. "He's an adventurer—"

"He's a scholar," Sybil interrupted.

"Maybe a bit of both."

Esme had known Sybil had a brother, but her imagined version of him didn't fit what either Maeve or Sybil was saying.

"When did you meet Lucien? I've not seen or heard from him since he left our father's house, over two years ago." Sybil twisted her key with each word.

Even as Esme tried to make sense of the strange truths Maeve was telling them, she struggled more to understand the truths of Sybil, her best friend and the girl she thought she knew so well.

Perhaps you never knew her at all.

"I met your brother not long after he arrived in Severon—around two years ago, in fact. He brought me through a door between my world and this one. He told me he had a sister, and she had a key like his, but I had no idea how to find you. When he disappeared, I put a small spell on the newest batch of Absinthe Underground posters, something for luring and tracking, hoping they'd somehow bring you to me. Or bring him back."

"Where's Lucien?" Sybil paled. "He's not here with you?"

Maeve sipped at her absinthe. "I've not seen him for weeks. I needed some gems from Fae, and your brother was helping me retrieve them—"

"You mean *steal* them?" Sybil blew out a long breath. "He was helping you steal gems from Fae?"

This was simply too much. Too many impossible things all at once. Esme turned to Sybil. "Why is your brother stealing things for a green faerie in another world? How does a *scholar* end up doing that?"

Sybil swallowed hard, as if she were pushing some truths down and sorting through others. "Lucien was always a scholar, that's true, but, as Maeve says, he was also a bit of an adventurer. He'd told me he was coming to Severon—we grew up in the country, many hours' ride from here—to learn more about magical items, but I had no idea his key would open doors between worlds. . . ." She looked around the dressing room like her brother might be lurking somewhere within it.

Why had Sybil never said more about Lucien? What was he doing opening doors between worlds with a key like Sybil's? What did it mean that Sybil had a key too? And how did all that connect to them? Esme's thoughts struggled to keep up as the absinthe made small starbursts appear at the edges of her vision.

"Lucien was indeed stealing things for me," Maeve cut in. "The jewels from Fae are very, very important. They let us make absinthe—"

"How?" Esme said, another sip of the drink already in her throat.

"We crush the jewels," Maeve said, "and then brew and distill a liquor from the dust. The magic in them is what gives those who drink it such a beautiful, ethereal experience. They're drinking a little magic and a part of Fae. I imagine you're feeling a bit of that now."

"Yes. . . ." A vision of stars whirling overhead and of herself walking through moss-carpeted moonlit forests filled Esme's mind. For one very clear moment, she felt utterly, entirely transported.

"Where's my brother?" Sybil demanded, fixing a glare on Maeve. Her knuckles were white around her key necklace.

Maeve shrugged. "I don't know. He went into Fae several weeks ago, and I haven't seen him since."

Sybil narrowed her eyes. "Is that why you need us then? To go find him?"

"Don't be silly. He's a grown man with a key of his own. He can find his way home if he chooses. What I need from you is to do the job he couldn't. I need you to go into Fae and steal more magical jewels for me."

Oh no. No. They couldn't go into Fae. Esme shut her eyes, holding them closed, as if that would make all this go away.

"Why? So you can make more absinthe?" Sybil spat out impatiently. "Is that all you care about?"

Esme opened her eyes, looking over at her friend. Sybil perched on the couch, her back straight, her shoulders rigid. She looked seconds away from leaping up and shaking Maeve.

"Of course not," Maeve said. "I make the absinthe out of the jewels, yes, but that's not why I need you to steal this particular set."

Here Maeve's voice got very serious. She cast a look toward the dressing room door, and her shoulders slumped. In that moment, she didn't look to Esme like her sophisticated self. She looked more like a scared kitten cowering in an alleyway. "This is very hard for me to say because of an enchantment, but there's one more secret I have to tell you. . . ."

"What is it?" Esme asked, leaning in closer. Something about Maeve's changed posture kicked at Esme's heart. Empathy pulled at her, as it always did when she saw another living creature suffering.

Maeve let out a long breath. "Well . . . the truth is . . . these particular jewels would help me go home."

"Why?" Sybil asked, gesturing at the lavish dressing room. "Why would you want to leave our world when you have all this?"

Maeve sniffed. "When I first came to your world I was curious, but Fae is so lovely . . . and this place? It's a pale shadow. The longer I've stayed, the more I've realized what I miss most about my home. . . ."

"Are you being held against your will?" Esme interrupted in a conspiratorial whisper. The villain of her favorite serial novel floated into her mind, and the absinthe in her blood sent all sorts of awful images whirling through her imagination. If stories about the Fae were to be believed, then Maeve couldn't lie. But who could possibly be holding her here?

Sybil stared at Esme with wide eyes. "*What* are you talking about?"

"Just that if she can't go home, maybe someone is keeping her here? Like in the stories." Why wasn't Sybil understanding this? She should probably drink some more of her absinthe, which was suddenly making everything so clear to Esme.

Sybil scoffed. "This *isn't* a story. Focus, Esme. This is real life!"

"Twenty minutes ago, I wouldn't have believed any of this was real," Esme shot back. "We have to help her!"

Maeve reached over and took Esme's hand in her own. "You can help me, lovelies. Truly. I—I can't say much more about it, though I want to tell you everything. What you need to know is I can't go back into Fae myself to get more jewels or look for Lucien, not unless you do this job for me." One tear ran down her cheek, and Maeve wiped it away.

That tear convinced Esme. Poor trapped Maeve! Esme wouldn't leave a kitten in such a terrible spot. "And that's why you need us? To help you get the jewels so you're free?"

"Exactly," Maeve said, another tear rolling down her cheek. She released Esme's hand to wipe it away. "But it's not just any jewels I need. There's one set of gems—the crown jewels of Queen Mab, the leader of the Moonshadow Court—that are rumored to be more powerful than all others combined. Those are the ones I need."

Esme caught Sybil's eye. Sybil raised one eyebrow, and Esme shrugged. Should they do it? Could they even? She wasn't sure, but she wanted to help Maeve.

"If we do this," Sybil said, "what will you give us?"

"More money than you can imagine. You can have all these clothes, all my wealth, anything you want. I promise you, if you bring me Queen Mab's crown jewels, you'll have enough money to never have to work again, and you'll be free to do whatever you like."

Enough money to never have to work again! Free to do whatever they liked! Esme's mind spun with the possibilities, and she held her glass in trembling fingers. It was so much to accept and think about all at once. She took another sip of absinthe, feeling almost as if she'd stumbled into a dream.

"Let us think about it?" Esme asked. "Can we give you our answer tomorrow, when we're clearheaded?"

Maeve refilled her own glass. "Absolutely. Tonight you should drink, dance, enjoy the club and the gifts of Fae. But let me know by tomorrow, or I'll have to find new thieves. We only have two days to get this done. I need Queen Mab's jewels by midnight on the Spring Equinox."

"Why? What's so important about the Spring Equinox?" Sybil asked a breath before Esme could voice the same question.

Maeve stood and considered her reflection in the mirror, as if they were talking about ordinary things, like the weather, not outrageous things like breaking into a Fae queen's palace. "The Spring Equinox is the only time of the year the jewels can brought out of the vault in Queen Mab's bedroom. The lock is tied to both the position of the moon on that day and something magical that unlocks it."

Esme spoke up. "What unlocks the vault?"

Safes and vaults were a bit like clocks—full of gears and levers and things that had to work together. Esme read an article just last month about safecracking, and, despite her general dislike of stealing things (current conversations and considerations about stealing a queen's jewels aside), her fingers itched to try it out.

Maeve waved a hand. "We'll discuss all the details once you've decided to work for me." She smiled at them. Gone was any hint of the fearful woman trapped in this world or the terrifying Fae beneath her glamour. Maeve once again looked like the elegant, fully-in-control beauty she'd been earlier in the evening. "Now, shall we drink to a magical evening?"

Sybil blew out a breath. "Might as well drink to magic," she muttered. "Maybe that's the best answer after all." She downed her glass of absinthe.

Esme lifted her glass. She should be worried about all of it— from Maeve, to the job, to the two-day timeline, and everything in between—but there was already too much Fae magic in the form of absinthe swirling through her body to make her listen to reason. Instead, for once, she let go of her plans, her lists, and the need to control the future. Tonight was about escape and enjoying the Absinthe Underground.

"To magic," Esme said, emptying her glass as well.

PART TWO

*Things That Guard
Against the Night*

Chapter Seven
Two days before the Spring Equinox

Sybil

The clock tower chimed six times, the noise bouncing around Sybil's skull, stirring her awake. Her head throbbed, pounding more with each boom. It was also heavy, fuzzy, and meowing.

Meowing?

No, that wasn't her head. That was the cat settled on *top* of her head. "Mercy," Sybil groaned, as she shifted the cat onto the couch beside Oliver, the gray kitten.

Mercy, an enormous tortoiseshell cat, stretched, yawned, and then went back to sleep. With the cat removed from her head, Sybil could now properly assess the headache last night's drinking had gifted her. Gingerly, she touched her temples, the bridge of her nose, her teeth. Her whole body ached, and her tongue was sticky from the sugary drinks. Her coat was on the floor, and she still wore the green dress Maeve had loaned her.

Maeve.

That's right.

Last night came back to Sybil in snatches. Maeve revealing the impossible truth of herself and asking them to help her. Lucien somehow being caught up in Maeve's story. The job Maeve needed Sybil and Esme to do. Sybil drinking many more glasses of absinthe and other gem-colored liquors. Dancing—so much dancing—with her arm wrapped around Esme's waist. The way Esme's cheek had brushed Sybil's as she whispered something in Sybil's ear. Esme leaning toward Sybil, her lips parted, her eyes bright, the two girls never quite kissing. Both of them whirling away with other partners. The band, the lights, the artists and poets. Maeve saying goodbye and then putting them into a cab so they got home safely. All of it was a kaleidoscope turning in Sybil's aching head.

Mercy, indeed.

Last night Esme had been glorious, radiant, laughing as she let herself have fun. But what would she say today? Would she even remember Maeve's job offer or the almost kisses she and Sybil had shared? Would she be full of questions about Sybil's brother and the key?

What did the key mean anyway? Sybil pulled it out from under her dress and turned it over in her hand. It was an ordinary-enough key—thin through the neck, seven teeth at the bottom. The top of it was ornately shaped, yes, but Sybil had seen keys similar to it before.

What made this one so special? Could it really open doors between worlds? Not for the first time, Sybil wished her mother were still alive so she could ask her all the questions that piled up in her mind, like dishes left unwashed in a sink.

Thinking of her mother, Sybil also remembered the way Maeve's glamour had dropped, revealing her true otherworldly appearance. Had Sybil's mother also looked like that beneath a layer of magic?

Sybil let out a long breath, trying to calm her thoughts. She wasn't going to solve anything without a cup of tea and something to eat. Yes, perhaps that was where she should start. By using a bit of the money they'd earned last night to bring home pastries. Then, when Esme woke up, at least she'd have baked goods to go with her inevitable questions.

Sitting up fully, Sybil shifted her gaze to her friend. Esme lay on her own couch, draped in cats and snoring softly. She still had on the black dress from Maeve's dressing room, but it was rumpled from the night of dancing. Feathers from the dress littered the floor, and Esme's feet were bare. Her hair made a dark pool around her head. One of her arms was flung across her forehead, and she looked peaceful. Usually, Esme was the first one up, and she got the tea going, but today she'd slept through all the clocks' chiming. A fierce warmth flowed through Sybil as she watched Esme sleep, and she hoped Esme would rest long enough for Sybil to take care of her for a change.

Sybil stood—slowly, so her brain didn't break in half—and went to the kitchen sink. After wiping her eyes, Sybil splashed water on her face. The chill of it made her hiss. They were lucky to have plumbing in this apartment, Sybil knew that, but for one very tired, very hungover moment, she longed for the comforts of the house she'd grown up in.

There'd be a private room, a hot bath, someone to help her dress and do her hair, a full breakfast laid out. . . .

But maybe that kind of life could be hers again—on her own terms this time. Maybe if Maeve was willing to pay them as much as she'd promised, Sybil and Esme might live comfortably in a town-home or get the cottage Esme had listed on her life-plan list.

Jean-Francois meowed at Sybil, as if he could read her thoughts. She put some water in a bowl for him.

"We'd bring all of the cats, of course," she whispered, trying to pet his head. He glared at her. "And yes, I'll get you some food this morning from the shops."

Seemingly satisfied at that, Jean-Francois began to lick his paws, ignoring Sybil completely.

As Sybil changed out of her extravagant green dress and into everyday clothing, more visions of the life she might make with Esme once they got Maeve's money filled her head. They'd have coffee every morning, and a cook would make them breakfast. There'd be no empty cupboards and no more long waitressing shifts. Esme could have an entire room for her books, and Sybil would have a studio where the light would come in perfectly as she painted. They'd stop sleeping on couches and actually have beds. Or a bed to share. Sybil wasn't sure how that would work, but they'd figure it out. There'd be enough money to go to the theater and the opera. To dress however they wanted. To travel.

It was wonderful to imagine, but even as the visions came, doubts crept in too. Their entire future depended on the very ridic-ulous fact that they had to somehow steal the crown jewels—which surely would be very heavily guarded—from a Fae queen and bring them into this world.

That didn't even sound possible, much less easy. As Sybil put her shoes and coat on and slipped out the front door, the questions continued. Was she really a good enough thief to help Maeve? Could she really go into Fae and steal something? How had Lucien done it, and where was he? Was it because Sybil was half Fae herself that Maeve had found her? Would Sybil ever have to tell Esme her secret? What would Esme say if she knew? She'd been so shocked by Maeve; what would she say about Sybil?

Sybil headed toward the closest bakery, thinking about the first time she'd ever stolen anything. She had been seven years old and at a spring fair with her mother at the village outside their estate. There was an old man with a wagon full of baubles there. A butterfly brooch, inlaid with colorful fake gems, caught Sybil's eye, reminding her of the stories her mother had told Sybil about her own childhood, growing up as a jeweler's daughter.

Sybil knew her mother would love that butterfly brooch. But she had no pocket money—rich girls could ask for what they wanted, her father believed, so they didn't need to be running around with income of their own—and she wanted that brooch painfully. So, when the old man was busy with another customer, Sybil snatched the brooch from his wagon and slipped it into her pocket.

Her heart galloped like one of her father's horses while she did so, but no one saw. She ran away from the old man's wagon, toward her mother a few stalls down, with a giddy, heady feeling flowing through her.

Sybil's mother clapped her hands in delight when Sybil presented the gift to her, and she never asked where Sybil got it. When she died a few years later, Sybil took the brooch back. It had been stolen, along with all of Sybil's other belongings, except for the key, when she'd arrived in Severon a year ago. Now the key was all she had left of her mother. It was the last tangible piece of her, but if it really did open a door to the world her mother had come from, perhaps it was so much more.

The bell on the bakery door rang as Sybil stepped into the warm room that smelled of yeast and sugar. A line of people waited at the counter, and piles of iced sweet buns, golden croissants, and other pastries sat in baskets behind the counter. Sybil's mouth watered as she looked at them. Esme loved iced buns and would eat at least four if given the chance. And so, Sybil would bring home as many as she could afford. After fishing in her coat, she pulled out the coins Antoine had given them for the cat poster. There was just enough for a few pastries and then some meat scraps for the cats. Not that she couldn't steal the cats some food, but Sybil liked to keep her thieving to items truly worth the risk when possible.

Was stealing Queen Mab's crown jewels truly worth the risk?

Sybil wasn't sure. As she joined the line near the back of the bakery, she recalled how that first brooch theft had sung to her—it was rebellion, risk, and freedom all in one. After her mother's death, her father's house became a strict place—young ladies didn't cry, and they didn't ask questions or run off to play in the woods with their brothers. They read appropriate books, sat up straight at the dinner table, didn't mind being bundled into squeeze-you-too-tight dresses, played the piano gracefully, embroidered delicately, and sketched landscapes and other suitable subjects with a drawing master. They certainly didn't dream of painting wild, colorful pictures full of beautiful women or living as an artist in cities like Severon.

And so amid that rigid, controlling life, Sybil stole things. To feel a bit more alive. To have some rule over her own days. To give gifts to people she loved. After the first brooch theft, she set herself on a training program in stealing. She pinched detective stories from the library and devoured them late into the night. She took her tutor's willow switch and broke it into pieces, which she then threw into the pond. (He always had a new one the next day, though.) When she visited other wealthy families' estates, she took decks of playing cards for Lucien and books and jewelry for herself. When Lucien had been in trouble and sent to his room without supper, Sybil stole food from the kitchen and picked the lock on his door to give it to him.

The bakery line moved forward again, and Sybil took one of the coins from her pocket and made it dance across her knuckles, a trick she'd learned after many hours of practice. A small boy standing in line in front Sybil watched the coin, wide-eyed. Sybil winked at him and then palmed the coin quickly, so it looked like it disappeared from her hand entirely. He made an excited noise, and his mother—a proper-looking woman in a striped gown—turned to frown at Sybil, taking in her ragged appearance and wild hair. Sybil glared back until the woman turned around, and then she winked at the little boy again. He beamed at her, reminding her again of her childhood.

As time had passed in her father's house, Sybil's fingers had become quick and precise from all the piano, needlework, and drawing. With practice, she became an ever more accomplished thief. By the time she was sixteen, she'd even stolen a few hearts among the maids and stable boys, but she'd always returned them unscathed because she couldn't be the girl those people wanted. She couldn't let her true self out—not in her father's house at least.

But she was able to do that in Severon. Here she could laugh loudly, stay up late into the night, read whatever dangerous books she wanted, hold Esme's hand on the street, and paint exuberant, bold canvases full of desire, secret hopes, and passion.

And so, if it took stealing things for Maeve to keep her freedom, Sybil wouldn't hesitate. She had to do this job, and perhaps in doing so, she'd both learn more about her own past and secure a future for herself and Esme.

The line at the bakery moved again, taking Sybil to the front. She ordered croissants and iced buns, spending all the money from Antoine. All her lingering doubts evaporated as she headed back home. She *was* a good enough thief to pull off Maeve's job, and now they had to do it, if for no other reason than they didn't have any money left for rent.

Sybil just hoped she could convince Esme to join her in this theft.

Chapter Eight
Two days before the Spring Equinox

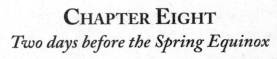

Esme

The front door creaked open, and Esme watched as Sybil crept into their apartment, the buttery morning light softening her features and landing on the white bag Sybil held from the bakery down the street. Esme's stomach rumbled at the sight of it.

"Morning." Esme sat up slowly. Her head felt like it'd been emptied out and then filled with something that churned, like a whirlpool. The room spun for a moment, and she took a deep breath.

"Morning." Sybil gave Esme a crooked grin. "Hope I didn't wake you."

"I've been up since eight. The chimes woke me. You?" Esme held her stomach, willing it to settle. Willing the room to stop spinning. Willing the pounding in her head to cease. She was never, ever drinking again.

"Since six. But it took me a while to get moving."

Sybil sat the bakery bag on the table, took two plates out of the cupboard, filled the kettle with water for tea, and put little pieces of fish and meat in all the cats' dishes. All seven of them rushed over as a yowling mob of fur, each fighting for a place to eat. Sybil separated them, gently pushing Jean-Francois and Mercy away from Oliver the kitten and Estella, a tiny, fluffy black-and-white cat. Pierre, a mottled brown cat, slunk away with his breakfast, while Ash, a gray-spotted cat, lapped at the bowl of water Sybil had put down for him. Jolie, the undisputed queen of the cats in the apartment, meowed impatiently at Sybil as she hurried to fill the bowls with food.

Guilt washed over Esme. "You don't have to do all that," she said, wrenching herself up from the sofa.

Oh. No. Too fast. She should move more slowly.

With careful steps, Esme walked to the cabinet, reaching to retrieve the tea cannister from the cupboard. Sybil put a hand over Esme's, closing the cabinet door firmly.

At the movement, a memory from last night danced through Esme's mind. Sybil's arm had been around her waist, their bodies pressed together, so near that the jutting bones of Esme's hips pressed into Sybil's softer curves. They swayed to the wild music, and when Sybil laughed, Esme felt the breath of it on her jawline.

A cat yowled, pulling Esme back into their kitchen. To Sybil's hand over her own against the cabinet door. "What are you doing?"

"Stopping you."

"I'm just helping with the tea."

Sybil shook her head. Her voice was soft, as if she too were aware of how very close they were standing in the kitchen. "Please, Ez, let me take care of you for once. You go get cleaned up and changed. I've got this."

Inexplicable tears rose in Esme's eyes at the words—probably because she was exhausted and wrung out from the night of dancing—but she nodded. "If you insist. But I'll do the dishes later."

"That I will agree to," Sybil said, as she reached for the tea cannister.

By the time Esme returned from washing up and exchanging last evening's dress for her favorite nightgown and silk robe, Sybil had tea brewed and a pile of pastries on the kitchen table. She'd pushed all of Esme's clock parts to one side, and the ghost of a smile rose on Esme's lips as she remembered when they'd talked about clocks outside the Absinthe Underground.

It had all felt so easy last night—to flirt, laugh, dance, and drink—but today, in the stark morning light, Esme didn't know how to once again bridge the distance between her and Sybil. They had more pressing matters to talk about anyhow.

"Tea?" Sybil held up the teapot.

"Buckets of it, please," Esme said, sinking bonelessly into a chair. She plucked her life-plan list from her coat pocket and put it on the table in front of her. "I think we might have had a tiny bit too much to drink last night."

Sybil's snort was quick, and Esme grinned up at her.

"Just a bit too much," Sybil agreed. "My headache is unrelenting this morning, but I'm trying to push through."

"It was the absinthe, I think. Did you like it?"

Sybil paused, a bite of croissant halfway to her mouth. "Yes. Did you?" Her voice was tense, as if so very much rode upon Esme's answer.

Esme was certain more was going on here, but her brain and body were too tired to poke at the parts and try to figure them out.

Instead, she took her teacup between her hands and blew on it, sending steam curling into her face. "Although I've already vowed to myself to never drink again, I did like it. I couldn't do that every night, but I enjoyed it, yes."

She'd done so much more than enjoyed it, but she couldn't confess it was divine, delightful, even delicious to hold her friend close all night. And so, she just drank more tea.

Sybil's eyes flashed to Esme's, intense and questioning. Heat flared low in Esme's belly. She wanted so very desperately in that moment to just lean over and kiss her friend, then maybe go back to bed with her and nap for the rest of the afternoon. Or not nap. Or kiss her, yes, but after a nap. Or something like that.

"I liked it too," Sybil said, her voice husky. She swallowed hard, picking up her own teacup. She took a long sip. "But . . . we do need to talk about Maeve's job. . . . She said we only have two days to do it, and, well, what do you think?"

Esme took a bite of iced bun, chewing slowly. Her thoughts were still on Sybil's lips, but she forced them back to Maeve's proposal. "What do I think about using a magic key to create a door into Fae and steal a queen's crown jewels? Or what do I think about how the beautiful woman we met last night is actually a Fae creature, in our world somehow? Or what do I think about how she's possibly being held here against her will and only we can save her through this theft? Or what do I think about how she wants us—us! Two ordinary thieves she just met—to do this job for her?"

And what do I think about you having a key to open the door to Fae and a mysterious brother who'd apparently been in Severon this whole time?

Well. Esme didn't know what to think about any of that, so she pushed those questions aside. At least for this morning.

"That about sums it," Sybil said wryly.

"Well, I think it's ridiculous, of course. I would say it was a dream or a hallucination if I hadn't seen Maeve change before my eyes and I didn't have blisters on my toes from running all over the city and dancing all night. I know it's true, but I just don't know if we should do it."

Sybil considered Esme. "You don't want to help Maeve? Or earn enough money for us to have a better life?"

"I like our life," Esme said, unable to keep a sharp note from her words. "And, of course, I want to help Maeve, but I don't understand why we're the ones she needs. How did she know you had the key, and how do we know that key will even work? Can I see it?"

Those weren't exactly the biggest questions Esme had, but they were getting closer at least.

After hesitating for just a moment, Sybil took the key from around her neck and handed it over. Setting down her teacup, Esme held the key in her palm, studying it as she'd done many times before. This time, though, she took the magnifying glass from her coat pocket and really peered at the key. There were no strange markings on it, no secret instructions engraved along its surface.

"How would you even get into Fae with this?" She handed the key back to Sybil. "We don't know where the entrance is."

Sybil slipped the key around her neck again, avoiding Esme's gaze. "We need to ask Maeve about that. Which is why I'm going back to the Absinthe Underground today. I'm going to steal the jewels for her."

"Sybil! You promised me you wouldn't steal anything again," Esme said, her voice brittle, remembering their conversation from last night. "Remember?"

"I promised I wouldn't steal *posters*. Stealing gems from a Fae queen is entirely different. Plus, we could have enough money to live the way we want to, without having to work terrible jobs or worry about rent or where our next meal comes from. Won't you help me, Ez? We could have so much . . ."

Sybil went on, spinning a lovely vision of the house they'd own, the books they'd buy, the places they'd travel, but Esme's mind clung to four of Sybil's words: *Won't you help me?*

From the first night she'd met Sybil, Esme knew she'd do whatever it took to help her friend. But she wasn't sure that extended into working for an actual Faerie and stealing things from another world. The thought of doing such things was so preposterous, Esme almost laughed, but Sybil looked so certain that this was the only way they'd be able to have a better life. How could Esme disagree with that?

She stirred her tea and thought about how they'd first met.

It had been a little over a year ago, on an evening in late February. A storm had blown in the night before, freezing Severon's river and sugaring the roofs with snow. The wind howled off the sea, sending flurries into every corner of the city; the streets and sidewalks were slick with ice. Esme was working a night shift when a girl whose hair hung in tired curtains around her face stumbled into the Rosemary Thistle café. She limped a little, as if her shoes pinched or she weren't used to walking much, and she blew on her gloveless hands as she surveyed the café.

The Rosemary Thistle wasn't fancy, and its owner, Claudine, was from a farm outside Severon. She was a great cook, however, and the café was busy most days, but this ice storm had kept people away. Esme hadn't made more than a few coins in tips, and her thin dress and sweater did little to keep her warm, even inside the café.

"You can sit anywhere you'd like," Esme told the girl, gesturing toward the many empty tables.

The girl cast Esme a grateful look and chose a table closest to the kitchen and far away from the other patrons.

Esme brought her a steaming mug of cider and a hunk of bread and cheese on a board.

A panicked look crept onto the girl's face as Esme sat the food in front of her. "I can't pay. . . ." she said haltingly. "I was robbed last night and needed to get warm for a moment." She pushed back the hair on the left side of her face, revealing a black eye, the bruised skin a dark purple.

"Oh, mercy," Esme said. "Did the ones who robbed you do that? Parts of the Vermilion District are dangerous, even in winter."

The girl shook her head. "They took my bag. This is from where I slipped down some frozen steps."

Esme made a sympathetic noise. "I've done that before myself. Here. Eat. Get warm, then we can see about some ice for that eye."

"But I can't pay you," the girl repeated, placing her hand on Esme's. A bolt of warmth shot right through Esme at that touch, making her feel something like longing and desire all at once. She ignored it immediately, as she always did, and focused on helping this girl. That was familiar territory. She knew how to help.

"First time is always free here," Esme said gruffly.

The girl hesitated for only a moment before gulping down some cider and then devouring the bread.

"My name's Esme. Just let me know if you need anything else."

"What time do you close?"

"Nine o'clock, so you've still got a few hours."

The girl nodded, taking another sip of cider. "If you don't mind then, I have nowhere to be, and I think I'll take my time eating."

Esme nodded and turned away to bring another customer more wine, but she carried with her the feeling of the girl's hand on her arm and the hope that she'd stay for the rest of the night—and maybe return the next day.

As it turned out, by the time Esme circled back to the girl's table, she'd fallen asleep, meal half eaten, with her head on her arms.

Slowly, the café emptied. Claudine went home, leaving Esme to clean up. She let the girl sleep. Finally, when the bells outside chimed nine, Esme nudged the girl.

"Where am I?" the girl said, bolting up abruptly. She looked around the now-empty café, her eyes frantic like she was running from something.

"It's time for me to go home," Esme said gently. "I can pack up your food if you'd like."

"You don't have to do that." The girl grabbed the mug of cider and finished it in one long draught. Then she stuffed the bread and cheese into the pocket of her coat.

"Thank you," she said, pausing as she stood to leave. "It was really nice of you to let me rest here, Esme."

Esme's heart had swelled at the look on the girl's face. It was somehow tragic, hopeful, and laced with regret all at once. Suddenly, the thought of never seeing her again, of letting her disappear into Severon to fall on more ice or get otherwise hurt was unbearable. Who was this girl, and why did she need to sleep in a café? What if she didn't have anywhere to go?

"You can come with me if you'd like," Esme said. "I mean, if you don't have any other plans. Not that I'm assuming you don't have anywhere to go. Because, of course, you could have a house all your own. And I don't know anything about you, not even your name, but still, if you don't have somewhere to go, then you can come stay with me. At my place, I mean. I have an extra sofa. At least for tonight. If you'd like."

Esme finished her disjointed speech a little breathless and unsure if she was making a great mistake.

It's never a mistake to help someone. Esme believed that with every part of herself, even if it got her into trouble sometimes.

The girl stared at Esme for a long fraught moment, as if she were considering all her options and weighing what kind of person Esme was.

"Sybil," she said at last. "My name is Sybil. And yes, I'd love to stay at your place tonight. I don't have anywhere else to go."

"It's decided then." Esme tried to keep a silly, delighted smile off her face. It broke through anyway, and she beamed at the girl—at Sybil. "My full name is Esme Rimbaud, and it's a pleasure to make your acquaintance." Esme curtsied then, in the dramatic way her mother had taught her.

Sybil laughed at the gesture and returned her curtsy. "The pleasure is all mine. I'm Sybil Clarion, aspiring artist and, as you might have guessed, new to Severon."

The two girls locked up the café, laughing, learning more about each other, and walking arm in arm because of the icy streets back to Esme's clock-tower apartment. That first night had passed quickly, and Sybil had just stayed after it.

And now here she was. Sitting in their kitchen, looking at Esme expectantly for an answer.

There was really only one thing Esme could say.

"Yes," Esme said. "Yes, of course, I'll come with you into Fae. Where you walk, I'll be right at your side. Even if it's into a Fae queen's castle."

Sybil let out a squeal of excited happiness and threw her arms around Esme. Esme leaned into the hug, just long enough to feel comforted, and then pulled away. "And now," she said, "let's eat our breakfast, then go talk to Maeve. We've got a lot of work to do in the next two days."

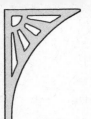

CHAPTER NINE
Two days before the Spring Equinox

Sybil

What had she done to deserve Esme?

Sybil still wasn't sure, and maybe she shouldn't be surprised Esme had agreed to help—Esme always wanted to help—but asking Ez to believe so many impossible things and then to commit a truly dangerous crime—in the Fae realm, no less!—went several steps above and beyond normal best friend duties.

Some part of Sybil wanted to tell Esme she didn't have to go through with it. But Sybil bit back those words. And so, there they were, standing in Maeve's dressing room in the Absinthe Underground, a few hours and many cups of tea after their breakfast. Bright midday sunlight slanted through the windows, casting golden daggers across the floor. Mercifully, Sybil's hangover wasn't as bad as it'd been earlier. Now she could at least turn her head without wincing. The air smelled like Maeve's orange blossom perfume, and lilting violin music played on a phonograph in the corner of the room.

Maeve sat at a dressing table, doing her makeup and looking perfectly ordinary today. None of her red curls were out of place, and her moss-green eyes were lined with a careful hand. Sybil stood behind Maeve, watching her every move in the dressing table mirror, looking for any sign of her Fae self to shine through. But there was nothing, just the lovely, elegant woman Maeve had first presented herself as.

Beside Sybil, Esme had a notebook out and was peppering Maeve with questions. She'd written the questions down before they'd left the apartment, neatly recording each in her tidy script.

Now Sybil glanced over, reading the questions again:

✦ *HOW DOES SYBIL'S KEY OPEN THE DOOR INTO FAE?*
✦ *WHAT—EXACTLY—DO YOU WANT US TO STEAL?*
✦ *HOW DO WE OPEN THE QUEEN'S VAULT?*
✦ *HOW ARE WE NOT GETTING CAUGHT ONCE WE'RE THERE?*

And the list went on from there. Sybil was relieved that nowhere on the list was the question she hoped Esme would never ask: Why does Sybil have a key that opens a door into Fae in the first place? That question carried with it so many others—most of which Sybil wasn't ready or able to answer.

Pushing through her anxieties, Sybil dragged her attention back to Maeve's explanation of what she needed them to steal.

"The main things I need you to take," Maeve said, "are Queen Mab's crown jewels—a magnificent jeweled tiara, two chokers, several ropes of pearls, earrings, bracelets, and thirteen rings—which are going to be in her bedroom, in a vault behind a painting above her fireplace."

"Is that all?" Sybil asked. "Just an enormous pile of jewels? Won't someone notice us carrying them out? Or that they're gone?"

"Not if you secure the three other things you'll need before you go to Fae."

"Three other things?" Esme said, shooting Sybil a worried look. "That wasn't what you told us originally."

Maeve shrugged and resumed powdering her face. "I'm telling you now: you'll need these small things in order to steal the larger one."

"What are they?" Sybil asked. "And how will they help us?"

Maeve glanced over at Sybil conspiratorially. "First, you'll need a book from Lucien's house so you know the words to open the door into Fae. I'd retrieve it for you, but the place is locked up tight, believe me." Here Maeve held up her left hand and took off her glove. A nasty bite mark, blue and black around the scabbed edges, stood out on it.

"What creature did that to you?" Bile rose in Sybil's throat. She hated the sight of blood. "We signed up to steal things, not fight monsters."

Maeve waved her injured hand casually. "It was one of Lucien's Hob-Locks. Hungry for blood, I suppose, since your brother has been gone. You share Lucien's blood, though, so you might be fine. Once you get into the house, Lucien's journal is on his desk, in the library."

"How do you know it's there if you couldn't get into the house?" Esme asked. "What if he took it with him?"

Sybil heard a note of hope in her friend's voice. Like this entire enterprise might hang on whether Lucien's journal was there or not. Sybil had her doubts about that. Surely, Maeve wouldn't let a little thing like a journal get in the way of her plans.

"He didn't," Maeve replied. "I peeked through the study window and saw it on his desk. I just can't get through his wards, but I think you two will do fine. Just look out for the traps in the house."

"Traps?" Esme put her pen down forcefully. Sybil shot her what she hoped was a reassuring smile.

Maeve painted her lips a deep raspberry color. "Oh yes, there are lots of magical snares in Lucien's house, but you'll figure them out."

Sybil wasn't so sure about that. Lucien had been making traps since they were children, and they'd grown increasingly more complex over the years. But how had he learned about making magical ones? Was her brother a magician? Was that how he'd opened a door between the worlds?

Calling Lucien a magician seemed silly, but what else could he be? He had Hob-Locks—whatever those were. He retrieved magical items in another realm, and he knew words for opening doors into that realm. All that sounded quite thoroughly magical. She longed to talk to him again, to hear about what he'd been up to for the past few years, and to demand explanations for why he had abandoned her in their father's house.

But first, of course, she had to find him.

Beside Sybil, Esme sighed and picked up her pen again. She wrote *Magical Traps?* on the page beneath her other questions.

"Right," Sybil said, fidgeting with her key. "So, first we steal a notebook from Lucien's library. What's next?"

"After you have Lucien's journal," Maeve said, finishing applying her lipstick and standing, "you'll need a magical bag, which will allow you to transport the crown jewels out of Fae undetected."

"How does that work?" Esme asked at the same time Sybil said, "What does this bag look like? Where will we get it?"

Maeve picked up a hat and pinned it onto her curls with a hatpin. "It's a small blue leather bag, embroidered with some flowers and birds. Quite unremarkable actually."

Something about the description rang a bell in Sybil's memory. She'd seen a bag like that recently, but where?

"It's got a charm on it," Maeve continued, "that hides magical items while you're in Fae. If anyone in Fae stops you, they'll just see a handful of pebbles in the bag. Collectors have been looking for it for centuries, ever since a story about it came out of Fae and made its way to this world. Lucien found it on a recent trip and mistakenly traded it for another item to a collector."

Sybil thought back to the night before, when she'd been selling the posters and looking over all the items on Antoine's shelves. "It's at Antoine's, isn't it?"

"Clever girl," Maeve said, nodding. "I would've stolen it myself, and was planning on doing so last night, but now, I'll have you take the bag instead."

"Can't we just buy it from Antoine?" Esme asked.

"Certainly not. If he knows we want it, he'll start to ask questions. If he were to discover its value, he'd never part with it."

"Even if it only works in Fae?" Esme pressed. "What use is it to him? Can't you just say you're smitten with the bag's design and you want it?"

Maeve shook her head. "Antoine is so desperate for anything that's collectible, he'd never let me have it, no matter how much money I offered."

"Won't the bag be much too small?" Sybil asked. The little bag in Antoine's study would barely hold one bracelet, much less the entire collection of crown jewels. "Do you really need all the jewels?"

Maeve frowned at Sybil, as if she were a teacher and Sybil were a student who wasn't paying attention. "Of course I need all the jewels! That's part of our deal. Once you open the vault in Queen Mab's room, grab the jewels, stuff them into the bag—they'll fit, trust me—and open another door back to this world. It should really be simple enough. I don't know why you're making such a fuss."

"Why we're making a fuss?" Esme repeated, then looked up from her notebook. "Won't the jewels be guarded? What if we get caught? If everyone in Fae looks like you—"

Sybil jumped in, knowing what she was really asking. "If everyone looks like your un-glamoured self—"

"My true self." Maeve sniffed.

Sybil nodded. "Your true self, yes. And we look like our very human selves, how will we not be caught immediately? Are there any other mortals in the Fae realm?"

Maeve trilled a laugh. "Of course there are mortals in Fae, ridiculous girl. There always have been. You're not the only mortal with a key between our worlds, and many centuries ago, there used to be thousands of doors between our worlds. The High Fae even used to send their children on grand tours in your world so they could enjoy themselves here. Why do you think there are so many half Fae and changeling children in your world?"

At that, Sybil bit hard on her tongue, holding back the question that had almost popped out about her own mother.

Maeve continued, oblivious. "Of course, there was eventually strife between our people and yours, and it was agreed between the human magicians and the High Fae that the doors would be closed. Only a few magician families were given keys—and those got passed down through the centuries. Any mortals in Fae now have either been there for generations, or they've stumbled through a forgotten door left unlocked. They are the companions of some Fae, the ensorcelled playthings of others, the adopted children of many—but you are correct that you two will draw attention, especially if you're in the palace. Which is why you must be quick, and which brings us to the third item you must steal before going into Fae. You need something to open the queen's vault. If Queen Mab's personal guards—the Nightshades, or just the Night as everyone else calls them—find you trying to steal the crown jewels, they'll throw you in the dungeon or kill you on the spot."

Esme's note-taking stopped abruptly.

"Kill us on the spot?" Dread sat like a cannon ball in Sybil's stomach. She'd known this job would be dangerous, but not deadly. Rather than meeting Esme's eye, Sybil asked the only logical question that she could form: "What could we possibly steal in our world that will open a queen's vault in Fae?"

Maeve picked up a perfume bottle and sprayed herself with it. More clouds of orange blossom scent filled the air. It was almost cloying, and Sybil yearned to open a window. "As I mentioned earlier, the queen's vault is locked in two ways—it's tied to the time of the year and can only be opened on the evening of the Spring Equinox, and it is secured with a scent lock."

"What's a scent lock?" Sybil asked.

"Exactly what it sounds like—only a rare perfume will open the vault."

Esme piped up a bit. "Fascinating! It's a mechanical sort of magic. Does this mean if we get the perfume, we can open the vault, as if we were Queen Mab herself?"

"Correct," Maeve said. "No one has been able to do it before now, however, because the perfume you need is an enchanted scent made from fruit grown under the moonlight in Queen Mab's orchards during the winter months, when no fruit should grow. It contains the essence of shadows and impossible things within it, and exactly two drops of it—and only it—will unlock the vault. Queen Mab wears a small bottle of the perfume around her neck at all times—"

"How in the world are we supposed to get it then?" Sybil burst out. "Steal it from the queen?" She was all for adventures and danger, but this sounded too risky even for her. Surely, the queen would be guarded. It was one thing to steal her jewels from a vault, another entirely to steal something from around the queen's neck.

"Ahh, there's the wonderful thing," Maeve said. "I believed for a very long time that Queen Mab had the only bottle of this perfume in both realms. But one of the queen's perfumiers went missing centuries ago. It was rumored he'd escaped to your world with his collection of scents, including one that unlocks the vault."

Understanding crashed over Sybil. "You've seen it then? Another bottle of Queen Mab's perfume?"

Maeve beamed at her. "Precisely! Lucien took me to the Severon Museum last month, and there's a bottle of it on display in one of their upper rooms—in the decorative arts galleries, near the clocks and starlight paintings. Those humans don't even know what they have. It's labeled incorrectly, but I'd know it anywhere. You're looking for a tiny midnight-blue perfume bottle inlaid with stars, and it has a crescent-moon-shaped stopper. There's a small bit of liquid inside it still, which should be enough for our purposes."

Esme had gone very pale. "You want us to break into the Severon Museum?"

Sybil wanted to say something reassuring, like surely stealing from the museum couldn't be harder than taking the crown jewels from Queen Mab, but she suspected that wouldn't sit well with Esme.

"As soon as possible." Maeve moved toward the door. "Do you have any other questions? I have a meeting before the club opens and must be going."

Sybil glanced down at the list of questions Esme had written out. Only one remained. "How are we not getting caught once we have the jewels?"

Maeve waved a hand. "You're clever enough to figure that out. I have complete trust in you. I've left Lucien's address on my dressing table. Do try to hurry with all this. Remember, if you don't get the jewels back to me in the next two days, I can't return home and you don't get paid."

Sybil started to reply to that, but Maeve hurried out of the room, leaving Sybil with the barest outlines of a plan and much less confidence in herself than Maeve seemed to harbor.

CHAPTER TEN

Two days before the Spring Equinox

Esme

"Y ou're telling me Lucien—your brother—lives here?"

They stood outside a three-story house that dominated a corner in the Lapis District. It was within walking distance of the Absinthe Underground, and they'd come right over after talking to Maeve. Esme's stomach flipped, and she tried not to gawk at the enormous mansion.

How could Sybil's brother afford such a place? What sort of life had Sybil run away from? What sort of traps might be waiting inside a place this large?

Esme nibbled on one of her fingernails and took in the details of Lucien's home. Carved flourishes and flowers framed the doorway. Even the door itself was ornate, with its brass flowers and a unique arched shape. Gold leaf decorated parts of the door, and the facade of the house was covered in the palest of green marble, like the entry hallway at the Absinthe Underground.

"Subtle," Sybil said, as she walked up the front steps.

Esme goggled at Sybil. "You think this is *subtle?*"

"For Lucien." Sybil shrugged. "I suppose that's the Hob-Lock?"

She pointed to a small scowling face made of bronze, placed above the doorknob. It looked like something out of a scary story— half demon and half elf—with rows of pointed teeth.

Esme shuddered at the nightmare creature, and she had no idea what to say about Lucien's extravagant house. Severon was a city where great wealth and crushing poverty lived side by side. How could someone spend so much money on a house, while children starved in the streets? That certainly didn't fit into the vision of Sybil's life Esme had imagined. But then, she was learning her friend had all sorts of secrets she would've never guessed.

Sybil studied the Hob-Lock. "Maybe we do this?" In the space between blinks, Sybil jammed her palm onto one of the Hob-Locks' teeth. Its eyes flew open, and it crunched its metal jaws down with a flourish, causing Sybil to cry out.

"Welcome home, Master," the Hob-Lock said in an unctuous voice. "Your blood is delicious as always."

Esme wrenched the Hob's mouth open and yanked Sybil's hand out of it. As she did so, the front door to Lucien's house swung open.

Sybil clutched her palm, which had a several teeth marks in it and dripped blood. She looked at the blood, her face paling. "We're in."

"At what cost?" Esme grumbled, handing Sybil a handkerchief to wrap her hand in.

"Worth it?" Sybil said.

"We'll see about that."

Esme closed the front door, and they stepped into a shadowy foyer. The air was musty, as if the windows hadn't been opened in weeks. Sybil banged into a table. Something toppled to the floor and shattered.

Esme pulled a candle stub and matchbook from her pocket. She struck a match, and the glow of flame illuminated her and Sybil's faces.

"Can't we just open a curtain?"

Esme shook her head. "And risk someone seeing us in here? Aren't you the experienced thief?"

Sybil snorted at that. "Let's hope so. Shall we go forward?"

"Careful. We don't know what else is waiting inside this house."

"You're just saying that because the door tried to eat me." Sybil grabbed a large black umbrella from the bronze bucket by the door and brandished it like a sword with her good hand. "Don't worry, I'm armed!"

Esme laughed and held the candle up, moving it slowly through the air. Gilded mirrors and paintings hung along the walls, wreathed in shadows. An ornate staircase curved upward in front of them, and dark rooms stretched along the first floor. Hopefully, Lucien's library was around here somewhere.

Esme's light fell on a stack of books resting on an entryway table. She picked up the closest one—*Eckleton's Guide to Fae for Travelers*. Well, that was certainly convenient. There wasn't enough light to read by here, but she intended to pore over it later. She slipped the book into her coat pocket. The other books piled on the table were also about Fae—some of them children's stories, others academic treatises—and they reminded Esme of the piles of library books she kept by the door of their apartment.

A pair of muddy boots lay at the bottom of the staircase, resting sloppily, as if they'd just been kicked off someone's feet. A man's plaid jacket was draped over a painter's ladder that looked very out of place, leaning against the banister in this fancy home. Sybil's hand lingered on the jacket in a way that made Esme feel very, very lonely. Over the past day, Sybil suddenly had a real family. One she might see again or go back to. One she might leave Esme for.

"Should we check upstairs first?" Esme asked, swallowing her worries, as Sybil moved toward one of the doorways on the right. Esme tried to keep her voice steady, though hot tears had risen in her eyes at the thought of family and her lack of anyone in the world besides Sybil.

"I'd wager the library is down there," Sybil said, pointing her umbrella toward the back of the house, down a long wide hallway covered in green wallpaper. She tapped the umbrella against the floor in a deliberate pattern, like someone looking for traps. With each tap, she edged a careful step forward.

"How do you know?" Esme's candle stub illuminated a vines-and-blossoms pattern laid out in marble pieces on the floor.

Sybil moved forward, still tapping the floor. She stepped on a purple flower and then a red one. "I just do. Follow—"

Suddenly, a crash rang out, cutting off the rest of Sybil's sentence. In one quick motion, the hallway floor tumbled away, opening into a yawning dark abyss. Esme dropped her candle in a porcelain dish on a nearby table and reached for Sybil. At the same moment, Sybil danced backward, so the two of them landed in a heap of skirts and elbows a few feet from the edge. They lay there for a moment, catching their breath.

"Well, we found one of the magical traps," Sybil said, offering a sideways smile as she hauled herself to her feet.

Esme swore as she stood up. "This house is going to be the death of us." She picked up the candle off the table and walked to the edge of the hole.

"Only if we're not careful," Sybil said cheerfully, joining her.

Together, they peered down into the abyss. It stretched from one side of the hallway to the other and looked to be at least ten feet long. There was no way around it, and the door they'd been trying to reach was on the other side. The darkness seemed to go on forever, and a salt-smelling breeze blew up from it, which was ludicrous since Lucien's house was many blocks away from Severon's coastline. But then it was also absurd that a chasm had opened in the middle of a hallway.

Leaden fear settled into Esme's bones. If Sybil had been one step farther down the hall, or if she hadn't been tapping the floor, she'd be gone, falling into that hole for who knows how long. Esme could've lost her in the space between two blinks. She took a shuddering breath,

"Remember, Maeve said this was the easy part of the job," Sybil said bracingly, as she retrieved her discarded umbrella. "I'm sure we'll face much worse in Fae."

Esme tried to give a confident laugh, but it came out as more of a groan. "If getting the journal from Lucien's library is the easy part of this entire job, according to Maeve, what else is waiting for us?"

"Adventure."

"Oh good, adventure." Esme muttered weakly. "My favorite. How are we going to get across?"

Sybil glanced over her shoulder, toward the entryway. A satisfied noise left her lips. "Of course." She hurried back to the painter's ladder and hauled it forward. "Lucien had a bridge like this to his treehouse when we were kids. We can get across this, no problem."

Lucien had a treehouse in childhood? That little glimpse of Sybil's life before Esme met her only raised more questions, but Esme didn't ask them, too scared perhaps of what she might learn. Instead she focused on the pseudobridge Sybil was proposing. Esme's clockmaker brain enjoyed a good bridge, and she'd often spent hours wandering Severon, admiring bridges and the complicated ways they were built to support so much weight. But this ladder was no sturdy bridge.

Warily, Esme watched as Sybil lowered the ladder across the gaping hole in the hallway floor. To call it a *bridge* would be generous. It was more like a child's attempt at placing a twig across a rushing river. Unsteady, dangerous, and assuredly not anywhere Esme wanted to be.

"Want to go first?" Sybil asked.

"Absolutely not. What happens if we fall into the hole? Where does it even go?" There was no way that hole led to the cellar, because if it did, surely they'd see the bottom of it. Perhaps, they'd just fall into darkness forever, never reaching the bottom of anything.

"It's only a few feet to the other side. Follow me." Sybil put her feet on either side of the ladder and started shuffling forward, her hands out like a tightrope walker, as she kept the ladder balanced. She couldn't reach the walls of the hallway on either side, but her steps didn't waver, even as another gust of wind swirled up from the abyss.

"Are you sure you need me to come with you?" Esme called, the candle flame in her hand flickered.

"Of course I need you!" Sybil hollered, not looking back. "I'll get to the other side and then hold the ladder steady!"

Sybil reached the other side quickly, hopped onto the floor with a bit of a flourish, and then kneeled to hold the ladder for Esme. "Keep your eyes on me!" she called. "Don't look down!"

Don't look down.

Wildly easier said than done. Still holding her candle stub, Esme exhaled, summoning all her courage. She took one wobbling step, putting her right foot on the ladder's right side. Then she slid her other foot on the ladder's left side. A cool wind blew up from the depths of the hole, extinguishing her candle flame. Darkness filled the hallway, and Esme could barely see Sybil on the other side.

"I don't think I can do it!" Esme shouted, panic clawing up her throat.

Nowhere on her life plan was *falling into a hole and facing certain death* listed. This was a terrible idea. She had to go back. They had to get out of here.

"Of course you can do it! You can do anything. Look at me."

"I can't see you!"

"Just don't look down! That's the important thing."

Esme took another long steadying breath. It was just one step in front of the other. She could do this. She would.

With fear making ribbons of her guts, Esme slid her feet forward, not gracefully, but getting there. She'd not really been afraid of heights until she was met with the possibility of endless darkness.

One step.

Then the next.

Another.

One more.

After what seemed like a lifetime, scuffling her feet the barest bit forward continuously, Esme reached the other side.

"I've got you." Sybil took both Esme's hands and guided her to the stretch of hallway floor beyond the chasm. "You did so good, Ez."

Esme collapsed on the solid ground, tears in her eyes at Sybil's touch and her gentle words. Esme's hands shook with the aftermath of adrenaline and fear. But she'd done it. It was only one very small obstacle crossed, but it was something.

Releasing Sybil's hand, Esme stood, steading herself against the wall. "I must insist we look for a back door or go out a window when we leave," she said, putting more lightness in her voice than she felt. There was no way she was crossing that void again.

Using a match from the small box Esme handed her, Sybil relit the candle stub. She shot Esme a half smile, one that told Esme she was far more stressed than she was letting on. "Not a problem at all."

A howl of wind came up from the hole in the floor, like the trap was angry they'd passed it, and Esme moved closer to Sybil, clinging to her arm. Holding on to each other, they stepped forward. With each step, Sybil tapped the floor with her umbrella, checking for traps. No more holes opened in the floor, and no flames shot from the ceiling. Esme slumped against the wall in relief when they reached the last door at the end of the hallway. She'd never been on a longer walk than the one from Lucien's front door.

Sybil rattled the doorknob. "Locked." She pulled her thief's tools from her coat pocket and inserted a slim piece of metal into the keyhole. She wriggled it around, but there was no satisfying click. "It feels like the lock is fighting me."

"How?"

"Like something in there is pushing my tool out."

Esme looked for another Hob-Lock, but there were no strange metal faces by the door.

Sybil took a few steps back and then ran at the door, slamming against it with her shoulder. Esme's body clenched as Sybil made impact. But the door remained closed, and Sybil thudded backward with a groan, landing on her backside.

"What are you doing? Do you want to break your shoulder? You're bleeding already!" Esme glanced down at the hand the Hob-Lock had bitten. Blood soaked through the handkerchief wrapped around it.

"Ahh! That's the answer, of course," Sybil said.

Quickly, she smeared some of her still-dripping blood across the keyhole to the library. There was a soft click, and the blood soaked into the metal, almost as if the lock were hungry for it.

Sybil rewrapped her hand, keeping her eyes averted from the blood. "Absolutely disgusting," she muttered.

"Let's agree that after this room, you don't feed more of yourself to this house."

"Let's just get Lucien's journal and get out of here," Sybil said, opening the door to the library. "How hard can that be?"

Esme wasn't sure she wanted to know.

A deep silence settled over them as their feet sunk into the library's rich carpet. The air smelled of paper, dust, and a faint woodsy scent. One curtain was open, and the afternoon light shone on a fireplace, a pair of armchairs, and a sofa. A small desk sat to Esme's left, and tall shelves ringed the room. A balcony cut the shelves in half. A portrait hung above the mantel, covered by a curtain. The light also glinted off dozens of small bronze frogs sitting on every surface.

"Does your brother collect paperweights?" Esme ran a finger over one of the frogs.

"Maybe? I haven't seen him in years. He steals things in Fae, so maybe his other hobbies include a fondness for paperweights. I have no idea, really." Still holding the umbrella and tapping the floor, Sybil walked over to the desk. She moved cautiously, but nothing jumped out at her. Esme exhaled in relief as Sybil stopped in front of the desk. Maybe this would be easy after all.

"I think this is it!" Sybil said, pointing to a small journal covered in brown leather. "Should I just pick it up?"

"What if there are more traps?"

"We have to try it. . . ." Gingerly, Sybil nudged the journal with her umbrella. Nothing happened. She rested a hand on the top of the journal. Still nothing happened. "See, it's fine," she said, as she lifted the journal from the desk.

The minute the journal left the surface of the desk, a tremendous croaking sound filled the library.

Croaking?

Esme whirled around as the noise grew louder. It was the beat of a hundred drums. It was a room full of clocks all chiming midnight in tandem. It was a swamp full of bullfrogs singing a deep-throated song.

It was terrifying.

The sound grew louder as all the bronze frogs—who were decidedly *not* paperweights—came to life at once, moving on creaking metal legs toward Esme and Sybil. The frogs leaped off bookshelves, chairs, tables, and the fireplace mantel. They rained down from the balcony, a bronze squall, knocking vases over and tearing away the curtains that covered the portrait. Everywhere the frogs touched, they left singeing holes, as if they were magma, burning away whatever was in their path. Smoke rose, filling the library.

Esme clambered onto Lucien's desk, offering Sybil a hand up after her. The frogs left a trail of destruction in their wake, and their beady little eyes focused on Esme and Sybil.

Esme looked around frantically as the mass of bronze frogs surged closer. "What are we going to do? Can we break a window?"

No, that wouldn't work. The frogs surrounded them. There was no way Esme and Sybil could run across the library to the windows, much less get one open quickly enough to escape.

Sybil's eyes were saucers. "It's one of Lucien's traps," she said, her voice wild. "We have to figure out how to best it!"

The bronze frogs clambered up the sides of the desk, like a wave chasing them up the beach. One of them landed heavily on Esme's shoe. The heat of its body ate through the leather, scalding her toes within. She screamed and kicked it away, but more frogs kept coming. Sybil slashed at the frogs with her umbrella, knocking some to the floor.

This was it. They were going to die here, caught under a swell of burning mechanical amphibians, and Esme's cats would have no one to feed them. She vowed then and there to always leave a window open when she left the house so the cats could go down the fire escape if she didn't come home.

"I don't want to die here!" she yelled, kicking away at more frogs. "Think, Sybil! Did your brother ever do magic for you or mention some word that might stop magic?"

That was how it happened in the faerie stories, at least. These magical frogs weren't clocks, but something had to be making them work, and if that was the case, then something could also stop them.

"There might be something in his journal!" Sybil said, tossing Esme the umbrella. As Sybil flipped through the pages, Esme stabbed at the frogs with the umbrella. Two of them landed on it, causing it to ignite.

"Any luck?" Esme shouted, discarding the flaming umbrella.

"That's it! Of course." Sybil stopped flipping through the journal. "I think I've got it!"

"I'm begging you, use it then! Stop these frogs!"

Sybil shot Esme a quick sheepish smile, and then she bellowed, "Éclairer!"

That *was* it.

All at once the bronze frogs jerked, and then every one of them transformed. Each suddenly, quietly, became a golden leaf, like the ones trees shed in autumn. All the fire and smoke their molten progression had left also cleared, and the destruction they caused appeared to be no more than a few books knocked off a shelf and a few vases tipped over. Nothing in the library was burned, and even Esme's shoe went back to normal.

Esme's jaw dropped at the speed of the transformation. She kicked at the closest pile of leaves. They fluttered to the floor, harmless. She hopped off the desk, her feet crunching more leaves.

A long silence stretched between Esme and Sybil.

"At least we got Lucien's journal," Esme finally offered because Sybil seemed too stunned to do anything.

"I told you this would be easy," Sybil said, grinning weakly. She gathered handfuls of the leaves, tucking them into her pockets and the pages of Lucien's journal. Maybe as a souvenir? Or for some other reason? Esme didn't ask what Sybil was doing because she wasn't sure she wanted to know.

"Want to go home?" Sybil asked.

Esme twisted her hair—which had come down from its bun in all the excitement—back up and stabbed a pencil through it. "More than anything. I'm at my limit of stealing and certain death for the day."

She was going to take a nap, then spend the rest of the day in her pajamas, petting her cats and reading the book about Fae she'd taken from Lucien's hallway.

As they were leaving the leaf-strewn library, Esme looked up, her eyes catching on the painting above the fireplace. Thanks to the bronze frogs, the curtain that had covered it was on the floor, and the image beneath stood out. Esme drew in a breath sharply, making Sybil turn around with a concerned look on her face.

"What is it, Ez? Are you hurt?"

Esme couldn't look away from the portrait. In it a young girl who had Sybil's wild curly hair and freckles was painted next to an older boy with sandy-blonde hair. Behind them stood a handsome, tall, dark-haired white man with a trim beard. In the center of the painting was a beautiful woman with forest-green eyes like Sybil's and white-blonde hair. She wore a choker of opals and held herself like a queen. Everyone in the family was dressed in expensive clothing, and the furniture they sat on looked like it should be in a museum. There was an ease between them, like all of them were tremendously happy to be together and they'd all been caught laughing over some shared secret only they knew.

"Is that your family?" Esme asked, in a strangled voice.

She glanced over at Sybil, who nodded even as her eyes brimmed with tears. Sybil held a hand over her key necklace, her voice soft. "It's from my father's estate. I didn't know Lucien had it. I haven't seen it in years."

Her father's estate? Esme wanted to ask so many questions, but anguish sat heavy on Sybil's features as she stared at the woman in the center of the painting. Esme knew what it meant to lose a mother, and even as negligent as hers had been, she would've given anything to see a photo or a painting of her again.

"Let's go," she said gently, taking Sybil's arm.

Sybil followed her out of the library, neither of them saying anything else.

✦

Esme couldn't stop thinking about the portrait of Lucien, Sybil, and their parents that hung above the fireplace in Lucien's library. She was trying to read from the book she'd taken while Sybil puzzled over Lucien's diary, but her mind kept wandering back to the painting, the wealth so clear in it, and Sybil's haunted look as she stared at her mother.

What had happened to them? How had Sybil ended up in Severon, broke and unwilling to talk about her family?

Also, had Sybil been lying about her past this whole time? If she'd secretly been a rich girl all along, why hadn't she told Esme that or written to her family in those long cold months when they'd desperately needed money?

Esme longed to ask, but maybe those weren't her secrets to learn. Maybe it was enough that she trusted her friend now, in this moment. Maybe that was what love was, trusting someone even when you didn't know everything about them. Esme knew Sybil was brave and kind, and she cared for Esme, even if only as a friend. That was more than Esme had ever had in her life, and it felt like enough. At least for now. Besides, she'd already promised she'd help Sybil always, no matter what secrets came out.

Esme knew from her own experieince that a person couldn't help where they came from. They could only control what they decided to do after they left. That was what was important. What one chose, not what was chosen for them. Even if Esme didn't know who Sybil had been, she knew who she was now.

Besides, they'd survived a plague of bronze frogs together, and that was no small feat. She couldn't afford any doubts about her best friend. Who knew what else was waiting for them in Fae? Who knew what would've happened had Sybil not remembered the words Lucien had enchanted the frogs with?

Esme got back to reading, hoping there was something useful in Lucien's book that would help them survive the next three thefts.

But she wasn't counting on it.

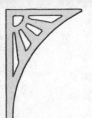

CHAPTER ELEVEN
One day before the Spring Equinox

Sybil

fter facing Lucien's traps and army of molten frogs, breaking into Antoine's townhouse for the enchanted leather bag should've been easy. And it was. Until everything went entirely wrong.

It was midmorning the day after their adventure at Lucien's. Much to their surprise, Sybil and Esme were huddled together in a wardrobe in Antoine's study. The wardrobe door was open just a crack, letting in a sliver of light. Holding as still as possible, they listened as Antoine paced the room, smoking a cigar and talking loudly to someone about an auction to sell posters.

The wardrobe was crammed full of jackets, furs, walking sticks, and other pieces of vintage clothing Antoine had collected. The musty smell of tobacco and mothballs was overwhelming.

Sybil glanced at Esme. They didn't have room to move, and their bodies were pressed so close, Sybil could feel each breath Esme took, as if it were expanding in Sybil's own chest. Because of her height,

Esme hunched, her spine curling like a question mark, to accommodate a shelf above them that sagged with books and boxes. This posture meant Esme's forehead leaned against Sybil's and that their lips were less than an inch apart.

It was excruciating.

Sybil longed to move forward, so she could kiss Esme, or step backward, so they could have distance between them again and Sybil could actually think. But neither of those things was possible—there simply wasn't room in the wardrobe, and Antoine was only a few feet away—and so she stayed still, breathing in Esme's air, trying not to think about kissing her. Sybil's left hand clenched the blue leather bag Maeve had sent them to steal, and sweat made her palm slick.

Forcing her attention from Esme, Sybil thought back on their morning so far. Having risen early and eaten the stale leftovers of yesterday's baked goods, the two of them had made their way to Antoine's neighborhood before sunrise. The plan was to sit on a bench down the street and watch his residence until Antoine went to his antique shop and his small staff left the house to run errands. Then they would hurry in, steal the magical bag, and have enough time to visit the Severon Museum later in the day to find the bottle of perfume. After that, they would head into Fae. Somehow. (Lucien's journal—which Sybil had spent the previous evening poring over—had exactly no information about how to open a door into Fae, but Sybil was hopeful she'd figure it out.)

It all went perfectly, until it didn't. Shortly after eight o'clock, Antoine left the house, getting into a carriage without sparing the two girls on the bench a second glance. Not long after that, his maid left with a shopping basket over her arm, and then his butler also went out.

"Now's our chance," Esme said, hopping up from the bench, her confidence surprising Sybil. She might've been faking it, but Sybil didn't care. She was just glad Esme was still at her side after everything that had happened at Lucien's yesterday.

They hurried to a back door of Antoine's house, and Sybil quickly picked the lock. From there, they ran upstairs to Antoine's study, located the blue leather bag, and lifted it off the shelf. They were just getting ready to go when the front door of the house creaked open.

Antoine's voice boomed up the stairs, talking to someone as he entered.

"What do we do?" Esme asked, all the confidence in her voice gone. She looked around frantically.

Antoine's footsteps and another person's sounded on the stairs, heavy and getting closer.

Desperation filled Sybil. If Antoine caught them in his study, when no one else was home, she wasn't sure she'd be able to talk her way out of it.

Gripping the magical leather bag, she pointed to the antique wardrobe that stood near the door. "There! Go!"

And so, they'd scrambled into the wardrobe, barely squeezing in seconds before Antoine and another man came into the study.

Now, as Antoine paced closer, a wave of cigar smoke wafted into the wardrobe, blending with the mothballs. He paused in front of the wardrobe, still talking. Sybil willed herself not to sneeze. Antoine leaned over, pushing the wardrobe door closed, trapping the smoke in the wooden box with Sybil and Esme. Sybil scrunched up her face to hold her sneeze. She needed to pinch her nose or cover her mouth, but she couldn't move without knocking something over.

The sneeze grew more insistent, begging to be let out. Sybil grimaced, gritting her teeth and closing her eyes against it.

"Are you okay?" Esme whispered, her voice brushing over Sybil's ear in a way that made her shiver.

"I have to sneeze."

"Don't sneeze. I beg you."

Sybil made a small wretched noise as the sneeze fought its way out.

"Please, don't sneeze." Esme shifted so her lips hovered a breath away from Sybil's.

Sybil scrunched her face again, desperately wanting not to alert Antoine. Sybil swallowed hard. "I'm okay. It's passing."

Esme shot Sybil a quick dangerous smile.

That look nearly killed Sybil. It made her knees weak and told her Esme was aware of exactly how close they were. Sybil almost wanted Antoine to accidentally bump into the wardrobe so she could have an excuse to tumble into Esme, their lips finally fully pressing against each other's, their hands tangling in each other's hair, their breaths merging as they figured out this thing between them with kisses rather than words.

Instead, Sybil stood there, rigid as if she were balancing a book on her head, barely daring to breathe. Her breasts, her belly, her hips, her forehead, and the toes of her shoes all rested against Esme's same parts. Together, they waited, each breath an eternity of wanting.

The things this girl does to me.

Sybil curled her toes in her shoes, trying to ignore the heat Esme's nearness sent through her entire body. They'd been close before, of course, in the apartment, on the dance floor, as they ran through the city hand in hand, but they'd never shared each other's air like this. It was delicious torture, intimate and urgent but also wildly distracting from why they were in this crowded wardrobe in the first place.

Wrenching her attention away from Esme, Sybil thought back to yesterday, when they'd been at Lucien's house. She hadn't been surprised to see him living well—he was used to money and had stolen most of their mother's jewels when he'd left the house—and he'd clearly been successful in whatever he'd been doing with Maeve. She also wasn't surprised to see the traps he'd laid throughout his house. If she was to believe their mother was from a magical other world—which Sybil did—then it didn't surprise her at all to know her brother had learned to do some magic of his own. What she *was* surprised about, however, was the family portrait.

It had been painted not long before their mother died, and Sybil could still remember how she and Lucien had giggled as their mother sang them a silly drinking song while they sat for the painter. Even Sybil's father had laughed along with them, making up verses of his own. To see the portrait yesterday—the only physical record of such a glowing moment from her old life, while Sybil was so solidly entrenched in this new one—was a shock. Why had Lucien hung it? Was it a reminder of what they'd lost? Of who they'd been? If that was the case, why had he never written to Sybil? Why had he totally abandoned her in their father's house?

Sybil flicked her eyes up to Esme's face, wondering what she was thinking about. For all that they were close—both literally in this moment and as best friends—Sybil was painfully aware of all the things she was keeping from Esme. That was the way of it, though, maybe. You could know someone so very well, but you'd never live inside their head.

What had Esme thought of that family portrait? She hadn't confronted Sybil, but that didn't mean she didn't have questions. Was she wondering why Sybil was so poor now? Would Sybil tell her the truth, even if Esme did ask? Could she bring herself to?

Esme shifted slightly, making the wardrobe creak as her body pushed against Sybil's more firmly.

"Would you believe me if I said there's a stuffed bird beak poking into my spine?" Esme whispered.

Sybil snickered under her breath and moved the tiniest step backward. Esme shifted again, her body still pressed against Sybil's but allowing more space behind her.

"Better?" Sybil asked.

"Better."

Outside the wardrobe, Antoine and the gentleman he was talking to droned on, discussing export prices and stock markets.

It reminded Sybil of the marriage negotiations her father had conducted. She protested every one, saying at sixteen she was far too young. He hadn't listened, and that was why she'd run away, fleeing to Severon to find Lucien.

With Esme, Sybil had found a soft place to land. She stopped looking for Lucien because she'd been so happy. In the tiny attic apartment, she'd found freedom, love, and a chance to be whoever she wanted. All things she hadn't in her own home after her mother's death.

Sybil looked up at Esme now, only to find Esme's eyes on her. They held each other's gaze. Desire wound through Sybil, stealing her breath.

Do it. Lean in. Kiss her.

"Esme," she whispered, her voice strangled, her mouth already so close to Esme's. "May I—"

Esme shook her head ever so slightly, her eyes shifting toward the door. Antoine was leaving. His steps moved past the wardrobe, and the study door creaked open.

Of course, she couldn't kiss Esme here, in Antoine's study, while they were in the middle of a theft. What was she thinking! Sybil gripped the leather bag in her hand, running her fingers over the stitching. *Stay focused.* There would be time for so many other things, including kisses perhaps, when this job for Maeve was complete.

Quiet filled the spaces where Antoine's voice had been. They waited several long, tense moments, and then Sybil pushed the wardrobe door open, peeking into the study. It was empty. She started to step out, but Esme circled a hand around Sybil's wrist, pulling her back into the narrow wardrobe again.

"Ask me some other time," Esme whispered, her lips brushing Sybil's ear. "When we're not stuck in a stinky wardrobe and on a deadline for a green faerie."

Her smile was like sunlight, filling Sybil's soul with hope and promise. Sybil returned it. Together, the two of them hurried out of Antoine's house.

Chapter Twelve
One day before the Spring Equinox

Esme

Thieving *was a hungry business. Esme's stomach grumbled as they* stood outside the Severon Museum. Which they were there to rob. The thought was so absurd, a wild laugh burst out of Esme.

Sybil shot her a glance. "What's the matter?"

"Nothing," Esme muttered. "Just hungry." Esme was no stranger to hunger, but normally she at least had soup or some bread at the café where she worked around this time of day. She'd been able to take a few shifts off from work, but the missed income made her nervous. Her stomach growled even louder, as if it too knew how much was riding on successfully completing Maeve's job.

"We'll get lunch before we go inside," Sybil said, not looking up from the gallery map in her hand. She had somehow talked a young woman leaving the museum into parting with it. "Maeve said the perfume bottle was on the fourth floor, in the decorative arts galleries, but there are five of those. . . ."

"She mentioned it's in the one next to the starlight painting galleries? Near the clocks?" Esme had never been to the Severon Museum, but Sybil seemed more than familiar with it.

"That's right! That means, according to this map, there's only one place that could be. I wonder if we'll need an escape route, in case we're caught. . . ."

Of course, they needed an escape route! But perhaps they wouldn't get caught. Was that too much to hope for? This entire job for Maeve was so incredibly complicated. Which, fine. Esme liked complicated things, but what she wouldn't give to be back in the wardrobe with Sybil, pressed so close to her friend, she could feel her heartbeat through her dress.

Ask me some other time.

Esme's heart still raced at her own words, so brave and perhaps so rash. Would it really be so wrong to kiss Sybil? Why?

Because people broke up, they fell out of love, and they moved on with their lives. Esme had learned that lesson from watching her mother. She had been a dancer and showgirl at La Lune, and she'd always had a new boyfriend. Esme didn't remember the men's names or faces; they were just a blurred carousel of heartbreak, always leaving her mother sobbing as they went away.

After the men left, Esme's mother would drink too much, get to work late, drink even more at the club, and forget about Esme for a few days. By six, Esme could make her own meals. By ten, she was doing all their laundry, cooking, and cleaning when she wasn't at school. One night, near Esme's eleventh birthday, her mother just didn't come home from the club. Esme waited a full day and then a night before she went to La Lune. Her mother was dead in her dressing room, a dozen empty bottles by her head.

Esme had been carted off to the Haven Orphanage that night, and she'd never even gotten a chance to go home for her things.

No. Love made you do silly, irrational things.

Like agree to steal things from the Severon Museum? whispered a voice in her head.

Esme definitely ignored that.

This wasn't about love; it was about protecting her friend—and having enough money to complete her life plan and be secure in her future.

"I'll get us lunch, and then we can find this perfume bottle," Esme said, pointing to a food cart that stood outside the museum. The smell of roasted meats and fresh bread made Esme's stomach growl even louder. "If we have enough money. . . ."

Sybil had spent all their coins from selling the cat poster on pastries yesterday, which was fine, but it also meant they had no plan for rent other than this outrageous one from Maeve. Esme was a girl who had lived far too close to the edge of destitution most of her life to throw money away on frivolous things, like meat pies from overpriced carts outside the museum. But she was so very hungry. And if this plan went awry, they might have to run away. And it was scientifically ill-advised to run on an empty stomach. . . .

"Lucien is buying us lunch today," Sybil said, pulling a pair of gold coins from her pocket. She flipped them through her fingers, smiling at Esme, all confidence and ease. "I swiped these from his desk."

"Well, thank you very much, Lucien," Esme said, some of her worry lifting.

Esme bought two vegetable-and-beef pies for each of them, and she and Sybil ate on a bench outside the museum, sitting in the sun. Groups of people streamed past, heading in and out of the building. There were well-dressed children laughing and chasing one another, mothers and nannies scolding them, and older couples strolling arm and arm. It was all very normal, and somehow—given what Esme now knew of green faeries and a Fae world just beyond theirs—it all seemed so precarious. So breakable. Like one of the many glass vases Antoine collected or the pink blossoms on the cherry trees above their heads.

A deep love for the world, with its fragility and changeableness, filled Esme, and she wanted to protect it too. Which was silly. She could barely protect her best friend, much less the world. Feeling immensely small and powerless, Esme took another bite of her lunch.

After they were done eating—Sybil wrapped up her second pie and tucked it into her coat pocket, and Esme wiped her greasy fingers on her skirts—they walked up the stairs to the museum. As they were paying admission, a guard stopped them, asking them to turn out their pockets.

"Why?" Sybil demanded, bristling.

Esme knew why. She watched as a group of well-dressed women breezed past the admissions desk. The guard, a tall white man with a pinched expression, eyebrows like caterpillars, and a thick brown beard, looked Esme and Sybil over, from their hatless heads to their scuffed shoes.

"It's standard policy," he said, deadpan, "when we check for thieves."

"We're not thieves." Sybil huffed.

"How would I know that without checking your pockets?" The man didn't budge, blocking their way. "Please, miss, don't make a scene. Just empty your pockets. We have had some . . . issues . . . with—"

"With people dressed like us?" Esme suggested. This wasn't the first time something like this had happened to her, and she was sure it wouldn't be the last. At least if they got the money from Maeve and moved up in the world, they wouldn't be stopped over their tattered hems or patched coats.

The man just nodded.

Sybil looked like she wanted to protest, and Esme thought back to the painted version of Sybil hanging in Lucien's study. That girl probably wouldn't have even seen them in a museum. Her eyes would slide right over their grubby coats and thin limbs, making them just one more part of a mass of people who were not rich.

"Empty your pockets, Syb," Esme said softly. "They won't let us in otherwise."

Grumbling, Sybil emptied her pockets into a small bin the man offered. The meat pie in its grease-soaked newspaper, two knives, a ball of twine, and other parts of her thief's kit came falling out. She held on to Lucien's diary, its pages stuffed with golden leaves.

"Okay to keep a book for sketching?" she snarled at the man. "Or am I too poor to do that too?"

He just eyed her knives and tools, his expression unchanging. "Sketch away. These things will be waiting for you when you leave." He then had Esme empty her pockets—some clock gears, the screwdriver, her life-plan list, and a cat toy fell into the bin—and handed them a paper ticket. "Use this to get your things back when you exit. Enjoy your visit."

He placed the bin with their belongings behind the admissions desk. Esme and Sybil moved toward the interior of the museum, joining the midday crowds filling its halls.

Esme turned to see the guard's eyes still on them. "How are we supposed to steal the perfume bottle without any of your tools?"

"Don't worry," Sybil said, her expression stony. "I have a plan." With those words, she dropped one golden leaf near the top of the stairs. Esme eyed it, fairly certain she knew what Sybil had in mind, but not at all certain it would work.

They hurried through the crowds admiring a famous portrait exhibit in the lower galleries and wound through countless small rooms. "Look at this painting, Esme!" Sybil would exclaim every few moments. In every room they passed through, Sybil dropped another golden leaf. As they hurried past treasures from around the world and through the centuries in Severon, Esme longed to linger. If she'd known there were so many clocks and mechanical items here, she would've visited the Severon Museum long ago.

She would come back someday. When she had a nicer dress and more time.

"Esme," Sybil whispered, glancing over her shoulder as they climbed a staircase leading to the fourth floor. "Look. The same guard from downstairs is following us now."

Esme glanced over her shoulder. Sybil was right. The man with the brown beard and regrettable eyebrows was on the stairs behind them. And he had two other museum guards—both athletic-looking young men—with him.

"Why are they following us?" Sybil hissed. "We paid our admission."

Esme's mouth was a grim line. "Besides our clothing and your confiscated thief's tools? Sport? Boredom? To scare us?"

"Well, I'm not scared of them." Sybil dropped another golden leaf on the staircase and marched forward.

Glancing over her shoulder one more time, Esme wished she could borrow just a bit of her friend's bravery.

The guards walked behind them, talking between themselves and with other museum patrons, always far enough away that they could deny actually following Esme and Sybil, but close enough to keep an eye on them. Under the guards' watchful eyes, Esme and Sybil moved across the fourth-floor landing and into the starlight galleries. Sybil paused in front of an enormous painting threaded through with silver starlight. It was a beach scene, and it looked like the water in the painting moved. There was also a silver starlight-lace dress on display within a glass case. A card on the outside of the case said, *Woven for the Casorina, for the Scholar's Ball, by Q, a starlight artist who disappeared shortly after making this dress.*

Esme longed to run her fingers through the starlight lace, and even through the glass, it felt magical somehow.

"Can you imagine wearing something like that?" Sybil asked.

"Never," Esme breathed. "But I'd love to."

"Me too." Sybil dropped another leaf at the foot of the starlight dress's display case.

They found the magical perfume bottle in a decorative arts gallery down the hall from the starlight one. As Maeve had said, it was between a room full of clocks (Esme swooned to see them and very much wished she could just linger in that room), and another room full of starlight-lace shawls, all of them yellow with age.

The room they stood in now was small and empty of other patrons. Fourteen long rectangular wood-and-glass display cases filled the space, making a maze of it. Sybil draped herself over the closest case, peering inside. Esme did the same, examining pens, vases, small golden statues, and dozens of other porcelain and gilded household items. There! Tucked in a back corner, hidden among a mess of dusty bottles and miscellany, was a midnight-blue perfume bottle inlaid with stars, with a crescent-moon-shaped stopper.

"Sybil! It's in here! I think I found it!"

Sybil hurried over. "Ahh, well done. That is it."

Relief made Esme slump against the case. "How are we supposed to—"

"Get off those cases!" boomed a loud voice behind them.

Esme and Sybil turned as one to see the scowling bearded guard stride into the room. The other two guards stood by the door.

"We were just looking," Sybil explained.

"Well, you're not supposed to lean on the cases," the guard barked.

"There are children in the next room practically licking the paintings," Esme blurted. She'd seen two well-dressed children with lollipops moving toward a painting and no one stopping them.

"That's certainly not true." The guard bristled. "You two are troublemakers, I can tell. You need to leave."

Esme glanced desperately between the guard and the perfume bottle still in the glass case. It was so close, but the guard was also right here. How could they snatch it from beneath his nose?

"We're not leaving," Esme said, putting more courage behind the words. Sybil shot her an approving look that made Esme stand a little straighter. "We paid our admission and have every right to be here."

The guard reached for Esme, and at the same moment, Sybil dropped Lucien's journal on the display case. Leaves scattered everywhere, covering the glass and the floor, and one even landed on the guard's shoe. The guard exclaimed in surprise, and Esme wrenched herself free.

Then, in a voice so quiet, Esme almost missed it, Sybil whispered, "Éclairer."

Many things happened all at once. The leaves on the case in front of them transformed into bronze frogs and began hopping across the glass, spreading cracks with each fiery step they took. The sound of screaming and more glass cracking rang out through the museum.

The guard spun around, yelling in surprise as the leaf on his shoe transformed into a bronze frog. The other guards also cried out. Esme's eyes met Sybil's, and Sybil winked at her. Then, in one quick motion, she pushed on the splintering glass of the case, sending it careening downward.

"Get the bottle," Sybil said, her voice urgent as she reached for one of the frogs.

Esme grabbed the perfume bottle and shoved it in her pocket. "How is that frog not burning you?" she asked Sybil.

"Magic!" Sybil called out cheerfully, as they ran out of the gallery.

They pushed past the bearded guard, who stood frozen as two bronze frogs hopped toward him. The other two guards kicked at the bronze frogs and cried out, blowing a whistle and shouting for Esme and Sybil to stop. The girls ignored them all and raced toward the main staircase. People were streaming out of the galleries, making a human river down the museum stairs. Broken glass was everywhere, and small bronze frogs hopped through the museum, leaving destruction in their wake. Screams and cries filled the building as people pushed to get out.

"Éclairer," Sybil whispered again, when they were nearly to the door. The frog in her hand transformed into a golden leaf. No one was behind the admissions desk, and Esme grabbed the things Sybil had left behind the counter and the contents of her own pockets. She left Sybil's meat pie, which had been smashed by other items piled on it. Together, they slipped outside, lost within the chaos of the crowd.

Hope and triumph soared in Esme as they ran down the steps of the Severon Museum. They had done it! Somehow, they had done it. They had the perfume bottle. She could've wept.

"You're a genius!" she said, throwing her arms around Sybil.

Sybil slipped the golden leaf into her pocket. "I hope no one was hurt."

"It was incredible!" Esme planted a kiss on Sybil's cheek.

Color rose in Sybil's cheeks. Esme's heart fluttered to see it.

You weren't supposed to kiss her! Ever.

It was just a friendly kiss. A shared moment of triumph. Nothing more.

Right.

"I wasn't sure it would work," Sybil confessed.

"I can't believe we have the book, the bag, and the perfume!" Esme was overcome by a racing swirl of reckless feelings. She took a deep breath, feeling her own cheeks heat as well.

Sybil's dimples deepened as she smiled at Esme. "Well, now that the easy part is done, I suppose we just have to figure out how to make a door into Fae, steal a Fae queen's crown jewels before a ball, and then find our way home so Maeve can pay us."

"But, before all that, dinner and a nap?"

"Of course," Sybil agreed, looping her arm through Esme's and pulling her close.

Which just made Esme's rash feelings dance with more wild hope and possibility. Perhaps a little bit of adventure wasn't so terrible after all.

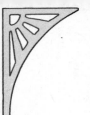

CHAPTER THIRTEEN
One day before the Spring Equinox

Sybil

*S*ybil *was exhausted. It had been hours since they'd fled from the* Severon Museum, and Esme was washing the dishes from their simple dinner of bread and cheese. Sybil sat at their kitchen table, Lucien's journal open in front of her, the perfume bottle and leather bag beside it. The book Esme had taken from Lucien's house, *Eckleton's Guide to Fae for Travelers*, was also on the table and marked with many slips of paper from Esme's reading. Sybil rubbed her eyes, making the words on the page swim, as if that would somehow reveal how to open a door into Fae.

The answers she needed were in this journal. They had to be! Otherwise, what was the point of all the other thefts they'd pulled off? If they couldn't get into Fae, then they would never be able to complete this job for Maeve.

Sybil ran a finger over the stitching along the spine of the journal and then over the flowers embroidered on the small leather bag, desperately hoping for a jolt of magic or some clue that might help. Nothing happened. She didn't dare open the perfume bottle—what if they only had enough scent to open Queen Mab's vault? Sybil couldn't waste any of the precious liquid to sate her curiosity.

Frustration filled her, and she twisted the key around her neck. What made this key work? How would it open a door between worlds? How had Lucien known what to do with *his* key?

Sybil longed to fling the journal across the room or yell at her brother or just do something! She got up and paced the apartment.

Outside their clock tower, the sky deepened to purple, and the first stars came out. Sybil marched to the window and back to the table, forcing herself to sit in front of the journal again. She desperately wanted a nap, but she couldn't sleep until she found the words that made the key work.

Yes, Lucien's journal was supposed to contain those exact words according to Maeve, and yes, Sybil had read it cover to cover four times already since they'd retrieved it yesterday, but she was no closer to an answer.

She slumped in her chair and slammed the journal shut.

"How's it going over there?" Esme asked, the teakettle in her hand.

"Magnificent. Just working out the details of our plan."

Esme seemed satisfied with that, and she hummed a song under her breath as she filled the kettle. Sybil blew out a breath. She hadn't told Esme she didn't know the words to open a door, and Esme seemed to have absolute trust in Sybil's ability to pull this off, whatever this was. The vote of confidence was nice but misplaced.

Swearing under her breath, Sybil flipped to the front of Lucien's journal, once more. She already knew the first sentence—scrawled in his cramped handwriting—by heart: *In the days after leaving my father's house, I began to explore the possibility that there were worlds beyond ours. . . .*

Sybil remembered the night Lucien had left like it was yesterday. It'd been storming outside, thunder pounding and lightning forking the broiling summer air. Sybil was walking past the library door when she heard Lucien and their father talking behind the closed library door.

"*We* are the guardians of the keys," Sybil's father said, his voice tense. "You know the Society of Magicians controls which magic gets in and out, and our family is in the unique position to keep the door closed—"

Lucien had interrupted. "But, Father, what's the point of having a key if we can't use it?"

"Not *can't*, Lucien. We *don't* use it because—"

She only caught snatches of their words before her father discovered her lurking outside the door with her ear to the keyhole.

There was a fierce fight after that, and Sybil's father decided she was a nuisance, headed on a path of no good. For her own sake—not for the sake of the secrets she'd overheard in the library or the way Lucien had stormed out and then disappeared the next day to Severon—Sybil's father had decided Sybil needed to marry, and fast.

"How *did* you get the door open, Lucien?" Sybil muttered, returning to her kitchen table and the question at hand. She flipped through the early entries. Lucien had written about buying his house in Severon and spending long hours in the Great Library, searching for books that would help him open a door.

One entry from a few months after he arrived in Severon snagged Sybil's attention. Somehow he'd gotten a door open—he didn't say how, curse him—but he did say this: *I opened a door into Fae today, and went walking in the woods. Met a lovely creature there. Her name is Maeve, and we got to talking. She told me she lived in a cottage in the deep woods and was curious about my world. I brought her through the door—she glamoured herself of course—and we spent many hours drinking and dancing in Severon's clubs. I offered to take her back home, but she wanted to stay longer, which was fine with me. . . ."*

Sybil searched the pages, moving past descriptions of magical items Lucien had found in Severon—starlight-lace fragments, small statues, Fae inventions, and pieces of jewelry—and how he'd bought, bargained, and stolen them. There was a whole section about how Maeve had been crushing her own jewels from Fae to make absinthe and how the stash of those was running low.

Lucien had also gone into some detail about the lands of Fae, and Sybil pored over these accounts, looking for traces of the brother she'd known in the diary. By his own account, Lucien was bold, fearless, and very curious about all things Fae. He included drawings and descriptions of Fae he'd met—from small mushroom-capped creatures who wove magical cloth to glittering moonshadow snakes. There were drawings of tree creatures and other Fae of all descriptions.

There were also notes on the High Fae and their courts—

The Fae land I've visited is like nothing I've read about in any of the books I've studied—especially Eckleton's Guide to Fae for Travelers, which is hopelessly out of date. Those

book's speak of eight different courts, but that information
is from many centuries ago. From what I can tell, now—for
whatever reasons, be it war, sickness, strife, or ending of
royal lines—this part of Fae is divided into three Kingdoms:
The Moonshadow Court in the mountains, the Starlight Court
in the northern realms, amid the ice, and the Solstice Court
by the sea. There is a place of learning called the Crescent
Atheneum in the middle of this world, in a city owned by all
the courts. Each court has its own queen, each is dangerous in
its own way. They come together each year on the Spring and
Autumnal Equinoxes and the Winter Solstice for a ball that
balances the courts and the powers. The Moonshadow Court
hosts the Spring Equinox ball . . .

"Wait, what's that?" Esme asked, coming over to the table with
two cups of tea in hand and peering over Sybil's shoulder.

Esme set the cups on the table and scrutinized the drawing
Sybil had stopped on. *The Moonshadow Court* was written at the top,
and a precise hand had marked roads, rivers, and other features. A
palace sat in the middle of the drawing, surrounded by a hedge maze.
At its back was a mountain, and beyond the maze, a small town
stretched to the edge of a forest. The forest bled to the edges of the
map, marked here and there with things like *Swamp Hag's Cabin* or
Will-O'-the-Wisps Hunting Grounds. A wide river ran through the
kingdom, disappearing into the forest. On the left and right sides,
Lucien had written *To the Starlight Court* and *To the Solstice Court*,
with arrows pointing in opposite directions. A road snaked through
the Moonshadow Kingdom, connecting it to the other parts of Fae.

Sybil pressed a finger near the palace. "I'm thinking we'll open a door here, sneak inside before the ball starts, and then return home through the closest door."

"Hmmm." Esme frowned, studying the map. "I'd feel better about all this if we had a map of the palace itself."

"Unfortunately, Lucien has not provided one." Sybil flipped through another section, near the back of the journal. "He says that he'd long wanted to go inside, but the only time of year it's open to outsiders is during the Spring Equinox ball. . . ."

"So, we're supposed to just stroll in, ask for directions to Queen Mab's room, and then steal the crown jewels out of her vault?"

Sybil picked up her cup of tea. "It's not a perfect plan."

"It hardly qualifies as a plan at all, much less a perfect one."

"But we have the other items—we're not walking in totally helpless. Once we get into the palace and find Queen Mab's room, we'll use the perfume to open the vault, hide the jewels in the bag, and get out of there."

Esme bit her bottom lip. "I know we have those magical items, but there's just so much room for mistakes."

"What would you do, Ez?"

Esme reached for the journal. "If I had my wish, I'd have schematics of the palace. Notes on how many guards there were, how often they changed out, and where they patrolled. I'd have our arrival spot and our exit clearly mapped out. I'd have at least two backup plans ready, just in case we couldn't—"

"But we have none of those things," Sybil interrupted. "And no way to get them."

"I know." Esme took a long sip of tea. "But you asked what I would do if I were planning this." She took out her life-plan list. "You know I like a plan."

"I do," Sybil conceded. "I'm just not sure we're going to get more than the bare outlines of one."

Esme nodded, still looking at the journal. "What does this mean?" she asked, pointing to a line Lucien had written below the map.

"Getting the door to Fae open is a family thing," Sybil read out loud. "I'm not sure, but I've been puzzling over it for hours."

Even as she said it, though, something in the words took her back to a place in her memory that she hadn't thought about for a very long time.

It was the night Sybil's mother had been thrown from her horse. She was in her room, her breath rattling in her chest, her head and arm bandaged from the fall. She'd asked to see Sybil alone.

Sybil went in, terrified. Her mother's eyes flickered open, and a small smile curved her lips.

"Darling Sybil," she whispered. "Come here, child."

Terror filled Sybil to see her beloved, beautiful, strong mother reduced to the frail wounded thing on the bed. Sybil glanced over her shoulder, but no one was there to stop her so, she clambered under the covers beside her mother.

"Will you be okay, Mama?" she asked.

Her mother shook her head. "I'm afraid not. My body is weaker in this world than in Fae. But I have something to give you before I go, my beloved."

With effort, she took a key on a long silver chain from around her neck. She handed it to Sybil. "This is in case you ever want to visit my home," she murmured. "Your brother has one too. He knows I'm giving you one, but don't tell your father about yours. It's just our secret."

"How does it work, Mama?"

Her mother started coughing then, bringing up blood. Sybil froze, terrified. When her mother finally caught her breath, she gestured to the blood on the handkerchief. "You can map your blood to find your way home, my darling," she whispered.

Sybil had no idea what that meant, and she cried then, watching as her mother fell back against the pillows, barely breathing.

Slowly, in a rasping voice laced with pain, she'd sang to Sybil of a forest, green and dark, with a river flowing through it.

A few words from that song danced through Sybil's mind.

"A willow, a word, a slip into the night. Your blood is a map to find your way home, little sprite. . . ."

Lucien had said opening a door to Fae was a family thing. Maybe these were the words Sybil needed to create a door between worlds. It was worth a try at least. She shut the book firmly and took a long sip of her tea. This had to work. It would work.

"What is it?" Esme asked.

"Let's get some rest, and then we'll leave in the morning. I think I know how to open the door into Fae."

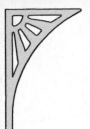

CHAPTER FOURTEEN
Spring Equinox

Esme

*W*hat *did one pack for traveling in the Fae world?*

After a night of fitful sleep, Esme was up early, shoving things into her bag. She was bringing everything she could think of: screwdrivers, a knife, a few clock gears, some dried mint leaves, her favorite knit sweater, her life-plan list, and, of course, the magical bag from Antoine's, and the perfume. She also had a small box full of white rowan tree blossoms—although Lucien said *Eckleton's Guide to Fae for Travelers* was out of date, Esme had read in it that rowan blossoms were welcome gifts for the High Fae. She'd plucked them that morning from the trees that grew down the road from their clock tower. She'd also left the apartment window out to the fire escape open a crack, letting in a cool morning breeze. It wasn't perfect, but if her cats needed to get out—or worse, if Esme and Sybil didn't come back—then at least they could get down to the trash cans at street level.

"We'll be back soon," Esme promised Jolie, picking her up and kissing her nose. She did the same for every cat and then retrieved her travel bag.

"Are you ready?" she asked Sybil, who was still studying the map in Lucien's book.

Sybil bounced on her toes as she slipped her own coat over her arms. "I am! This is going to be great. We've gotten all the items we needed, and we're ready for this, Ez. In a few hours, we're going to be richer than you can possibly imagine."

"That sounds wonderful," Esme admitted as she closed her bag.

"Are you seriously bringing a suitcase into Fae?" Sybil asked, staring at the bag Esme gripped.

Esme scowled at her. "It's not a suitcase. It's a traveling bag."

It was a cheap one, made from scraps of fabric. The same one every orphan who aged out of Haven was given when they left. Some charity in town—a group who thought it was better to stitch bags rather than help orphans find jobs once they were thrown into the streets—made the bags for the orphanage. Esme had reinforced it over the years, fixing holes, adding a shoulder strap, and weaving in tighter threads. Now the ugly green-and-gray bag, once a hated thing, was covered in colorful patches, sturdy and strong. It was a testament to all Esme could do on her own, and she most certainly was taking it into Fae.

"Suitcase, traveling bag, whatever," Sybil said. "We're supposed to be traveling light and not getting noticed. Can't you just fit everything you need in your coat pockets?"

Annoyance flared in Esme. She took a long steadying breath. For whatever reason, the patchwork bag was the hill she was going to die on. "I cannot and I will not. I've gone along with all this, despite our lack of a plan, but I absolutely refuse to be less prepared than necessary. I'm bringing the bag. End of discussion."

A surprised look flashed across Sybil's face, and it sent a snicker of dread through Esme. Had she been too harsh? Would Sybil be mad at her now? Esme hated that this was where her thoughts went, but she couldn't help it. A lifetime spent trying to guess at other people's moods and trying to please them was a hard habit to unlearn. She slipped the bag over her shoulder and stood as tall as she could.

"Fair enough." Sybil smiled at Esme. "The bag goes with us. Just, please, don't put a cat in there."

"That I can promise," Esme said, relief filling every part of her. Sybil wasn't angry at her for standing up for herself. Not that she'd really thought Sybil would be, but still. Esme couldn't help the anxiety.

"Let's go over the scrap of a plan we have again?" Esme asked. Here, Sybil opened Lucien's diary and turned to the page with a map on it.

"I'm hoping we come out here, by the palace," Sybil said, pointing to the spot she'd identified last night. "If for some reason we get separated, meet me here, by the hedge maze."

"We cannot get separated." Esme swallowed hard. What was she going to do if they got separated in Fae? Not a possibility she liked to imagine.

"We won't get separated," Sybil said. "I promise, but still, you wanted a bit more security, so that's our backup plan."

"Fae is enormous," Esme said, peering closer at all the parts of the map. Worry filled her at the scope of the dark woods, towering mountains, and the many places they knew nothing about.

"It'll be quite an adventure," Sybil agreed, her voice laced with eagerness. "Let's just hope we open the door near the palace, as I'm planning to do, not in the middle of the woods."

"What happens if we open a door in the woods?"

Sybil raised an eyebrow. "Lucien only mentioned wandering in the woods once, but he barely made it out of there. According to him, the woods are crawling with wild creatures, most of them outside the Moonshadow Court's influence."

Esme swallowed the lump in her throat. "Perfect. Maybe I'll pack another knife."

"Couldn't hurt," Sybil said, far more cheerfully than she had a right to.

As Esme added more knives and another knit scarf—who knew what the weather would be like?—to her travel bag, Sybil continued to discuss their plan. First, Sybil would open the door. She'd direct the magic to land them near the palace, preferably in a hidden spot so no one would see them arrive. From there, they'd sneak in with the other Spring Equinox ball guests, and then, they'd find Queen Mab's room.

Well, Esme had to admit it was a strategy. Not a good one. Not a careful one that accounted for all the variables or that was made after much research and study. But it was something. She hoped there weren't too many guards between them and the jewels, they didn't run into Queen Mab or any other High Fae, and everything else went perfectly.

Which Esme knew was incredibly unlikely, but Sybil was looking at her with such confidence, Esme just nodded. "Sounds like a good plan."

Relief lit Sybil's face. "Thank you. And really, once we get this done and get home with the jewels and Maeve pays us, that's it. No more stealing for me, I promise. If I need to, I'll find a proper job, maybe at another artist's studio or maybe just working in a place like the Absinthe Underground."

"Or maybe you won't have to," Esme said, a warm rush of feeling for her friend going through her. "Maybe if this all works out, we really will have enough money to not have to work again."

"Now that's a plan," Sybil said. "Are you ready to go?"

No.

Esme looked around the apartment, taking in her books, her clocks, the comfy couch that was her bed, her cats, and she desperately hoped they found their way back.

She gave Jolie one last snuggle and then checked again that all the cats had food and water and that the window was open enough for them to get out if they needed to.

"I'm ready," she said, trying to keep the tremble from her voice.

Sybil put an arm around her, the touch warm and welcoming. "Don't worry, Ez. We'll look out for each other, okay?"

Esme wasn't sure if it was okay, but she nodded. That was what they did: looked out for each other.

PART THREE
The Crown Jewels

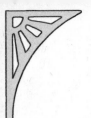

CHAPTER FIFTEEN
Spring Equinox

Sybil

Sybil *took the key from around her neck and moved toward the* apartment door. Lucien said in his journal that, as far as he knew, any door would work for this magic; you just had to have the right words and focus on where you wanted to go. Which seemed like a challenging task, given that they were heading into Fae, a place Sybil had never been. Still. She would visualize the hedge maze near Queen Mab's palace. That should do the trick.

Esme shifted the bag on her shoulder beside Sybil, her nervousness radiating in every gesture. Sybil knew she should be worried, but all she felt was excitement. Something about going into Fae felt like going home, or maybe that was just because it reminded her of her mother. Whatever it was, Sybil's heart raced. She had left her father's house to see the city and new places—and here she was on the cusp of entering a new world!

Her hands shook as she moved her key toward the lock of the apartment door. Behind her, Jean-Francois yowled grumpily, but

Sybil ignored him, focusing on the key. It slipped into the lock, like it was made for it.

"So fascinating," Esme murmured, looking over Sybil's shoulder. Sybil could practically hear the gears turning in Esme's mind as she tried to figure out how it worked.

Sybil turned the key and whispered the phrase from her mother's song: "A willow, a word, a slip into the night. Your blood is a map to find your way home, little sprite. . . ."

There was a loud click, and Sybil's heart soared.

This was it.

She flung the apartment door open—only to find the same hallway that was always there, waiting on the other side. The gas bulbs flickered. Their milk bottles were outside their door. There was still that suspicious stain near the stairs.

Sybil swore loudly.

"Did you do it wrong?" Esme asked, peering into the hallway.

Sybil wasn't sure. She had the key. She'd said the words. Why wasn't it working? Were there other words? Something else she had to do?

She tried it again, singing the words this time. Again, the lock clicked. Again, when she opened it, the apartment building hallway waited on the other side.

She tried a third time. A fourth. A fifth.

The clock struck nine times, shaking the apartment, sending cats skittering, and reminding Sybil it was officially the Spring Equinox, the day they had to steal the jewels and return to Maeve. Sybil swore again, slamming the door shut and pacing away from it. She pulled the key from the lock and twisted it through her fingers.

What was she doing wrong?

She drew Lucien's journal from her pocket and flipped through it, angrily looking for something, anything that would help. One of the golden leaves from Lucien's study—the only one left after their escapade at the Severon Museum—fell to the floor, and Oliver, the kitten, began batting it around.

"Don't mess with that," Esme said, plucking the leaf away from Oliver and handing it back to Sybil.

Sybil tucked it into the journal and bit her lip, trying to think. The golden leaf stood out like a bookmark among Lucien's words. When they'd been in Lucien's house, how had they opened the doors? Securing the journal in her pocket, Sybil looked at her hand, moving away the bandage and staring at the bite from the Hob-Lock. It was still healing, and the flesh was barely scabbed over.

Blood. Each door in Lucien's house had wanted her blood to open. Maybe that was the trick. What had her mother said about the key?

Your blood is a map to find your way home. . . .

Yes, that had to be it. Sybil pulled one of her knives from her pocket and sliced the end of her thumb.

"What are you doing?" Esme asked, staring in horror.

"Opening a door." Sybil ran her bleeding thumb over the end of the key, the lock, the inside of the keyhole. "Please, please," she whispered, "take me to my mother's home."

Then she slipped the key into the lock and whispered the words, "A willow, a word, a slip into the night. Your blood is a map to find your way home, little sprite. . . ."

The lock clicked, and Sybil's pulse raced. She almost didn't dare turn the doorknob, not wanting to see what was on the other side.

Please be Fae, please be Fae, please be Fae, she thought, putting a hand on the doorknob.

Esme stood shoulder to shoulder with Sybil as she started to turn the knob. "Aren't you supposed to tell it where you want to come out in Fae?" Esme asked.

Right. She *was* supposed to do that. She turned the doorknob and began to open the door. As she did so, she closed her eyes and focused all her energy on pleading with the magic. "Please put us out near Queen Mab's—"

"Wait!" Esme shouted. "Oliver! No! Get back here!"

Sybil's eyes flew open, right as Oliver pushed through a crack between the door and the frame. There was a flash of silver light, then the door creaked all the way open. Esme grabbed for Oliver, but he rolled away, as if they were playing a game.

"Oh my," Esme breathed, looking through the doorway.

Sybil took a step forward, too stunned to speak.

No milk bottles and dimly lit stairwells this time. Finally, the blood-smeared apartment door had opened into a new world. In front of Sybil stood a dense grove of towering pine trees, their trunks wider than the columns that held up the Severon Museum's entrance. Their heavy branches creaked in the breeze, sounding like ships in Severon's harbor. Sybil reached out a hand, lightly touching the rough bark of the tree that held the door she'd created. Her fingers came away sticky with sap. The smell of damp earth and evergreens filled her nose. At her feet, a carpet of moss and dried needles covered the ground. Something skittered through the underbrush, and above her somewhere, a creature chittered indignantly, as if it too were wondering why a door had suddenly opened in a pine trunk.

Sybil turned around. Behind her, through the door, was their very ordinary, very cozy apartment, with its cats, teacups, kitchen table, and empty cupboards. But in front of her, a whole new world waited.

"Close the door," Esme called out, stepping across the threshold to grab Oliver. "Before any of the other cats get through!"

Even if Sybil hadn't wanted to shut the door, it was closing on its own, shrinking rapidly to nothing. She grabbed her key out of the lock right as the door disappeared. That was close. What would've happened had she not remembered the key? Would they have been stuck in Fae?

Sybil tried not to let those worries settle, and she looked over at Esme, who chased Oliver through a mound of pine needles. Esme made a triumphant noise as she finally got her hands on the kitten, and she held him close to her chest. It was only then that Esme looked up. Sybil followed her gaze, taking in the dark purple shadows beneath the lowest boughs that seemed to slither somehow.

"Where are we?" Esme asked, her voice soft with wonder.

Sybil breathed in deeply, feeling something in her settle as the cool earth-scented air filled her lungs. "Fae." Sybil wished her mother were with her to welcome them to her homeland.

"But where in Fae?" Esme insisted, clinging to Oliver. His eyes were wide too, as if also realizing how strange and unlike home this place was.

"I think," Sybil said, "we ended up in the forest around Queen Mab's castle."

"The enormous forest full of monsters?"

"Let's hope Lucien was exaggerating."

Esme blew out a breath and tucked Oliver into her bag. He mewled loudly as she stroked his head. "How are we going to find our way to the palace?"

"We start walking," Sybil said, nodding toward a break in the pines where blue smoke curled above the trees. "Maybe someone up there can tell us where the palace is."

◆

They walked through the pines longer than it seemed possible. There was a path of sorts, and occasionally, the tree canopy thinned to let flashes of morning sunlight through. Each time Sybil thought they were getting closer to the smoke, the wind shifted, making the pine trees rustle with unseen faces and secret words. Sybil's dress snagged on undergrowth, and gnarled twigs caught in her hair.

"How long have we been walking?" Sybil asked, looking over at Esme, who was feeding Oliver a bit of water from her cupped palms. They'd stopped beside a burbling stream that twisted through the woods. Piles of boulders littered the stream's shores, and Sybil leaned against one, shaking a pebble out of her shoe.

"Don't know," Esme said. "Water?" She shook the water out of her palms, then offered Sybil a glass milk bottle, rinsed and now filled with water.

Sybil took it happily and drank the cool liquid. "I retract my earlier statement about bringing a bag. I'm glad you thought to do so."

Esme's eyebrows flew up. "Oh! Are you admitting I was right and you were wrong?"

"Nonsense. I'm just saying it was a good idea—"

"Hello, children," crooned someone from the deep shadows of the trees.

Sybil jumped, dropping the water bottle. Half its contents glugged out before Sybil could grab it again. "Who's there?" she called out, clutching her knife.

Beside Sybil, Esme armed herself with her screwdriver. "We have weapons!"

"Ohhhh, you have weapons," said the person, delight lacing their vowels. "Very good then. This should be fun. I have a knife too!"

Sybil gasped as a tall, willowy woman of sorts stepped out from behind a pine. Her skin was knobbled like tree bark, and mushrooms grew in her long green hair. Her hands were bony, each knuckle the size of a pebble, and long yellow claws curled at the ends of her fingers. The smell of pond water—a bog full of rotting plants and decomposing things—wafted off the woman. A wicked-looking serrated knife glinted from her right hand.

"Who—or what—are you?" Sybil wracked her brain, thinking back to the pages of Lucien's journal. She'd not seen any description of a creature like this, but that didn't mean anything. Lucien probably always opened doors exactly where he intended, never getting lost in impossible woods.

"Swamp Hag," Esme whispered, her knuckles white as she clenched the screwdriver. "Remember from the map?"

That was right. Lucien had marked the Swamp Hag's cabin near a stream, but he'd not left any indication of what to do if one met said Swamp Hag.

The hag was now circling them, eyeing them as if they were pieces of meat she was buying from a corner shop. "Yes, you'll do nicely," she said, her voice like the cries of a dying animal. "Let's go back to my cottage, children."

"In faerie stories," Esme said, "it never goes well for anyone who goes back to a mysterious cottage in the woods with a strange creature."

"Should we run?" Sybil asked, turning so she was back-to-back with Esme. The hag circled closer, and Sybil waved her knife. Which only made the hag laugh.

"Where can we run to? She certainly knows the woods better than we do."

"I won't hurt you, girls," the creature said. "I'm Mordgran, Auntie of the Forest. Protector of lost Fae who wander too deeply into the woods. There are terrible things in these trees, you know." She looked at them, her lichen eyes not blinking. Then she leaned in, sniffing Esme, long and deep. "Ahhhh, but you are mortal? Well, that changes things . . ."

The hag stepped closer, her teeth as sharp as her knife. "We don't have any rules about protecting *mortals* we catch in our woods."

Terror held Sybil in place. Part of her wanted to shout she was half Fae so Mordgran would leave them alone. The other part still wasn't able to reveal that to Esme. But, if she had to, she would. If that was what it took to save Esme's life.

The Swamp Hag took a step closer, her rotten marsh breath moving hot and damp over them. "You'll be delicious," she sang under her breath. "Perfect feast for the Spring Equinox celebrations."

Esme stepped in front of Sybil, brandishing her screwdriver. "Leave us alone."

"Esme, get back! You can't protect me from everything."

"Watch me," Esme muttered. She pulled a knife from her bag, waving it toward Mordgran. "Stay away!" she shouted.

As she did so, Oliver's gray head peered out of the bag. Mordgran's eyes fell on him, and she screeched, leaping backward.

"What is that?" she shouted in her teeth-crunching-stone voice.

Sybil and Esme looked down at the same time. Oliver blinked back at them with innocent wide eyes.

"This creature?" Sybil said, pulling him out of Esme's bag.

"Sybil! No! Put him back," Esme whispered. "He's too small!"

"I don't think she knows that."

Mordgran stared at the tiny cat in Sybil's hands. She whimpered as Sybil took a step closer. "Keep it away," Mordgran pleaded.

Oliver opened his mouth, showing his needle-sharp teeth as he yawned. The hag flinched. Sybil stepped closer. "Drop your knife," Sybil ordered, "or I'll put this terrible, awful, monstrous creature in your arms."

Oliver finished his yawn and blinked at Mordgran. She dropped her knife and took another step back. "Please let me go," she whispered. "I didn't mean any disrespect, Your Majesty," she said, her eyes still on Oliver.

Your Majesty?

At this, Sybil looked over at Esme, who was smothering a laugh. The thought of Oliver as anything royal was ridiculous. Though perhaps no more ridiculous than Maeve really being a green faerie or Sybil and Esme having gone through a door into Fae.

"Tell us how to reach Queen Mab's castle," Sybil said. "And we'll let you go."

As if on cue, Oliver gave a tremendous meow. The noise made Mordgran cover her ears.

"Of course, my liege." Her voice was all oil and rot. "I'll help you find the palace, if you'll only leave me alone. Follow the golden threads out of the woods, and then you'll reach the edge of the royal maze. From there, you'll see the castle."

Oliver gave another meow, which Mordgran seemed to take as a dismissal. Not looking up at Sybil or Esme, the hag shuffled backward, disappearing into the woods until she was out of sight.

Chapter Sixteen
Spring Equinox

Esme

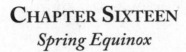

Once Mordgran was gone, taking with her the smell of hidden swamps, Esme began to breathe normally again. She held Oliver to her face, rubbing his little pink nose against her own.

"You're such a good little kitten, aren't you! Scaring away that big mean forest hag."

Sybil snorted, causing Esme to look up. "Maybe he can steal Queen Mab's jewels for us too."

Esme laughed, but it sounded forced, even to her. If Mordgran was representative of the type of creatures in Fae, how were Esme and Sybil going to sneak into a guarded palace, steal a queen's jewels, and get out unscathed?

"I think Oliver has done about all he can for now," Esme said as the kitten yawned again. Esme settled him into her bag, making him a comfy bed on the extra scarf she'd brought and securing the bag so he wouldn't fall out.

"What did Mordgran mean, 'follow the golden threads'?" Esme asked, looking around the woods.

"Up there," Sybil said, pointing into the canopy, where sunlight danced through the trees. The light made a long golden trail. Esme had missed it before because she'd been looking down rather than up.

Leaving the stream, they started walking through the woods, twisting and turning along an unseen path, directed by the golden light. Their feet sunk into deep piles of fallen leaves as the pines gave way to ancient oak trees, whose roots made tall arches for them to pass under. Crows croaked to each other as Esme and Sybil slipped under their trees, and the whisper of unseen feet through underbrush filled the air. Long curtains of moss hung from the oak branches, and within the trees, Esme could make out houses—some no bigger than a book, others the size of carriages—built of moss and wood and connected by rope bridges. Bobbing lights in colorful glass jars lit the shadowy canopy. Red-capped and silver-hued mushrooms grew under the trees, and Esme longed to study them. For a time, as they paused beside a wide pond covered in lily pads and surrounded by cattails that waved in the wind, winged creatures the size of dragonflies and wearing dresses made of flower petals flitted around their heads. Sybil sketched a few of them in Lucien's journal.

"Why do you think Mordgran was so afraid of Oliver?" Sybil asked as they resumed walking. "She kept calling him 'Your Majesty'?"

Esme thought back on all the Fae tales she'd read over the years. "There was a story of a Fae king who could shift his shape into a cat," she said. "It was something I read about in school, before the orphanage. He'd travel around in a cat shape to check on his subjects and to visit other kingdoms. Maybe that's what Mordgran thought was happening?"

"Perhaps she thought he was a High Fae from another court, and we were his mortal servants," Sybil suggested.

That made both of them giggle, and as they walked, they talked more about the bits of lore Esme had read and what Sybil had found in Lucien's journal.

"Did you know," Esme said, as the ancient oak trees began to thin and pines appeared again—now they were more like those in Severon's parks rather than the enormous ones Esme and Sybil had encountered earlier—"that according to the book I found in Lucien's house, there's supposed to an oracle somewhere in the mountains of Fae who is famous for—"

A loud crack split the air. Esme froze, grabbing Sybil's arm. Feminine voices swelled ahead, bickering loudly from around the bend.

Esme looked around, seeking a hiding spot among the rocks— all too small to crouch behind—or tree trunks—too narrow to really offer any cover.

"What are we going to do?" Esme's mouth was dry, her palms sweaty. She shifted the bag on her shoulder, gripping its strap.

Sybil pointed to a stand of pine trees whose branches grew low enough to create a ladder. "Climb?"

Esme swallowed hard. The thought of being up high—especially after standing on a ladder bridge over the chasm in Lucien's house—still made her feel woozy, but what choice did they have? The voices were coming closer. She nodded at Sybil, who ran toward the closest tree.

Making sure her bag—and Oliver inside it—was secure on her shoulder, Esme swung her leg over a tree branch and stepped upward. Rough bark scraped her legs, and sap made her fingers sticky, but she kept climbing. Only once she was near the top, where the wind swayed the trees, did she pause and look over at Sybil, who clung to the tree next to Esme's, her eyes wide. She pointed down to the forest floor. Esme followed her gaze, her heart thumping.

Two girls had stopped under Esme's tree. One of them wore a pale blue dress and a wide leather bracelet around her wrist. Her skin was bone white, and her pomegranate hair was cut short, her bangs falling across her forehead in a severe line. She had a sword strapped to her hip and wore scuffed black boots. The other girl had a waterfall of brown curls, light-purple skin, and delicately pointed ears. Her gray dress was simple but elegant. A belt woven with silver threads around her waist accentuated her curves, and she carried a basket on her arm. Its shadowy contents writhed, and Esme decidedly didn't want to know what it contained.

"There's nothing here," the girl in the gray dress said. Frustration laced her voice. She peered under the trees, moving her hand through the shadows.

"How many moonshadow snakes does Queen Mab really need?" asked the girl in the blue dress. She slumped against the trunk of a tree and took a long drink from a small metal bottle. She offered it to the other girl, who shook her head.

"Who can say? Mother just said to gather more before the feast." The girl in the gray dress stooped beside the tree next to the one Esme was hiding in.

One of the girls below them was Queen Mab's daughter? Esme's fingers dug into the pine's rough bark, and she bit her lip to hold back a gasp. She looked over at Sybil, who met her gaze and raised one eyebrow.

"Ahh! There's one!" called the girl in the gray dress. She pointed upward, toward Esme's branch.

"I'll get it," the girl in the blue dress said.

"If you insist."

The girl in the blue dress tossed her water bottle to the other girl and then put her feet on the first branches. She scaled the tree with easy confidence.

Esme tried not to move. Closer, then closer still, the girl in the blue dress climbed. Esme shifted slightly, which made pine needles rain down. She hugged the pine and peered around it. As she did so, an enormous snake slithered from the shadows, like it was made from them. Its long fangs glinted, and it reared its head.

The snake lunged toward Esme's face. A scream tore from her lips as she lurched away, releasing the branch she was holding. Her foot scrambled off the tree, flailing in the air. She flung out her hands, desperately reaching for the thin pine boughs, but they slipped through her fingers. From somewhere behind her, Esme heard Sybil call her name, and she saw the girl in the blue dress fling out a hand, but it was too late. Cradling her bag with Oliver inside it to her chest, Esme fell—down, down, down to the forest floor.

✦

Esme lay in a soft bed of moss, stretched underneath a canopy of trees. Stars swam in her vision, like fireflies dancing on a dark night.

Her bones hurt, but her head was cushioned by something soft. She stirred.

"Hush, hush," someone whispered. "Stay still. That was quite a fall."

Esme blinked. Three shapes hovered over her: Sybil, whose brow was knit with concern, and the two girls in the blue and silver dresses. Sybil clutched Oliver.

"Is he hurt?" Esme asked. Her back ached, but she was able to move her arms and legs.

Sybil shook her head. "You missed him as you fell. And these two did something to help slow your fall."

Esme groaned. "I'm not sure what happened? There was a snake?"

The girl in the silver dress flashed Esme a smile. "You're right. Quite the moonshadow beastie. But he's captured now." She gestured to the basket on the ground. A tangled mass of other snakes writhed there. As far as Esme could see, there was nothing keeping them in the basket.

"Why don't they flee?" Sybil asked. Much to Esme's relief, she was holding Oliver away from the snakes.

"It's an enchanted basket," said the girl in the blue dress. "From Queen Mab's workshops."

Ahh, that made sense. Or did it? Esme wasn't sure anymore, and at the word *workshop*, a pang for her clocks, faraway in another world, went through her. "Is Queen Mab's palace far from here?"

The two girls shared a look. "It's close enough. Where are you both from? Are you here for the ball?"

Esme looked to Sybil, who nodded slightly. "Yes. That's why we're here," Esme confirmed.

"We're from the Starlight Kingdom," Sybil said quickly. "We took a wrong turn and got lost in the forest."

The girl in the blue dress looked between them, her eyes narrowed. "Does the Starlight Kingdom not believe in fashion?" She took a bit of Esme's dress in her hands and rubbed the rough fabric.

The other girl laughed, flipping her curls over one shoulder. "Be nice, Chloe!"

Sybil answered before Esme could: "Of course we have fashion, but we're traveling."

"Are you part of Queen Mab's court?" Esme asked.

The girl in the gray dress pushed back her hair and sighed. "Regrettably. But I also work in the library."

A library! What would a Fae library look like? What might Esme learn there?

"And I work in the stables," said the other girl. She put one hand on the pommel of her sword.

Esme eyebrows flew up. In her world, stable girls didn't walk around with swords. There was clearly more going on here than it seemed.

"I'm Hyacinth," said the girl in the gray dress.

"*Princess* Hyacinth," the girl in the blue dress amended, giving a mocking bow. "Queen Mab's youngest daughter."

Hyacinth scowled. "And this is my nemesis, Chloe."

"Nemesis?" Esme asked. "Why are you hunting moonshadow snakes together?"

Hyacinth shrugged. "Queen Mab demands gifts from all her court for the Equinox ball."

"Queen Mab asked *me* to get them," Chloe corrected. "Her Royal Highness, Princess Hyacinth, just can't stay away from me."

Hyacinth rolled her eyes. "I didn't trust you'd actually bring anything back."

"I was doing just fine without—"

"Can you take us to the palace?" Sybil interrupted, her voice eager. "We're here for the Equinox ball, but we got lost in the woods. . . ."

"Where are your possessions?" Chloe asked, her eyes narrowed.

"A swamp hag took all our things, except for our coats and my bag," Esme said at the same time Sybil said, "The horse carrying our things ran off, disappearing into the woods."

Chloe raised an eyebrow, looking between them.

"Both those things happened," Sybil amended hastily. "In succession. It was awful."

"I see," Chloe said flatly. Then she shrugged. "What do you make of it, Princess? Would you like to bring these travelers to your mother's ball?"

Hyacinth bit her lip. "It's strange that you're so lost in the forest. I've read that members of the Starlight Court are excellent navigators, but . . ."

"We are!" Esme interjected. "We just hadn't planned on our horse running off. . . ."

"And we're terribly excited about the ball," Sybil added. "Please? Can you help us get to the palace at least?"

Hyacinth blew out a breath. "I suppose we can help. For the sake of diplomatic relations between our courts, if nothing else. I have obligations as soon as we return to the palace—Mother expects my sisters and I to help greet guests—but Chloe can find you some dresses. You'll need to stay close to her. It's not feast time yet, so everyone should be enjoying the garden party before the ball. But we don't want you to be seen in this attire."

Esme got to her feet stiffly, helped up by Sybil. She slung the bag over her shoulder, secured Oliver back in it, and started walking. Although each step hurt, it could've been much worse—*should've* been after falling from such a height.

The four of them wended through the forest, walking along a path that took them under a silvery waterfall that sprayed their clothing with mist, and along a ridge that showed them snow-capped mountains in the distance. They walked until the sun was high in the sky and Esme's stomach grumbled, reminding her that it was well past lunchtime. Eventually, they reached the edge of the forest. To their left, tucked into a valley between the mountains, sprawled a small village. But that wasn't what made Esme gasp.

"Welcome to the Moonshadow Court." Hyacinth waved a hand, like a tour guide. "My mother's grand palace awaits."

Beside Esme, Sybil swore softly.

"Absolutely overblown pile of rocks," Chloe muttered.

Esme tried to take the palace in. It was so much larger than she'd expected. How were they ever going to find Queen Mab's jewels in it?

She had no idea, but she forced herself to study the details, cataloguing them like she would do with clock parts.

The Moonshadow Queen's Palace was made of dark polished stone, and it looked like it had been pulled from the bones of the mountain itself. At the palace's back, jagged granite peaks covered with dark pines and capped with snow soared into the clouds. The castle itself ran right up to the back of the mountain, resting against it like a woman leaning against her lover. A central tower dominated the palace, and obsidian steps led up to the palace doors. Ornate columns, midnight blue and wrapped with carved moonshadow snakes, held up the portico. Towering hedge mazes filled the yard in front of the castle, and a long driveway ran between them. Carriages pulled by horses, large horned stags, bears, griffins, unicorns, and skeletal creatures trundled over the bridge.

"Those are the High Fae gentry from the other courts," Chloe said, pointing toward Fae in magnificent gowns or suits that shone silver, gold, amethyst, and other colors, who stepped out of the carriages, mingling with one another or making their way up the palace steps. "But of course you knew that, yes? Since you're traveling from the Starlight Court?"

"Of course we knew that." Sybil huffed. "And we'd be arriving with them, had we not gotten lost. As we already told you."

Chloe clucked her tongue against her teeth, but Hyacinth nudged her. "Leave them alone, Chloe. They've had a long day."

"I know that. I just think it's strange that—"

"Is that Queen Mab?" Esme asked, interrupting Chloe and pointing toward a gorgeous Fae who stood at the top of the palace steps. She glowed with silver light, and her long blue hair was twisted upward. A silver headpiece sat on her head, the shape of a crescent moon crowning it. A pair of black-and-silver wings folded at her back, and even from this distance, Esme was mesmerized by her deliberate, regal movements.

"It is indeed," Chloe said as she followed Esme's gaze.

Sybil bit her lip beside Esme. "What is she doing? Is this part of the Equinox celebrations?"

Chloe nodded. "She greets all her guests as they arrive, then hosts a feast, and later this evening, she puts on her best dress and the crown jewels for the ball."

Sybil nudged Esme at the mention of the crown jewels, and Esme nodded, ever so slightly. At least they knew the jewels were here. Somewhere.

Hyacinth shifted the basket of moonshadow snakes on her arm. "I better get back to the palace. I'm already late, and Mother will flay me—or at least bar me from the library for a month—if I show up to the feast with pine sap in my hair."

"Poor baby princess," Chloe said, making a face at Hyacinth. "Your life is nothing but torment."

Hyacinth plucked a glowing silver mushroom from the ground and threw it at Chloe. She ducked, and the mushroom hit Esme on the arm, leaving a shimmering spray of silver behind.

"Missed me." Chloe grinned at Hyacinth.

"I'll find you later tonight," Hyacinth promised. "And I shall have my revenge!"

Chloe laughed, and Hyacinth waved to them as she hurried over the bridge.

"This way," said Chloe. "Stay close." She led them away from the central palace driveway, along a narrow path tucked between the edge of the hedges and the forest. "We'll cut through the hedge maze—fewer prying eyes than along the main paths—to get to the stables where my quarters are. I'm sure I have something suitable you can borrow for the evening."

As they slipped through a gap in the hedge, Esme gasped. Silver lights threaded through rustling willow leaves, which blew on a warm breeze and made an aching, magical sound. As Chloe hurried forward, urging them along, Esme forced herself to keep up, only allowing herself quick glances of the wonders they passed.

Every few feet, the hedges opened, revealing spacious courtyards filled with stone follies, reflecting ponds, burbling fountains that shot jets of water into the air, and hundreds of plants Esme had never seen. Purple orchids towered over the Fae who lounged on blankets beneath them. Delicate trees with blue leaves made music when the wind blew through them. Entire sections were carpeted in the most delicate white and pink flowers.

Sybil gripped Esme's hand. "Isn't it marvelous?" she whispered. "I never imagined it would be so . . . so lovely."

Esme had only imagined Fae in the confines of the stories she'd read. She'd never considered how a Fae garden might look or how the wind in Fae would sound. But, now that she was here, wonder filled her. "It's incredible," she said to Sybil.

Chloe knew her way through the hedge maze and constantly issued directions as they walked—"Watch out for the fire fungus; step over the gnome's garden path, please; don't linger at the moonlight pool unless you'd like to talk to the water sprites, though they're always temperamental, especially on the Equinox!"—and eventually she marched them to the back edge of the garden, a shadowy space nestled right against the mountain. They slipped through another gap in the hedge and walked toward a sprawling crystal greenhouse within a ring of ancient oaks.

"The queen's stables are over here," Chloe said, ducking out of the hedge maze, and gesturing toward a wide meadow full of fenced paddocks. Bordering the paddocks, right at the foothills of the mountains, was a complex of buildings easily the size of several city blocks. "Over a thousand people work in them—including grooms, trainers, pages, coachmen, blacksmiths, musicians, animal doctors, saddlers, and, of course, me."

They were staggering and Esme marveled at the sheer amount of logistics it took to keep everything running.

"What do you do in the stables?" Sybil asked, as they started to walk toward the stables.

"Lots of things," Chloe said. "Though I'm partial to the baby dragons."

"Baby . . . dragons?" Esme said, as they approached one of the paddocks.

Beside her, Sybil gave a little squeal of excitement. "Look at them, Ez!"

Delight filled Esme as an emerald-green creature, the size of Jean-Francois, chased a larger dragon around a stone enclosure. Little jets of green flame erupted from the dragon's mouth, making its playmate flap their own wings in annoyance. Oliver took one look at the dragons and then ducked his head back into Esme's satchel.

"Queen Mab is known for breeding the best dragons in Fae," Chloe said, leaning against the fence. "I'm sure half the people at the ball tonight are hoping to take home a hatchling or secure the promise of one down the line."

Spotting them, the emerald hatchling hurried over to the fence, spitting fire and shrieking. Chloe whistled a quick tune, and the dragon stopped spitting fire. It gave Chloe a tiny bow, then turned back to its playmate.

Esme's heart was going to melt. It bowed! The little dragon bowed!

"What was that you whistled?" Sybil asked.

"Just a lullaby we teach all the dragons when they're small," Chloe said. "We teach them all sorts of songs, but that's the starter one. This stable is a nursery of sorts where we train the dragons so their riders can control them. Those first few notes are basically me saying hello to the dragon and telling her all is well. Eventually, we'll teach her melodies for flying, fighting, and other such things."

"Amazing," Esme murmured, adding dragon upbringing to her list of unexpected things she was learning today.

"Do you train dragons?" Sybil asked, as Chloe led them away from the enclosure and down a boulevard between stone buildings. "Or ride them?"

"I wish," Chloe said. "When I'm lucky enough to be given dragon duty, I'm usually stuck cleaning up after them. But I like being around them, and I managed to learn a few of the songs. Now, follow me. My rooms are this way. In the older section of the stable."

They twisted through a few more alleys between the stables, and Esme glimpsed long paddocks full of horses and other creatures. Chloe stopped at a two-story cottage that backed right along the side of the mountain. Its roof sloped, and ivy grew up the side.

Chloe opened the cottage's door and beckoned Esme and Sybil into a well-lit cheerful room that smelled of baking bread. Colorful quilts hung from the walls, and a horseshoe was tacked above the door leading from the main room into the kitchen. The furniture was simple but well-worn. A wooden staircase split the lower level of the cottage, leading to more rooms upstairs. "Wendell, I'm home," she called.

"Wendell?" Sybil asked, looking around the room.

Chloe hung her sword on the wall and nodded. "Wendell Moorstone, the queen's favorite stablemaster, who retired a decade ago. He was given this cottage for his many years of service. He's my friend and lets me live here."

As she spoke, an ancient old man, with long white hair, weather-worn tan skin, and sharp features, shuffled into the front room, carrying a tea tray piled with several cups, a steaming porcelain teapot, a pot of jam, and slices of bread.

"Ahhh, Chloe, child," he said in a watery voice. "There you are. Just in time for tea."

Esme nearly cheered at the mention of tea.

Chloe took the tea tray from Wendell and kissed his papery cheek. "I've brought some friends for tea too, Wendell. Please meet Esme and Sybil. They're here for the queen's ball."

"The queen's ball?" Wendell pushed a piece of thin white hair away from his face, revealing pointed ears.

Surprise filled Esme to see he was Fae, but that really shouldn't have been shocking, should it? Since he was Queen Mab's stable-master, and they were in a Fae realm. Even as she thought this, the aroma from the teapot, something spiced with a hint of green grass and the deep woods, wound around her. What kind of tea would a Fae stablemaster serve? Esme longed to find out.

"The Spring Equinox ball is tonight, remember?" Chloe said, in answer to Wendell's question. "It starts in a few hours, shortly after the feast."

"Ah yes, yes, of course," Wendell said. He cast a crooked smile at Esme. "My memory was once the most feared in all the realms, but these days, it's a bit sneaky. Much like a young dragon, trying slip out of its bridle."

Wendell laughed, and Chloe steered him into a chair. "I need to show our guests some dresses, Wendell, but you sit. Enjoy some tea. We'll join you soon." She patted his hands tenderly, making Esme like her a bit more.

"Sounds lovely," Wendell said. "But I insist this girl stays here with me," he pointed to Esme. "And, please, let me have a look at that creature you've got in your bag. I can smell it from here, and I'd love to say hello."

Esme glimpsed Sybil, who smiled at her.

"Enjoy your tea," Sybil whispered. "I'll find us dresses and see if I can learn more about getting into Queen Mab's room."

"Thank you," Esme said as she sunk gratefully into the chair across from Wendell. As Sybil and Chloe walked up the stairs, Esme pulled Oliver from her bag and set him on her lap. Wendell poured her a cup of tea, and Esme handed him Oliver, who purred under his touch.

They might be in another world, ready to rob a powerful queen of her jewels, but at least Esme would have a cup of tea to fortify her nerves. It might not have been part of the plan, but it was a most welcome part of the afternoon.

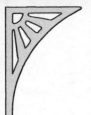

Chapter Seventeen
Spring Equinox

Sybil

Sybil *had so many questions, all of them sitting on the tip of her tongue.* She didn't know where to begin, however. The personal things she ached to know seemed far less urgent than getting into Queen Mab's room. All she really knew was that she and Esme needed dresses that would let them blend in as they snuck into Queen Mab's castle. Sybil still wasn't sure walking into the palace was the best idea, but what other choice did they have?

"What do you think of this one?" Chloe said, holding up a pale blue dress. "It's made from spider's silk and dewdrops. . . . Simple, I know, but it should fit you."

They were in Chloe's room, a small, cozy chamber under the eaves of the cottage. There was a narrow bed, a window that overlooked the stables, a wardrobe, and piles of books and papers spread out over a small desk.

Sybil stepped forward, reaching for the dress Chloe held out. It was dazzling, and Sybil had never worn anything so fine in her life.

Not in her father's home or even the green dress Maeve had loaned her that first night in the Absinthe Underground. "I love it. But how does a girl who works in the stables get such things?"

Chloe stopped rummaging through the wardrobe and turned to Sybil, a pair of silver shoes in hand. "Hyacinth gives me her cast-off dresses sometimes. I modify them to better suit myself. I was a seamstress once, many years ago, far away from here. . . ." Chloe shuddered at the words.

Sybil took the dress from Chloe and held it up to her body. Chloe was taller than she was, and the train dragged on the floor. "This one will be perfect for Esme."

"And this one should fit you," Chloe said, pulling out a midnight-blue velvet dress woven with silver threads. Silver lace decorated the top of the dress.

"What's this made from?" Sybil asked, touching the collar.

"Starlight lace, of course. Dreadful stuff, but I suspect you are quite familiar with it, coming from the Starlight Court."

"I . . . uh . . . of course . . . I am."

"What does it do?"

Desperately, Sybil searched her memory for what Lucien or her mother had told her about magic and starlight lace. She gripped the key around her neck. Before she could reply, Chloe pressed on.

"Why are you really here?"

The question sent a spike of fear through her. "What do you mean? We told you, we're here for the ball."

Chloe snorted. "Really? Where's your invitation? What part of the Starlight Court are you from? Do you align more with the struggles of the Duke of the Silver Cups or the Lady Joycell Alderwood?

Do you eat starlight for breakfast, or have you given that up recently and that's why you've lost your glow?"

Sybil's mouth opened and then closed again as her brain whirred, trying to think of answers. "I . . ."

"You don't know what I'm talking about, do you? Because you're not really Fae!"

"Of course we are!" Sybil summoned every ounce of her breeding and background. "I told you we were traveling and our horses ran off and we got lost in the woods. We're great ladies in the Starlight Court."

Chloe raised an eyebrow. "Where's your carriage? What kind of great ladies arrive on horses?"

"Ones who wanted to see the countryside."

Chloe scoffed. "I've never met a Starlight Court member who doesn't have a glowing silver star at the base of the neck. Lift your hair and show me."

"No."

"It should be the easiest thing, if you're who you say you are."

Sybil hesitated. Could they just make a run for it? They could, but where would they go? Besides, Esme was currently drinking tea with Wendell, and Chloe had been a friend to them so far. She deserved at least a little bit of the truth.

"Fine." Sybil blew out a breath. "We're not Fae. Or at least I'm not fully Fae and Esme is definitely human. How did you know?"

Chloe made a triumphant noise. "You might've tricked Hyacinth, who is Fae through and through, but I can smell the city streets on you."

"That's impossible. There are other mortals in Fae, so how do you know we're not them?"

"Have you seen the other mortals in Fae?"

Sybil shook her head.

"They're a sorry bunch. Thin-skinned, entirely enchanted, always happy to do the Fae's bidding. But you smell like the sea, and smoke from gas lamps, and the sweat of machines. You're not from this world, which means you must've come through one of the doors between our worlds. But how and when?"

Sybil blinked at Chloe. "Wait—I thought you were Fae too. Does this mean—does Hyacinth think you're Fae? But you're really—" She whispered the last part, as if Hyacinth might be nearby to hear it.

Chloe held up a finger to Sybil's lips. "Don't say it."

"Does Wendell know?"

Chloe shook her head and removed her finger.

"How did you get here?" Sybil whispered.

"It's a long story, but the quick version is that I stumbled into this world while I was mapping dragons. That's how I met Wendell. I've been trying to find a way back to my world for the past year using these books, but there's nothing in them. Do you have a way to open a door between our worlds?"

Sybil wrapped her hand around her key protectively. "I might."

Chloe bit the inside of her cheek, considering. "Why are you really here?"

Sybil blew out a breath. What did she have to lose if she told Chloe the whole truth? Maybe Chloe could help them get into Queen Mab's room? They'd certainly have a better chance of success with more information. They barely knew anything about the palace at all. It was a risk, but she had to take it.

Quickly, Sybil filled Chloe in on why they were in Fae. She left out Maeve, saying instead that someone had hired them to steal something from Queen Mab.

When she was done, Chloe sat down hard on her bed. She blinked at Sybil. "You want to get into Queen Mab's room, steal something, and leave? Do you know how impossible that's going to be?"

Sybil had an idea, but not knowing exactly how difficult it was had kept her brave. She twisted her key. "We can do it," she said, with far more confidence than she felt. "And if you help us, then, when I open the door back into my world, you can come with us."

"What's stopping me from just stealing the key from you now and opening a door myself?" Chloe asked.

"Because you won't be able to open one," Sybil said. "My mother gave me this. It only works for me or someone of my blood. But if you help us, then you can come too."

Chloe only paused for a small moment, considering, and then she nodded. "It's a deal. Now, listen, we have to do this before the feast. As soon as it's over, Queen Mab will be getting ready for the ball, and you need to be in and out of her room before then."

◆

An hour or so later, Sybil and Esme were dressed in Chloe's ethereal dresses, their hair was woven with colorful stones and flowers, and they slipped their ragged coats on over the gowns. Esme also put her bag over her shoulder; it looked out of place with her Fae dress, but she refused to leave Oliver or anything else in the stable. There was no guarantee they'd have time to come back for them.

Esme said goodbye to Wendell, who sent them with leftover bread slices, and Chloe led them away from the stables and into the hedge maze once again. This part of the gardens was full of night-blooming flowers. The sounds of water falling over stone, music, laughter, and the clinking of glasses drifted from the garden's shadows.

"They're having a garden party through there," Chloe called out, indicating the direction of the noise. "In the main part of the garden. It'll go on all night, sort of the less formal version of the Equinox ball in the palace."

Had Lucien ever been to a garden party like this? For just a moment, Sybil longed to change directions and walk toward that party, just to see what it was like or perhaps find her brother. Of course, finding Lucien wasn't a possibility she'd allowed herself to imagine. No. They were here for Queen Mab's crown jewels. Going to garden parties wasn't going to secure their futures or help Maeve.

"Do you trust Chloe?" Esme asked, leaning in close to Sybil as they walked. She shifted her bag.

"Well enough." Quickly, Sybil explained the bargain she'd made with Chloe. "It's in her interests to help us. Plus, we don't have much of a choice."

Esme frowned, and her very visible worry made Sybil nervous. Not for the first time that day, she wondered what she'd gotten her best friend into. There was still a thorn of fear in her for Esme's well-being—one that had stabbed her through the heart as Esme had fallen from that tree. Despite Esme saying she was fine, Sybil wished she'd stayed back with Wendell, drinking more tea. But, of course, Esme had insisted on coming.

"I can still do this myself," Sybil had whispered. "If you're not feeling up to it or if you're—"

"Sybil."

"Yes?"

"Shut up, please. I'm coming with you. We have been over this so many times, I'm bored talking about it." Esme pinched her elbow.

Sybil had to smile at that. "Fine," she grumbled. "Shutting up now."

They walked along the edge of the maze, passing a pair of Fae—tall, willowy women with pointed ears, light-orange skin, and tiny deer horns sprouting from their heads—who were wandering through the gardens, deep in a conversation interspersed with kisses. Neither of them stopped to stare at Sybil and Esme, which Sybil supposed meant the dresses they'd borrowed from Chloe helped them fit in.

"Here," Chloe said, stopping suddenly at a shadowy alcove in the hedge. She slipped behind it, and Sybil and Esme followed. They were in a very narrow gap between the hedge and the stone of the mountain. Long hanging vines, heavy with purple flowers that smelled like rotting fruit, fell over the stone. "Pull these back," Chloe said, wrenching the vines aside.

"Oh!" Sybil said, unable to contain her surprise as she pulled away some vines.

Behind the vines was a round wooden door built into the side of the mountain itself. Moss furred it, and a rusty metal knob stood in the middle of the door.

"What's this?" Sybil asked, looking over her shoulder to make sure no one was looking at them.

"I call it the Hyacinth Door," Chloe said, her voice full of wry amusement. "It's ancient—Hyacinth thinks it's from a time before the High Fae were even here. It leads to a tunnel under the mountain, which eventually runs into the palace. Hyacinth uses it to sneak to and from the royal apartments. She doesn't think anyone else remembers it's here, and it's how she's able to get out her most tedious royal engagements. She's put a small enchantment on it so others don't find their way in."

"But you know how to open it?" Sybil asked.

"Of course."

What a funny pair of nemeses Hyacinth and Chloe were. Sybil bit back a smile.

Whispering a word, Chloe pulled the door open. It creaked, and a musty under-the-earth smell wafted out of the darkness.

"This way," Chloe said, stepping forward. Beside Sybil, Esme swore softly.

"I hate dark places," she muttered.

"We'll be okay," Sybil said, reaching for Esme's hand. Their fingers wove together.

Chloe pulled the door shut behind them—it clanged loudly—and then darkness deep and entire blanketed them. Sybil could feel Esme's hand shake, and Sybil's own breath hitched in her chest. Chloe whispered another word. A small silver light flickered on the wall beside her, coming from a palm-sized lantern. Relief filled Sybil. Its silvery light softened the angles of their faces.

"Is there gas in the lantern?" Esme asked, releasing Sybil's hand and moving closer to study it.

"Starlight," Chloe said, shuddering slightly. "Like I said, dreadful stuff, but useful sometimes."

"Did Hyacinth discover this lantern in the tunnel as well?" Sybil asked.

Chloe shook her head. "She made it. Hyacinth is extremely good at starlight magic, but don't tell her I told you that. It's not fitting for a Moonshadow princess to know such things, but she found the way in an old book and couldn't help trying it."

Chloe picked up the lamp and gestured to the tunnel that stretched into the darkness in front of them. "Now, we better get moving. It's a long walk to the royal apartments."

She wasn't kidding. They walked for what seemed like hours, as the tunnel twisted through the mountain. It narrowed at points, so they had to squeeze through, and sometimes it opened into wide caverns hung with stone formations hanging from the ceiling. The stone walls were slick, and water dripped from somewhere in the tunnel. Eventually, the tunnel intersected with a twisting staircase.

"This is the start of the palace," Chloe said, her silver light illuminating rough, well-worn stone stairs. "We go up exactly one hundred and seventeen stairs, and then we're at Hyacinth's room. Not much longer now."

After all the walking, Sybil's breath came in ragged gasps. She was extremely grateful when Esme handed her the bottle of water she'd brought from home.

"Did I ever tell you how brilliant you are to have packed this?" Sybil asked, taking a long swig.

"Tell me again?" Esme said, grinning.

"Absolutely brilliant."

They stopped again at a small landing near the top of the stairs. Chloe pushed against the wall, smashing her fingers into various stones and bricks. Finally, one clicked, and the wall swung open slightly, letting in a long finger of light.

Chloe peered into the room on the other side and then turned to face Sybil and Esme. "Hyacinth is probably with her mother and sisters at the Equinox feast already, but that doesn't mean her attendants are gone. Be careful. This is the princesses' hallway, so there are seven bedrooms on this floor. Queen Mab's room is on the next floor, up the main stairs and to the left. Big doors with snakes on them. You can't miss it."

Sybil swallowed her glug of water. "Aren't you coming with us?"

Chloe shook her head. "I told you I'd get you this far, not help you rob the queen. That was our deal. I'm desperate to get home, but I don't have a death wish. Do you know what Queen Mab does to people who steal from her?"

Sybil decidedly did not want to know.

"What?" Esme asked.

Chloe frowned. "Best you don't find out. Now hurry. I'll be waiting on this landing for half an hour, and then I have to go. I have obligations tonight too." She fished a small silver hourglass out of her pocket and turned it over.

Esme pulled Oliver from her bag. "Can you hold him? Please? I don't want him running away in the palace."

Chloe looked warily at the cat. Then Oliver stretched and yawned, his little pink tongue sticking out slightly as he did so.

"Fine," Chloe said, relenting, "but hurry." She cradled the cat to her chest, humming a melody to him.

Taking a deep breath, Sybil pushed open the door. This was it. There was no going back now. They were stepping into Queen Mab's palace.

"Ready?" she asked Esme.

Esme shook her head. "Not at all."

"Just stick to the plan. We'll be okay."

"We don't really have a plan for this part."

Sybil squeezed Esme's hand. "Sure we do. Get to the queen's room, steal the jewels, run away."

Esme blew out a long breath. "Not even remotely a plan."

"We're going to be fine, Ez. Trust me. And by the end of this evening, we'll be richer than you can possibly imagine."

"Let's just get it over with."

As they stepped forward, the hidden door shut softly behind them. Sybil ran her fingers over the small gap in the pink-flowered wallpaper that outlined the door. As she watched, the line wavered and then disappeared. More of Hyacinth's enchantments, probably.

Hyacinth's room was large, nearly twice the size of Sybil and Esme's entire apartment, and the walls were painted with a riot of flowers. All the furniture was upholstered in shades of pink, and books were piled on every surface. Even the pillows were covered in books.

"She has more books than you, Ez," Sybil said, looking around.

"Only because she's royalty. And works in Queen Mab's library. When we do this job for Maeve, and we're rich beyond our wildest dreams, you have no idea how many books I'm going to buy. And clocks. We're going to have so many clocks."

"Goody. We can always use more clocks."

Esme swatted Sybil on the arm as they moved through Hyacinth's room, opening the main door cautiously. Outside Hyacinth's door, long hallways stretched in both directions, built around a central palace courtyard. At their feet, the wooden floor was inlaid with celestial designs and polished to a shine. There were two closed doors beside Hyacinth's and four others along the hall. Tall mirrors hung between the doors to the princesses' rooms, and ornate silver candelabra stood in front of the mirrors, reflecting dancing golden candlelight into the hall.

"Look at this," Sybil breathed, walking to the onyx balustrade across from Hyacinth's room. Three levels below, the High Fae of the Moonshadow Court feasted at long tables, their lips painted red from wine. A swell of noise floated upward. A long line of guards in deep-purple uniforms stood between the queen and an ornate staircase leading to the upper levels of the palace. Sybil watched, fascinated, as Queen Mab raised a glass to toast, and the hall fell silent.

"This is our chance," Esme whispered, pulling Sybil away from the railing. "Let's find the queen's room while she's talking."

Sybil wrenched her attention away from the feast and lifted her skirts. Together, she and Esme moved as quickly as they dared through the princesses' hallway. Their reflections were caught again and again in the glittering mirrors. They hugged the wall, in the hopes of avoiding the eyes of the Fae at the feast, but they would be totally exposed on the steps. They stopped at the edge of the staircase, peeking around a pillar.

"What do we do?" Esme asked.

Sybil held a finger to her lips. Queen Mab had stopped speaking, and the noise of the feast resumed. Wild music began to play, and servers brought out platters of roasted meats and elaborate baked pies.

Sybil looked to the bottom of the staircase. A pair of girls with shining ice-blue dresses and black hair had walked up to Queen Mab's table, bowing low. The queen fell into conversation with the girls, and the attention of all the guests seemed to be on them.

"Go! Now!" Sybil urged, grabbing Esme's hand. As one, they ran up the stairway. Sybil slipped for a moment, but Esme hauled her upward. Sybil fought the urge to look over her shoulder, but in a breathless blur, they arrived at the top of the staircase. They collapsed behind a tall marble pillar, breaths coming in ragged gasps.

"We made it!"

"Up a staircase," Sybil said dryly. "We're practically in the vault."

Esme groaned and peered into the hallway. "First door on the left," she said. "I see it. That's got to be Queen Mab's room."

Sybil looked over Esme's shoulder. A set of tall obsidian doors— carved with flowers, stars, moons, and snakes—sat in the middle of the hallway. They radiated regality, authority, and security. It was absurd to think two thieves from another world could just walk into Queen Mab's room, but that was exactly what Sybil planned to do. She glanced farther down the hall. Two guards patrolled there.

"We can't get past those guards," Esme whispered.

"We have to try!" If they didn't, then there was no point to this whole mission. Sybil might as well open a door and send them and Chloe back home now. But, if she did that, they would never get Maeve's reward.

"Of course we're going to try!" Esme snapped. "I just don't know how we're going to get it."

"Watch the guards—they're moving away from the queen's door, pacing in a circle. Wait for it. . . ."

The guards turned so their backs were to Queen Mab's door; that was Sybil and Esme's chance.

"Now go!" Sybil said, barreling toward the door without looking back. As quietly as possible, she tried Queen Mab's doorknob—locked, of course—and then pulled out her thief's kit.

"Hurry!" Esme arrived a second after Sybil and looked toward the guards.

Sybil nodded, focusing on the keyhole in front of her. She pushed her metal thief's tools into it, moving them around.

Mercifully, the queen's door clicked open, and Sybil and Esme rushed inside before they could see if the guards had noticed them or the door opening. Shutting the door softly, Sybil locked it behind them.

She glanced around the room, stopping suddenly. There was a fireplace shaped like an open maw, two sofas, silver and black, sat in front of it, and a raised platform with an enormous bed dominated the middle of the room. A large mirror and gilded dressing table were on one side of the room.

"It looks like Maeve's dressing room," Esme said, turning around.

It did. Almost exactly. "Maybe it's just a Fae style?" Sybil guessed, not sure what to make of the similarity, but certain they didn't have time to give it much thought. "Let's find the safe."

Sybil moved to the fireplace, gazing upward at the painting above it. Maeve had said the vault was behind the painting, but she hadn't said it would be a painting of Queen Mab in a glittering black dress, wearing her crown jewels. Something about her pose was familiar, but Sybil didn't have time to think on it.

"Help me," Sybil said, tugging one of the couches over so it stood in front of the fireplace. Esme shoved the couch, leaving long treads in the carpet.

Sybil clambered onto the sofa, but Esme stopped her. "I'm taller, let me."

"I'm a better climber."

"Fine. But if you fall—"

"I'm not going to fall. Now hand me the perfume."

Esme fished the perfume bottle from her bag and handed it over. Perfume in hand, Sybil scurried onto the back of the sofa, balancing on her tiptoes. She ran her fingers along the back of the painting, feeling for a moment like she was stealing a poster. Wedging her fingers behind it, she pulled. It stuck for a moment and then swung outward. Behind it was an obsidian panel carved with stars and flowers. It hummed with magic, as if it were waiting to be opened. Sybil traced her fingers along the stone. She uncorked the perfume bottle, and the smell of fruit, spice, and something otherworldly rose in the room.

"Where are you going to put the perfume?"

It was a good question. The tiny bottle had a glass wand in it, meant for applying perfume to a wrist.

"I'm not sure. . . ."

"Remember, Maeve said just two drops."

"I know. But if I put those in the wrong—"

Outside the door, there was a rattling noise, like someone was turning a key in the lock. In one quick motion, Sybil shut the painting over the vault. It clicked softly. She leaped off the sofa, and she and Esme shoved it into place. They barely had time to dive behind the sofa when the queen's door opened.

"No one in here," reported a gruff voice.

"Sorry, Captain. I swear I heard voices, but it might have just been echoes from the feast."

Sybil dared a glance over the top of the sofa. Two guards in purple uniforms stood in the queen's doorway, their swords out. One was a thin Fae man with long white hair and dark eyes. He had silver ribbons pinned to his chest and held himself with authority. The other guard was stocky, with red hair, pointed ears, and no decorations on his uniform.

"The room looks as it always does, Captain," said the redheaded guard. "But I can check it over again." He took a few steps into the room, and Sybil ducked.

"No. Leave it, Woodsfire. But double the patrols on this floor after the feast." There was the sound of a sword being sheathed. "Now let's go. The queen said to keep watch over the guests from the Starlight Court after that incident last year. She expects this year to be—"

The door to Queen Mab's room slammed shut, cutting off the guard captain's words.

Sybil slumped against the couch, her heart thumping. That had been too close. She turned to Esme. "Are you okay?"

"I didn't have a heart attack, if that's what you mean, but otherwise, no, I'm not okay. Let's get the jewels and get out of here."

Wordlessly, they pushed the sofa back against the fireplace. Sybil clambered up it, and Esme joined her there, both balancing on the cushions.

"We still haven't figured out where to put the drops of perfume."

"Anywhere," Esme urged. "It's magic. It should be fine. Just hurry!"

Sybil pulled the painting open again and picked up the perfume bottle. She dripped two drops of the blue liquid on the vault, right in the middle. The smell of oranges and petrichor and something smoky filled the room, making a small blue cloud. For one moment, the perfume hung in the air, and then it was sucked into the stone.

With a sound like a wine bottle being uncorked, the obsidian vault in front of them cracked in half down the middle. Two doors swung open, revealing Queen Mab's crown jewels. Long ropes of pearls; stunning bracelets studded with diamonds, emeralds, rubies, and other gems; rings; chokers; and a dazzling tiara sat inside the vault on a tray of purple velvet.

Esme gasped. "They're incredible. Are these really magical?"

"I hope so." Sybil scooped up an emerald and opal bracelet, holding it out to Esme. A jolt went through Sybil as she picked up a strand of pearls and held it beneath her collarbones where it skimmed her key. Yes. These were magical, no doubt about it. She handed the necklace to Esme.

Esme set the necklace against her skin.

"Do you feel anything?"

"No. Should I?"

Sybil shook her head. "It doesn't matter." Shoving the perfume bottle into her pocket and the rest of the crown jewels into the enchanted bag, she grabbed Esme's hand. "Let's go!"

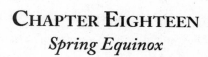

CHAPTER EIGHTEEN
Spring Equinox

Esme

If only they could use Queen Mab's door to make a portal back to their world. But no. That was impossible. They had to get back to the tunnel in Hyacinth's room. Esme couldn't leave Oliver, and Sybil had promised Chloe she could come with them back to their world.

"See any guards?" Esme asked.

Sybil had Queen Mab's door open a crack, and she was staring down the hallway. "They're farther down, near the top of the staircase."

"Should we go?"

"If we don't now, we'll be stuck in the queen's room. Ready?"

Esme hadn't really been ready for any of today, but they were so close to escaping with the queen's jewels. "Yes."

Swiftly, she and Sybil slipped through the gap in Queen Mab's door. Sybil, who had the enchanted bag of stolen jewels looped around her wrist, shut the door softly.

"Walk normally," Sybil said. "Stick to the shadows."

Esme nodded, and the two of them moved along the queen's hallway, hugging the walls, as if that would hide them from the guards. They turned a corner, and Sybil pulled up short, swearing.

Oh no.

Walking toward them, surrounded by palace guards, including the two who'd checked the queen's bedroom not long ago, was Queen Mab. She walked with the grace of one of the big cats Esme had seen at the Severon zoological park, all barely contained power and lithe danger. Her dress shone with onyx, diamonds, and deep-blue sapphires, and her hair was woven with gems. Her dark blue wings were folded at her back, and she had a sword belted at her waist. A small bottle filled with silver liquid hung on a chain around her neck.

"What do we do?" Esme's heart had lodged in her throat. What kind of queen wore a sword to a feast?

A Fae one, who can do whatever she likes. We're so dead. Queen Mab is going to see us, and then I'll never get my cottage by the sea or the chance to tell Sybil—

"Follow my lead," Sybil muttered seconds before the queen stopped in front of them.

"Hello, little ones," Queen Mab said, her voice smooth as a looking glass. "What brings you to my hallway?"

Sybil sunk into a low curtsy, and Esme copied her. She kept her eyes down, focusing on the silver gleam of Queen Mab's shoes.

"Hello, Your Majesty," Sybil said, her voice quavering slightly. "We're here as guests, from the Starlight Court, and we got a bit turned around in the palace."

Follow Sybil's lead. That's what Esme needed to do. But what did that even mean? Her throat was dry, her hands shaking. She exhaled softly, trying to stay calm, as befitted someone from a Fae court.

"Hmmm," the queen said, stepping closer to Sybil. Esme darted her eyes toward her friend as Queen Mab ran one bloodred nail along Sybil's ragged coat, stopping at the leather bag dangling from her wrist. "I've never seen such interesting fashion choices from the Starlight Court. Though I like your reticule. May I look inside?"

No! Esme bit back the word. They couldn't tell a Fae queen no. But what if the magical bag was a fraud? Yes, it had somehow accommodated all the crown jewels, but Esme hadn't checked that the magic made them look like pebbles. There hadn't been time! But she really should've checked that.

"Of course, Your Majesty," Sybil breathed. "Please." She pulled open the little bag and offered it to the queen.

"Pebbles?" said Queen Mab, poking a long nail into the bag. The sound of stones clinking together filled the air.

Esme closed her eyes with relief. The magical bag had worked. They would be fine as long as the queen didn't pull out any of the stones and see them transform into her own crown jewels.

"Pebbles, Your Majesty," Sybil said rather weakly. "I like to travel with something from my own homeland."

The queen withdrew her finger, as if satisfied with that answer. "Very well. Very strange, but we've certainly seen odder things in this court." She put her finger under Esme's chin, now, the nail biting into Esme's flesh as the queen tilted her face upward. "But that still doesn't explain what you're doing in my private hallway."

"We got lost, and—"

Esme cut Sybil off as an idea came to her. She reached into her bag, pulling out the small box containing the white rowan flowers she'd gathered earlier. Opening the box, she offered it and the flowers to the queen. "We wanted to give you a gift, Your Majesty," she said quickly. "Something as lovely as you are. You were so busy with the feast, and I . . . well, I suggested we bring the blossoms to you up here, in the hopes we might leave them outside your door. It was a silly idea, I see that now, but we wanted to gift these to you."

Esme heaved in a breath, anxiety making her knees wobble. She could feel Sybil's eyes on her, but she kept her gaze on Queen Mab.

The queen raised an eyebrow and plucked a rowan blossom from Esme's hand. She held it to her nose, inhaling. "Ahhhh, one of my favorite scents. I've not smelled this in a long time, as one of our dragons burned my rowan grove many years ago. Thank you."

She put the rowan blossom into her hair and then pocketed the box of flowers. Esme bowed her head.

"Now I must get ready for the Equinox ball," the queen said. "But you have pleased me. Find me tonight, and I'll give you one boon, as a gift for these rowan blossoms."

She moved away, taking most of her guards with her. Only one, the older captain with the long silver hair, loomed over Sybil and Esme as they got to their feet.

"You're lucky the queen is in a good mood," he snarled. "I've seen people lose their eyes for looking at her askew. Now, you've given your gift, so get away from here. You won't be so lucky if you're caught wandering this level again."

Esme didn't need to be told twice. With a small nod to the guard, she and Sybil turned, hurrying down the staircase. They were halfway down the stairs when the doors to Queen Mab's room crashed open.

"Thieves!" bellowed Queen Mab. "Nightshades! Stop them!"

Esme glanced upward to see Queen Mab standing at the top of the stairs, pointing at them. *Oh no.* The slim measure of triumph she'd felt at giving the queen the rowan blossoms evaporated, replaced by panic.

"Run!" Sybil urged, pulling at Esme's hand.

Esme's feet flew along the marble stairs. Loud voices and footsteps pounded after them, getting closer. In a blur, Esme and Sybil were at the bottom of the stairs. They turned to the right, racing along the princesses' hallway.

"Wait! Sybil! Hyacinth's room is that way!" Esme pointed toward the pink door at the end of the left hallway.

Sybil swore, letting go of Esme's hand as they reversed course, running as fast as they could toward Hyacinth's room. The Nightshades were nearing the bottom of the stairs. Adrenaline spiked through Esme. This was why she hated stealing! There was always—always!—the possibility of getting caught. What was going to happen to them if they were? Would the queen pull out their teeth, one at a time over the course of a week? Would she enchant them somehow and get them to kill each other? Esme had read enough faerie stories to know that common punishments among the Fae were beyond what she could even imagine.

"We're almost free!" Sybil yelled as they reached Hyacinth's door. "Don't worry!"

Of course she was going to worry.

Sybil rattled the knob, but it must've locked behind them when they'd gone through it before.

"Stop! Thieves!" someone yelled behind them.

The Nightshades ran toward them. "I've got them!" yelled the captain. "Over here!"

"What do we do?" Terror spiked through Esme.

"Escape!" Sybil pounded on Hyacinth's door. "C'mon, Chloe, where are you?"

Esme joined Sybil in pounding on the locked door.

It opened suddenly, and Chloe was there, a terrified look in her eyes. She glanced at the guards. "Get in here!" she said, fear making her voice shaky. She held Oliver close to her chest. "Now! Hurry!"

Esme stepped forward, and then an arrow flew past her, crunching into the doorframe with a loud thump. Wood splintered. Chloe yelped, squeezing Oliver. The poor, terrified cat leaped out of Chloe's arms, landing in the hallway behind them.

"Oliver!" Esme spun around, reaching out to grab him.

"Leave him!" Sybil called, tugging at Esme's arm. "We have to go!"

The guards were steps away, one of them already fitting another arrow in a wicked-looking crossbow.

Esme shook out of Sybil's grip. "We can't leave Oliver!"

Right as she got hold of his small furry body, the guards reached her.

"Esme!" Sybil shouted. "Get in here!"

"Go! Keep him safe!" Still on her knees, Esme tossed Oliver to Sybil, who caught him a moment before Chloe slammed Hyacinth's bedroom door.

Esme stared at the door, her breath coming in ragged gasps.

Sybil and Oliver were protected. That was what was important.

What about you?

A blade of fear, quick and deadly, sliced through Esme. What about her?

"Get up, thief!" shouted one of the guards.

Esme got to her feet, turning slowly.

The Nightshade captain grabbed Esme, wrenching her arm. "What were you *really* doing in the royal hallway?"

Esme glanced at Hyacinth's door, which the guards were now pounding on. One of them called a warning—"Princess Hyacinth—it's the Nightshades, we're coming in!"—then the other kicked the door open.

The hands around Esme's arms tightened. Three guards ran into Hyacinth's room, opening doors and looking behind curtains. Anxiety twisted Esme's guts. Her breath came in shallow gasps.

"It's empty," one of the guards called out.

The Nightshade holding Esme kicked her legs out from under her, forcing her to her knees. "I swear I saw another creature with this one. Look again."

Please let Sybil and Chloe get away. Please let them escape.

One of the Nightshades came back, shaking his head. "No signs of anyone, Captain."

Esme sagged with brittle relief, adrenaline flooding her limbs. The weight on her chest lifted, letting her take a deep breath.

The Nightshade captain holding her pulled a sharp silver knife from his belt. At the sight of it, Esme flinched. Suddenly, she was eleven years old again, and another orphan was standing over her with a knife. The scar on Esme's cheek twinged. She swallowed hard against her terror.

"Where are the queen's crown jewels?" the Nightshade with the knife said. "Where did they go?"

Esme drew up her courage, summoning every ounce of bravery and all her desire to protect Sybil. She could do this.

"I don't know what you mean," she said, pushing her shoulders back. "I was just here to give the queen a gift before the ball. A gift she *liked*, I might add." The queen had liked it so much, she'd promised Esme a boon, whatever that meant.

"So you're innocent then?" the Nightshade captain demanded, turning his knife over in his hand.

"Entirely."

"Why did you run?"

"What would you do if a squad of guards appeared behind you?" Esme fought to keep a tremble from her voice. "I couldn't think with the queen's shouting in my ears, so I panicked and ran."

"Turn out your bag," said the guard, gesturing with his knife to Esme's satchel. She'd almost forgotten she was wearing it.

With shaking fingers, she started to open the bag, but the Nightshade commander made an irritated noise. He sliced through the strap, and the bag tumbled to the ground. He shook out the contents: The nearly empty bottle of water, two pencils, three clock gears, the book of Fae stories from Lucien's house, a bundle of food, and Esme's extra scarf tumbled onto the floor.

"What's all this?" asked the guard, poking at the items with the tip of his knife. He picked up the book. "*Eckleton's Guide to Fae for Travelers?*"

"For research," Esme said, hoping this book looked like something a lower member of the Starlight Court might have.

The Nightshade frowned. "Why do you have this ugly bag? What is all this stuff for?"

"Traveling."

"Huh," said the captain, looking again at Esme and then at her bag.

Thankfully, Sybil had the perfume bottle, the enchanted bag containing the queen's jewelry, and Lucien's journal. Who knew what the Nightshades would have done if they'd caught Esme with those? Best not to think of it.

The Nightshade captain turned to one of the other guards. "Check Queen Mab's room for the jewels again. I'm taking this one to the dungeons for questioning."

The dungeons? What are they going to do to me in the dungeons? Esme glanced again at Hyacinth's door. Where had Sybil and Chloe gone? Could they help her? Did she even want them to?

Protect Sybil. No matter what happens, protect the girl you love.

It was that thought that gave her enough strength to bite back sobs as the Nightshade captain dragged her away from the royal hallway and down the palace stairs.

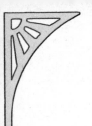

CHAPTER NINETEEN
Spring Equinox

Sybil

Darkness surrounded Sybil, dense and heavy, but it was nothing compared to the despair surging through her. She clutched Oliver to her chest and tried not to cry.

Esme had been taken. Queen Mab's guards had her. She was no longer at Sybil's side, and it was all Sybil's fault. She inhaled, trying to breathe through the panic wrapping sharp claws around her heart. She'd failed Esme. It was a terrible thing to fail someone you loved. How could she ever make this right?

"Be careful on the stairs," Chloe said, as they raced down the dark twisting flights, her starlight lamp bobbing in the darkness.

The stairs became the mountain tunnel. Sybil kept one hand on Oliver and the other on the wall, her fingers tracing over rough stone, slime, and other things she didn't want to imagine. She kept an ear out for the sounds of guards, but all noise from the outside or within the palace was muffled in the mountain tunnel. There was only the sound of their feet on the stone, their ragged breathing, and a steady drip of water from somewhere in the distance.

Sybil reached in her pocket again, checking that the leather bag with the queen's jewels was still in it. It was, and the bag felt as small as ever, disguising its precious, priceless contents.

It was done. This should've been a triumphant moment, with Sybil and Esme celebrating as they made a door and went back into their world with Chloe. They should've been handing the jewels over to Maeve, getting paid, and then finally—finally—returning home for some well-earned rest. A pang went through Sybil as she thought of their cozy apartment, so far away. Normally, all she wanted to do was leave it and be out in the world, but now she'd give anything to just be back there with Esme.

If you failed someone, could you show up again and keep trying? Did you get another chance?

Sybil had to try. She had to rescue Esme. But how?

"Chloe, stop," Sybil said, as they snaked through a narrow stone passageway.

Chloe turned, her face lit by the silver lantern. "What is it?"

"We might have the jewels, but I can't open a door back into our world until we save my friend!"

Chloe snorted. "Of course. Did you really think I was going to leave her in Queen Mab's dungeons? Don't be ridiculous."

A combination of relief and misery filled Sybil. Relief that she wasn't doing this alone, but misery at the thought of Esme in a Fae dungeon, having who knew what awful things done to her.

"How are we going to save her?" Sybil's voice was small, nearly lost in the gloom of the tunnel.

"Break into the dungeons, of course."

"So, we—two humans, one who has just stolen the queen's jewels—need to break another thief out of the dungeons? All without getting caught?"

"Exactly," Chloe said, tilting her head and shooting Sybil a wry smile. "Easy, right?"

✦

Chloe led Sybil out of the secret door in the mountain and into the garden. As they walked through the hedge maze, she kept handing Sybil flowers, leaves, and long vines to weave into her hair to make her look more Fae or in case they ran into more of the queen's guards.

"How do you hide yourself among them?" Sybil asked.

Chloe held a finger to her lips, and they darted off the main path and back into the shadows of the hedge as two Fae—one with goat legs and horns wearing a yellow velvet vest and the other with light-pink skin and a tail poking out from under her mushroom-and-moss gown—ambled past them, goblets in hand, deep in conversation.

Chloe pulled up her sleeve and took off the leather bracelet she wore around her wrist. Underneath it was a small, raised metal bump in the shape of a crescent moon that looked to be fused with Chloe's skin. "It's a banned item, made by human hands with Fae materials, to disguise us among them if needed. I bought it from a trader not long after I arrived here, at great cost. To the Fae, it lets me glitter with magic and enchantment. But if any of them find me with it, they'd kill me on the spot."

Sybil had so many questions, but there wasn't time to ask. She had to stay focused on rescuing Esme. Once they did that, Sybil could open a door and bring Chloe back into their world, and then there'd be time to talk and tell stories.

Up ahead of them, in the center of the maze, a ring of silver and gold lights hung in the air. Energetic fiddle and flute music filled the grove, and a group of Fae with pearly wings swayed in a ring. There were other dancers too: a blonde girl dancing with a tall bear of a man who had pointed ears and jet-black hair bound in a silver circuit. A dark-skinned human with an arm around another Fae with a long red beard and tall boots. Nymphs dancing around a teenage boy with golden-brown skin who played a set of bagpipes for them. Satyrs moving gracefully on their hooves while beautiful women held their hands.

"Are those humans?" Sybil asked Chloe, as she watched the blonde girl spin faster and faster.

Chloe cast the girl a glance and shuddered. "Yes. Some of them were born here, to mortals trapped behind the doors. Others came willingly through doors that were accidentally left open. Likely, the ones who are dancing are in the thrall of Fae magic, and they've forgotten who they are and why they're here."

"Could they leave, though, if they wanted to?"

Chloe nodded. "Anytime. There are stories of Fae, many centuries ago, who held mortals here against their will, but those days ended when the doors closed. Now there are so few mortals in this world, the Fae don't use them for sport as they once did. They mostly dance with them or ignore them—"

"Unless they're stealing jewels or pretending to be friends with the princess?"

"Not a friend," Chloe corrected. "Hyacinth is my most loathed enemy. But yes, that's exactly it. These mortals are here willingly, losing themselves in Fae food and drink."

Sybil clutched Oliver to her chest, watching the dancers and those surrounding them. Some deep part of her, the part that thrummed with her mother's blood, desperately wanted to join in. The music was intoxicating and a touch feral, and Sybil longed to lose herself and her problems in it.

"Is this the Spring Equinox ball?" she asked. For all that the party in the garden was delicious, it wasn't as grand as some of the balls Sybil had been to when living in her father's house.

Chloe laughed. "Of course not. This is the pre-party, which is always a bit wilder than the formal ball. Mortals are allowed to come to this party but not the ball, which is only for High Fae and members of the courts."

Sybil turned her attention back to the dancers. Had her mother ever been to a garden party like this? Would she have danced here, her long chestnut hair falling below her waist as she turned and swayed to the music? Had Sybil's father ever joined her, coming back through the door for a night of dancing and merriment?

Those were all questions Sybil would never have an answer to, but she liked to think of her parents dancing with bare feet in this garden, while the moon rose above them. It was a very different picture from the people they'd been when Sybil and Lucien were in their house. Then they had been mostly serious, respectable, and living for their children. But what a wild thing to consider, that her parents had had lives, loves, hopes, and entire worlds of their own before they'd had children.

In her arms, Oliver meowed plaintively.

"I miss Esme too," Sybil said, wrenching her attention away from the dancers. Oliver meowed again, and Chloe pulled a small piece of dried meat from her pocket.

"I normally keep something for the baby dragons," she said. "But kittens get hungry too."

Oliver happily accepted the food and devoured it. Sybil's stomach rumbled, reminding her it had been many hours since she'd last eaten. Near where they were standing, a long table was piled with jeweled fruits, sugary confections, roasted meats, fresh-looking bread, and dozens of other delicacies. She stepped toward it, but Chloe gripped her hand.

"Don't eat those," she said, her voice all warning. "Not unless you want to taste the enchantments of three kingdoms."

Curiosity filled Sybil, and she longed to try something. Would eating that sweet bun be like drinking absinthe, where each bite filled her with distilled magic? Or would it be different somehow?

"Never eat at their feasts," Chloe warned. "It was one of the first things I learned here."

"What *do* you eat then?" Sybil looked more closely at Chloe, noting how the bones in her wrists stood out and how her cheekbones were sharp as cliffsides.

"What I can forage or fruit I grow myself. Or the things Wendell bakes at home, since I'm under his protection as his guest. Sometimes a little meat, but nothing made in High Fae kitchens. That's one of the only ways I've kept myself hidden in plain sight for the past year. I tried some once . . . and it was a very close shave that I didn't get caught. . . ."

Before Sybil could reply or ask more questions, she spotted a girl with curly hair and light-purple skin in a glowing black-and-silver gown across the garden from where they stood. The girl was standing next to what looked like a giant hedgehog in an emerald-green dress, and she was laughing loudly.

"Is that Hyacinth?" Sybil asked, pointing.

Chloe looked up, her eyes falling on Hyacinth. Her gaze softened, and in that moment, Sybil knew all she needed to know about how Chloe really felt about her "nemesis."

Had Esme ever caught that look on Sybil's face? Or had Sybil always been too busy looking away, out into the world, to really see the amazing person in front of her?

Self-loathing and shame snaked through Sybil, wiggling as violently as Oliver in her arms. Sybil vowed to herself, even as she tucked Oliver into one of her coat pockets, that when they found Esme and got home, she'd never take her friend for granted again. That she'd actually be brave enough to tell her how she really felt, and that—if Esme would let her—Sybil would march across that space between them, and finally, finally kiss her best friend.

Though, of course, they had to find her first.

"Yes, that's Hyacinth," Chloe said. Her face shuttered again, the warmth gone as quickly as it had arrived. She turned to Sybil, biting her bottom lip. "Though now I'm not sure she'll be able to help us. She gets odd at the court events. All her focus turns to pleasing her mother."

Sybil felt something tangled in those words, but she didn't have time to unravel it. "Well, we have to try. Let's go talk to her."

Sybil started cutting a path across the dance floor, tired of skulking in the shadows, and determined to go rescue the girl she loved.

CHAPTER TWENTY
Spring Equinox

Esme

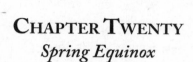

The Nightshade captain threw Esme into a small cell, in a dungeon far below Queen Mab's palace. She landed roughly on her hands and knees on a pile of moldering straw. Bits of it clung to her hands, her dress. The room was narrow but deep, the back half of it a tangled mess of shadows. It smelled like mildew and rotting things, reminding Esme of the orphanage basement, where she'd get sent for asking too many questions or reading after lights out or eating her porridge too fast or a dozen other small crimes she could never keep track of.

"What's going to happen to me?" She scrambled to her feet as the wooden door of the cell clanged shut. She gripped the metal bars that covered the small window at the top of the door.

"Queen Mab will question you after the ball," the Nightshade captain barked.

"But I told you! I'm a visitor from the Solstice Court!"

"Thought you said you were from the *Starlight* Court."

Esme swore under her breath. She had said that. Along with a lot of other things, as she'd tried to explain her presence in the royal hallway.

"You have a few hours to get your story straight," the Nightshade said. "You better hope we find Queen Mab's jewels by then and that she's in a merciful mood."

Esme's stomach plummeted at the words. What was she supposed to say, *Oh, my friend and I were just here to rob you. We wanted to take—no, correction, we took—the crown jewels. But I have no idea where my friend is. Sorry about that, and yes, could you please let me go?*

"You've made a mistake!" she called, banging on the door. "Let me out! I'm here for the ball, and my . . . uhm . . . court will be furious if they find out I'm in here!"

The Nightshade captain just laughed and walked away. Esme hit the door one last time and then blew out a frustrated breath. How was she going to get out of here? She still had her bag—minus her knife and milk bottle, which the guards confiscated, but they declared the rest of the contents useless. Maybe she could jam a clock gear in the door and somehow get it to unlock that way?

She pulled at the door handle and banged on the wood for a few moments longer before finally kicking it, which sent a dagger of pain through her toes and up her shin.

"You're not going to be able to open the door," someone said in a low voice from the shadowy part of the cell. "It's enchanted so it only ever opens from the outside."

Esme turned at the words, horrified to see a shape rising from the gloom at the back of the cell. Was it some nightmare thing like Mordgran? Or something else with teeth and claws that could rip her to shreds? Esme stepped back so her shoulder blades pressed into the rough wood of the cell door. The figure was built like a man, but it moved unsteadily, like it was drunk or injured.

Esme dug in her bag, looking for something, anything, she could use to defend herself. She had a knit scarf, the bread from Wendell, and a book. Right! The book.

The figure stepped forward into the flickering torchlight coming through the small barred window. It was a man—he was taller than Esme, and sticks and leaves matted his thick beard. His sandy-colored hair hung in dirty tangles, and one of his eyes was blackened. He'd clearly been well muscled at one point, but now his skin stretched over his bones, looking too tight. His shirt was torn, his collarbones like rudders. There was a smattering of freckles across his nose, or maybe that was just grime. A powerful smell rolled off him—a combination of sweat, human waste, blood, and the damp of the cell.

"Don't come any closer!" Esme whipped the book out of her bag. She brandished it in front of her like it was a weapon. "I'm armed!"

The man stopped, looking at the book. He quirked his head to one side in a gesture that was somehow very familiar.

"Is that, perchance, *Eckleton's Guide to Fae for Travelers?*" he asked, his voice rasping like it hadn't been used in a while.

Stunned, Esme looked at the title, though she already knew the answer. "It is."

"Can I see it?" the man asked. He took a step backward, holding his hands up. "I won't hurt you, I promise."

Esme wasn't sure about this promise or about giving up her only weapon, but beyond the metaphorical power of a book, how good a weapon was it anyway? If this man wanted to hurt her, what was a book going to do besides give him a papercut? Or a light bruising if she managed to hit him with it? Perhaps, if she gave him the book, he'd leave her alone. It was something to hope for at least.

Esme tossed the man the book. He caught it easily and then held it like it was something very precious. Moving closer to the light coming in through the door—Esme stepped a few paces away—he flipped to the front papers. His breathing hitched as he turned to Esme.

The man gripped the book with white knuckles. He took a step closer, and Esme's fear returned. She pulled her scarf from her bag, not sure how helpful it would be, but ready to fight for her life if needed.

"Who are you," he said very slowly, "and how did you get my book?"

He turned the book toward Esme, where she saw a name scrawled there in familiar handwriting: *Lucien Clarion.*

"Lucien?" Esme said, dropping her scarf on the filthy floor of the cell. "*You're* Lucien Clarion?"

This man was Sybil's brother? All at once, his wrinkled brow and freckles and the way he tilted his head came into context, and Esme saw her best friend mapped into a larger male version.

"Do I know you?" A dimple on his cheek deepened, nearly lost under his beard as he considered her.

Esme shook her head. *How to explain this? Maybe just from the beginning?* She might not have much time. "You don't know me," she said slowly, "but I know your sister."

"Sybil?" Lucien's voice twisted with surprise. "How? She should be at home, married to a duke by now if I know our father at all."

That information hit Esme square in the face. Married? To a duke? All the questions Esme had squashed at Lucien's elaborate home, when she saw the painting in his study, came flooding back, threatening to overwhelm her.

"Sybil is here," Esme managed to say. "In Fae, at the Moonshadow Court. We were hired to steal Queen Mab's crown jewels. . . ."

"You're going to steal Mab's *crown jewels*?" Lucien repeated, his voice full of disbelief. He scrubbed a hand over his face, as if trying to discern whether Esme were real. "How does a human—I'm assuming you're human—"

Esme nodded and Lucien continued.

"How does a human end up in the Moonshadow Court, with my sister and one of my books, which, if I'm remembering correctly, was in my front hallway, unless—"

"Sybil has a key," Esme said, finding that the simplest explanation for the entire complicated business. "It opens up doors between this world and ours."

Lucien's mouth had fallen open. "I knew she had a key . . . but how did she know to use it? Who are you to her?"

Esme blew out a breath, running her hands over her skirt. "I . . . I met your sister about a year ago. She came into my café after leaving home . . . and . . ." Esme found herself suddenly shy as she tried to explain everything Sybil was to a man she'd just met, especially a man who had known Sybil for many more years than Esme had. "And we're roommates," she finished rather sullenly. A fierce protectiveness went through Esme, followed by anger, since *we're roommates* barely scratched the surface of their complicated relationship.

"Ahhhh," Lucien said, his eyes meeting Esme's. "I'm glad she got away from Father, to be honest, though I wish she'd come to find me in the city. I can't imagine it was easy, staying alive and fed in Severon."

Esme shrugged. "We managed." Her voice guarded the secret of their cozy apartment and the home they'd made.

"You said someone hired you to steal Queen Mab's jewels?" Lucien pressed, scratching at his beard again. "Can you tell me who that was?"

Lucien had worked with Maeve, so what was the harm in telling him, especially since they were going to be stuck in this cell until the guards came back to haul Esme off to torture her? Might as well put the whole story out there.

"Her name is Maeve. She's a—um—a woman, or really she's Fae—who owns a club called the Absinthe Underground. Though I'm pretty sure you already know that. We met her one night, after Sybil stole a poster for the club, and Maeve hired us to steal Queen Mab's jewels."

Lucien made a disbelieving noise, part scoff, part bitter laugh. "Maeve hired you. Of course she did." He slumped against the wall, sitting and resting the book on his knees. He looked suddenly exhausted.

In her mind, Esme sifted through parts of Lucien's journal Sybil had read to her and through absinthe-hued memories from the night they'd met Maeve, trying to recall everything she knew about Maeve and Lucien. "You were working with her, right?" Esme said, phrasing her words carefully. "To steal jewels for the Absinthe Underground?"

"Correct."

"She also told us she's stuck there, or well, stuck in our world. . . ."

Lucien scoffed vehemently. It was a cynical sound, too big for the small space of the cell. "That's what she told you? That she's *stuck* at the Absinthe Underground?"

"It's what she said, along with many other things." Quickly, Esme filled Lucien in on everything that had happened—from the first night they'd met Maeve to her offer of paying them so much that they could start a new life to stealing the journal from his house—

"Did you encounter any of my traps?" he asked eagerly, interrupting Esme's story.

Esme groaned. "The abyss and the frogs. Oh, and the Hob-Lock, which opened after it bit Sybil."

Lucien's eyes grew wide. "Ahhh, of course it did. It's enchanted to only be opened with *my* blood, but being a Fae creature, the Hob-Lock likely heard it could open for anyone *with* my blood, as in my family. Fascinating!"

Esme continued, telling him about the thefts of the magical leather bag and the perfume from the Severon Museum. Lucien beamed at hearing how Sybil had used the bronze frogs, saying, "She always was an excellent thief! Even when we were kids!"

Esme then told him about Maeve's timeline and how she needed the jewels by the end of the Spring Equinox, or she'd be stuck in their world—

"Because she's trapped there?" Lucien clarified.

Esme nodded.

Lucien scoffed again and waved for her to continue. Esme wrapped up by telling him how Sybil opened a door into Fae, how they eventually ended up at the palace, and how they'd gotten the jewels, but Esme had been caught. She left Chloe and Hyacinth out of the story, not wanting to get them into trouble.

By the end of the tale, Lucien's mouth was hanging open, though he promptly closed it, hauled himself to his feet, and paced a loop around the cell. Esme stayed tucked into one corner. "So," Lucien said, "you're telling me Sybil is somewhere out there, running around Queen Mab's castle, with the Moonshadow Court's crown jewels in her pocket?"

"Well, not exactly in her pocket. . . ."

"In a magical leather bag that expands to fit them," Lucien corrected.

"Yes." It sounded ridiculous when put like that, but it was the truth. "Unless she already made a door back to our world, which I don't think she'll do because . . ."

"Because you're here," Lucien said softly. His warm hazel eyes met Esme's, and the look was so full of understanding and compassion, it made tears rise in her own.

Of course, Sybil wouldn't leave without her, would she? But how was Sybil supposed to help Esme? She was a thief, yes, but Esme was in the dungeon of a Fae queen. It was very possible she might never see Sybil again. As tears ran down her cheeks, Esme bowed her head, putting a hand to her mouth to hold back the sob that filled her throat, taking away her air. Swallowing once, she inhaled raggedly.

"Can I tell you something, Esme?" Lucien stopped his pacing. She nodded.

"Maeve is a liar. A good one—a beautiful one—but a liar nonetheless."

"What do you mean?" she asked roughly, swiping at her tears. "I thought the Fae couldn't lie."

Lucien blew out a breath. "That's true, in a way. They can't lie directly, but they can dance so wildly around the truth, it's nearly impossible to make sense of where a lie begins and the truth ends."

Esme took that in, trying to separate the tangled threads of Maeve's story. Was it true? Or was Lucien lying?

"Let me try to explain another way," he said. "Did you ever wonder why Sybil was able to open a door into Fae?"

Esme nodded again; of course she had wondered that. "She just said the key was from her mother—your mother—"

Lucien gave her a long measured look. "Did she ever tell you anything about our mother?"

"No."

"Ahhh." Lucien started pacing again. "I suppose that's her story to tell, but you know our mother left us keys that open doors into Fae. I used one after I left home and ended up in the woods surrounding the Moonshadow Court. I met Maeve there, and we fell in love—or at least I thought we did. I was wild for her, absolutely willing to do anything she said. I stole things from all over Severon, and we built the Absinthe Underground together."

"How did you end up here?" Esme gestured to the dungeon.

Lucien ran a hand through his beard. "We were running out of Fae gems to make absinthe with. That part of Maeve's story is true.

So I agreed to come into Fae and steal more. Maeve didn't want to come with me, saying she was needed to run the business, but that wasn't the entire truth of it."

"What do you mean?"

"When I got here, I learned Maeve hadn't been telling me everything about herself. Yes, she's a green faerie, but she isn't just a forest Fae, living in the woods on her own. She's one of Queen Mab's daughters—"

"She can't be!" Esme gasped. Or could she be? Esme thought back to Maeve and the way she'd seemed to hold court in the Absinthe Underground.

"I felt the same way when I found out," Lucien said. "I overheard some Fae talking about it in a tavern, and I asked them some questions. They told me the story of Queen Mab's fourth daughter, an ambitious, unloved thing, who was banished by her mother to the far reaches of the Moonshadow woods for some petty crime or another. Her six sisters—the other princesses, Iris, Amaryllis, Beryl, Jade, Luna, and Hyacinth—were forbidden from seeking her out, and Queen Mab erased Maeve's name from all the histories, at least until the sentence was lifted."

Esme tried to make sense of all this. "If she's a princess, why is she in Severon? Wouldn't a life in exile in Fae be better than a life in the mortal world?"

Lucien raised an eyebrow. "Think about the opportunity our world offers. There's a whole realm to be seen and enjoyed there."

Esme wasn't sure about any of this. Was Lucien telling the truth? Maeve had seemed so terrified when she'd told them about being trapped. Esme had felt tremendous empathy for her—she knew what it was like to be stuck somewhere and willing to do anything to get free—but was Maeve really a scared being trapped in their world? Or was she what Lucien said, a princess in exile? *Or was Lucien himself the person who'd trapped her?*

"What happened between you two?" Esme asked. "I thought you were in love?"

Lucian grimaced. "I did too. But, as the Absinthe Underground grew, so did Maeve's ambitions. I found myself more her errand boy than her lover. I promised myself I'd go on one last trip to Fae, to steal more jewels. The money was flowing in, and I confess I love the adventure of it all."

"That's something you and Sybil have in common," Esme said. There was a sound of footsteps in the dungeon hallway and a scratching sound at the cell door. Esme forced herself not to consider what it might be.

Lucien looked surprised. "Really? Sybil? The girl who'd rather paint landscapes or play the piano than ride a horse or jump off a cliff into the sea?"

In these words, Esme had a perfectly clear portrait of her best friend, a wild thing trapped in a rich lady's world. A girl desperate to escape to Severon. "She loves adventure," Esme said. "In fact—"

Esme was cut off by a loud clanging on the cell door. She leaped away, pulling the now-filthy scarf off the floor. Lucien stood behind her, gripping the book.

"If they try to give you any faerie food or drink, don't take it," he whispered. "It will let them do whatever they want to you. . . ."

Before Esme could reply, the cell door slammed open.

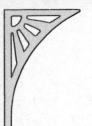

CHAPTER TWENTY-ONE
Spring Equinox

Sybil

S *ybil had never been so happy to see a stinking, filthy jail cell in her* life. Not that she'd ever seen a jail cell, though she'd imagined one—something full of rats and piss buckets and spare wooden cots. But the one in front of her was far worse than what she'd imagined.

The dungeon beneath Queen Mab's palace was a low-ceilinged, clammy place. A pair of torches sat near the front, their light flickering off the mildew that streaked the stone walls and pools of rank water covering the ground. The stale tang of urine blended with smoke from the torches, the damp, and other unsavory underground smells. Rusted metal rings with chains attached hung along the walls. There were only three cells—Chloe had said this was because Queen Mab kept few prisoners, preferring to make offenders compete in trials or executing them outright, a fact that made Sybil's skin crawl. The cells were carved into the belly of the mountain, and each had a thick wooden door on it. One guard was posted in a guard room near the front of the dungeon. While Chloe and Hyacinth distracted the guard, offering her liquor from the queen's own table, Sybil tucked Oliver into her coat pocket and grabbed a set of keys from a hook on the wall, then snuck into the cell area. She'd stood on her tiptoes to peer into each cell. Two were empty, but she could just make out the outline of Esme's head and back through the third.

"Esme!" she hissed, as she unlocked the door and rushed into the cell where her best friend waited. Oliver gave a happy meow.

"Sybil?" Esme's eyebrows flew upward. "What are you—"

Sybil didn't let her finish. She grabbed Esme into a tight hug, squeezing everything she couldn't say into it: *I'm so sorry for leaving you. I missed you. I need you. Please don't be mad at me. I love you. . . .*

Sybil gripped Esme's back, clinging to her, then Oliver, who was squished between them, made a loud noise of protest. Esme and Sybil broke apart, laughing.

"I wasn't sure I'd see you again, Ez. I'm so glad we found you." Tears rose in Sybil's eyes.

Esme reached out a hand, taking Oliver and snuggling him close.

"Sorry to interrupt this touching moment," someone said in a rough voice behind Esme. It was heavy with barely restrained merriment. "But we should probably save reunions for after we've escaped."

Sybil would've known that voice anywhere. But it couldn't be. Could it?

Releasing Esme, Sybil turned to the figure behind her. He was stooped, stinking, and covered in a beard that looked more like an enormous lichen than anything else, but she'd know him anywhere. "Lucien?"

What was her brother doing here? In the cell with Esme?

Sybil had hoped—in the far-off part of her mind that wasn't focused on the theft of Queen Mab's jewels—she might run into Lucien in Fae, but the world was so big and the chances so small, she hadn't really given it much thought. Now here he was. Grinning at her like a dog happy to see its fellow lost puppy. She flung herself into his arms, not caring that he reeked. He wobbled at the impact and then hugged her close.

"Didn't expect to meet you here, sis," Lucien said, his voice craggy. "Truly thought we'd meet next in a drawing room, not a dungeon."

Sybil pulled away, staring at her brother in astonishment. "How? How are you here?" It was a question that contained others within it, and she stumbled over the words.

"The very short answer to that question is that I got caught."

Ahh, so that was why he hadn't returned to their world. "How long have you been in this cell?" she asked, taking in his dirty, emaciated appearance. "Maeve said she hadn't seen you in weeks."

"Far too long," Lucien said. "They brought food at first, and then I think they forgot me down here. I've lost track of how long I've really been gone."

Sybil looked between Lucien and Esme, trying to put it all together. "How did you two end up in the same cell?"

"Good luck?" Esme said. "Or laziness? They just threw me into the first one."

"Same," Lucien said, nodding. He held out a hand to Oliver. The kitten sniffed it, then licked it once, making a surprised face. Lucien grinned. It was that same easy, confident smile Sybil remembered so well.

"Esme told me all about your job from Maeve," Lucien said, petting Oliver again.

Sybil shot Esme a look. "You told him about Maeve?"

Esme shrugged, still holding Oliver close. "We talked about a lot."

Sybil didn't like the strange note in Esme's voice. What had Lucien told her? What would Esme think of Sybil if he'd revealed the truth about their mother?

"Ahem." Someone cleared their throat behind Sybil. She turned to Chloe, who leaned against the doorway of the cell, watching the hall. "Hyacinth is still drinking with the guard, but I'm not sure how long she'll be able to hold her attention. We should go."

Sybil nodded. She wasn't entirely sure how Chloe had managed to convince Hyacinth to help or what she must have said or promised—though she'd certainly left out the part about the stolen jewels—but thankfully Hyacinth had agreed. And the guard had been all too happy to see a princess bringing her wine, which Hyacinth had claimed was a "gift of gratitude from the royal family on this Equinox."

"Right," Sybil said. "Let's go now. I'll use my key to open the door between worlds, and we can get out of here." She started to close the jail cell door, but Lucien reached out a hand to stop her.

"Don't be so quick to lock us all in here again, sis. This door only opens from the outside, and you can't open a door between worlds within Queen Mab's palace."

Sybil paused, catching the door before it slammed shut. "I thought I could use any door for this?"

Lucien shook his head. "That's what I thought too, on my first trips into this world, but don't you think I would've escaped already if I could open a door from this cell?" He pulled his own key—identical to Sybil's—from under his shirt.

"You've had that with you the whole time?" Sybil couldn't keep a note of accusation from her voice.

Lucien nodded. "Like I said, it doesn't work on any door in Queen Mab's palace. When they caught me, I'd made the mistake of drinking Fae concoctions in a tavern. They're about a thousand times stronger than the absinthe we make, and I was totally ensorcelled. I suppose I was making an ass of myself or trying to steal something, because one minute I remember drinking something frothy and blue green, and the next I woke up in this jail cell. The first thing I did was try to open a door between worlds, but I couldn't."

"That would make sense," Chloe said, glancing at the keys Sybil and Lucien wore. "In the times before, when all the doors between the worlds were open, I suppose the Fae monarchs wouldn't want just anyone to be able to open a door into their homes."

Lucien nodded. "Exactly. Imagine you're Queen Mab, in your bath, and a door appears, and out stumbles a mortal magician, looking for some answers to his scholarly questions. From what I have gathered from my research, the doors back into our world are built into natural formations—trees, hillsides, things like that. From our side, with our keys, we can use any door and open it to Fae, but here, we have to use a door that's built into something already."

Sybil knew then where they had to go to escape. "Lucky for us, we know exactly that kind of door."

"Not so lucky," Chloe amended. "We're going to have to go through the Equinox garden party to get there, and he smells terrible."

Lucien grinned, making Sybil's heart warm to see it. "We'll figure it out. And when we're back in Severon, I'm going to bathe for at least a day and then eat everything on the menu at my favorite café."

"That sounds like an excellent plan," Sybil said, returning Lucien's smile.

CHAPTER TWENTY-TWO
Spring Equinox

Esme

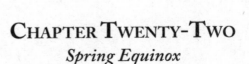

Esme glanced between Sybil and Lucien as they hurried down the long torchlit corridor of the dungeon. They looked so much alike, it was uncanny. She slipped on a slick patch of stone and stumbled, catching herself against a wall. Oliver meowed from inside her coat pocket.

"Esme?" Sybil turned, frowning. She offered a hand, but Esme pushed off the wall, ignoring it. "Are you okay?"

"I'm fine, keep going."

Why had Sybil not told her more about Lucien? Something else whispered at Esme's mind, some missing piece, like the last gear needed to finally make a clock start ticking. What was it Lucien had said? That Sybil's secrets were her own?

At the main door of the dungeon, Chloe paused, glancing both ways as she peeked outside. There would be time for questions and answers once they got back to Severon and had given the jewels to Maeve. Because, no matter what Lucien said, Esme wasn't just willing to take his word on everything. What if he was lying and Maeve really was trapped?

"Hyacinth and the guard are over there," Chloe said, nodding toward one side of a long room. Esme glimpsed a uniformed woman at a rough wooden table, holding a bottle while Hyacinth stood nearby, laughing at something the guard said.

Chloe pointed toward a staircase. "Go up that way. Now!"

Esme didn't need to be told a second time. Head down, she ran toward the stairs that led out of the dungeon. They were the same stairs the Nightshades had dragged her down what felt like hours ago but couldn't have been that long. Injuries from her tumble out of the tree and rough treatment by the guards slowed her down, and she stumbled over a step.

This time, Sybil caught her arm, saving Esme from a nasty fall.

"Are you hurt?" Sybil whispered. "What did they do to you?" Concern was written all over her face.

Esme wanted to sink into that fretfulness and just let herself be fussed over and cared for, but she wasn't in the habit of letting someone else take care of her. Plus, Sybil had left her once already. Esme could walk on her own.

She shook off Sybil's hand. "Keep moving."

Sybil nodded tightly, looking as if she wanted to say more, but Lucien urged them forward.

They ran up the dungeon steps, ending up on the far side of the palace, opposite the door hidden in the mountain. It was full night now, and the moon rose on the eastern horizon.

Chloe glanced at the stars. "It'll be midnight soon," she said. "Which means Queen Mab's ball will be starting. She's got to be frantic to find her jewels."

"Let's not dally here any longer," Lucien said. "Where's this door?"

"Across the lawn and through the garden labyrinth," Chloe said. "Follow me and stay close. The night is wilder already."

Esme shivered at her tone, but she didn't need telling. She could taste ecstatic unruliness in the air. Fae creatures—human-sized foxes in well-tailored suits, beautiful faeries with lithe limbs and glittering wings, High Fae with ice-blue lips and bloodred eyes, stout gray-haired crones with mushroom-shaped hats, almost-human-looking people with feathered wings and sharp gazes, trees with the faces of women and long green hair, and so many others—spilled out of the garden and onto the palace lawn. Some of them glanced at Esme and the others, but their gaze quickly moved on, as if they were too ordinary to actually pay attention to. They hurried through the garden, only stopping when they got to the door that was built into the mountain.

"Isn't this part of the palace?" Lucien asked, looking up at the castle looming over them. "Can you even open a door here?"

"I don't think it is," Sybil replied. "We had to go through many underground passages to get to a stairway."

Chloe nodded. "It's built into the stone itself, so not technically part of the palace like the dungeons or stables are. I think it should work."

Lucien nodded. "One way to find out, I guess. Sybil, would you like to do the honors?"

Sybil pulled out her key. Esme exhaled, excitement lighting her nerves. This was it, time to go home.

Suddenly, a loud feminine voice sent Esme's heart plummeting into her stomach.

"Where are you all going?" Hyacinth called out, making them pause right as Chloe pulled back the vines hiding the mountain door. "Chloe, wait!"

Chloe swore under her breath as she turned. Esme clutched her bag, with its broken strap, and petted Oliver in her pocket.

"Why are you heading toward my room?" Hyacinth asked, looking them over.

Esme felt Hyacinth's gaze sear into her. No longer did the princess look at them with curiosity or welcome. Now, there was something wary in her posture.

"We . . ." Chloe paused, the truth dying on her lips.

Esme shot Sybil a look. Sybil clutched her key.

"Chloe, what's going on?" Hyacinth's voice was sharp, regal in that moment. "I thought you needed me to distract the dungeon guard because the Nightshades had gotten too zealous and started throwing guests in cells. Who is this, though?" She glared at Lucien. "And why are you all going into the secret door to the palace? I've not seen Mother, but the ball will be starting at any moment. I thought we were going to—"

"Stop right there!" someone shouted behind them. Esme turned to see a troop of Nightshades running toward them down the hedge-maze corridor. The silver-haired Nightshade captain had his sword out, and the guards shoved aside party guests, who made noises of protest.

Esme grabbed Sybil's arm. "Put the key in the door. Now!"

"Why are they after you?" Hyacinth demanded, stamping her foot. "Chloe? Talk to me! Someone please tell me what's going on."

Chloe opened and closed her mouth.

The guards were closer. "In the name of the queen, we demand you stop!"

"What is the meaning of this?" Hyacinth said, stepping in front of the guards.

"Your Highness," said one of them, bowing. "Your mother's crown jewels have been stolen. These people were seen leaving her chambers—"

"The crown jewels?" Hyacinth spun around and gripped Chloe's arms. "Do you know anything about this?"

"Hurry!" Esme said, nudging Sybil, who seemed to be frozen.

"Sybil! Get moving! Do you need me to open the door?" Lucien asked, pulling his own key from his neck.

"I've got it," Sybil said. Pulling out her knife, she sliced her finger open and smeared the keyhole with blood.

Esme had never wanted to be home more than in that moment. She held her breath as Sybil whispered the rhyme her mother had taught her. The guards were right behind them, stepping around Hyacinth and Chloe. Reaching for them.

"Take us home," Sybil begged, turning the key in the door and flinging it open.

It creaked loudly, metal on rock, but there, waiting on the other side, was their home. Esme started breathing again. It was so close, she could weep. There was their cozy clock tower apartment with its mismatched furniture and cats and mint plants. Esme looked over her shoulder, seeing only the chaos of Queen Mab's party and the guards rushing toward them.

"You did it!" she said, so relieved to see her home, she plopped a quick kiss on Sybil's cheek.

Surprise crossed Sybil's features, and then she gave Esme a small shove. "Get in there," Sybil said. "You first this time." Sybil grabbed her key from the keyhole.

Esme stumbled over the threshold between the worlds, banging into her kitchen table as she did so. Clock parts rained to the floor, and Jean-Francois yowled at her. Esme turned. Sybil stood in the doorway between the worlds. Just beyond her, the Nightshades had nearly reached the door.

"Lucien, Chloe, come on!" Sybil called out, grabbing for her brother.

But the guards already had their hands on Lucien, even as Sybil pulled at him. In another second, the guards would take Sybil too. Maybe they'd even be coming through the door!

Esme couldn't let that happen.

"Just go, all of you!" Chloe yelled.

Esme saw her clutch Hyacinth by the hand, pulling her away from the door, sprinting toward the maze. Chloe threw one last longing look over her shoulder, and then she disappeared around a corner.

"Lucien!" Sybil screamed again, as one of the guards threw a punch that knocked him to the ground.

"Don't worry about me!" he yelled, blood painting his teeth. He struggled to his feet only to be knocked down a second time. Another guard kicked him in the ribs.

Sybil surged forward, leaving the doorway as if to grab Lucien, but Esme was faster. She caught Sybil's hand and pulled her through the door, back into their home. Then, before any Nightshades or Fae could come through, Esme slammed the door between their world and the Fae kingdom.

✦

Silence filled the apartment. Or not really silence, because there was the ticking of the clocks, and the sound of cats meowing at having been awakened by two girls landing in a heap from another world and the noise of Oliver leaping from Esme's coat pocket and hurrying over to slurp from his water bowl. But after the tumbling chaos of the Fae world—the music, laughter, and shouts at the garden party; the brutal violence of the Nightshades breaking Lucien—these ordinary sounds were so very quiet in comparison.

Sybil's soft, gutting, heartbreaking sobs cut through all of it.

Oh no.

Esme turned to her friend, who lay on the floor in a pile of skirts and hair and sorrow. Carefully, she put a hand on Sybil's back.

"Syb?" Esme said, as if Sybil were a lost kitten. "Are you hurt?"

"Why did you close the door?" Sybil wailed, turning a tear-streaked face toward Esme. "I almost had Lucien, but you pulled me away!"

"You didn't almost have him," Esme said softly. "The guards almost had you. If I hadn't pulled you away, they'd be hauling you off to prison right now, or they'd be in this apartment with us."

"I don't care! Did you see what they were doing to him? I'd only just found my brother again, and now he's gone, thanks to you!"

Those words hit Esme like a slap.

"Thanks to me?" Her mouth opened and closed as she tried to form a reply. "It's thanks to me we found Lucien in the first place!"

She wanted to say more—to remind Sybil that Esme was the one Sybil had left behind. The one the guards had caught and thrown into prison. But she didn't have the words. All she had was hurt and a great blooming anger.

"You should've let me help him." Sybil hauled herself to her feet. "And Chloe was supposed to come with us too." Sybil picked up her key, which had fallen to the floor. "I'm going back. I don't care what happens. I'm going to get my brother."

She started to put the key in the lock, but Esme grabbed her hand. "Wait. Please. We can go back for him, but first, let's take Maeve the jewels. Then we can get paid for the job and not be running around Queen Mab's palace with her stolen jewelry."

"Why can't we leave it here and go back into Fae?" Sybil said.

Esme glanced at the clock tower. It was half past eleven. "We have to help Maeve before midnight, remember? And it's already almost eleven. We have to complete this job, so it all was worth something."

Sybil swiped at the tears on her face and blew out a breath. A long moment passed between them, and Esme wanted so desperately to hug her friend. She didn't want Sybil to go back into Fae ever again, but how could she stop her? Instead of touching her or reaching out to comfort Sybil, though, Esme just stood very still, waiting for her friend to say something.

"Fine," Sybil said at last. "But the minute Maeve pays us, I'm going back to get Lucien, and maybe Chloe. You can come with me if you want or stay here with your precious cats and clocks."

Her words carved into Esme. Each one cut away the threads that bound them together.

Slowly, Esme looked around their home, seeing it for the first time through Sybil's eyes, the eyes of a girl who might've married a duke and who'd grown up in a world of wealth and privilege. It looked small, dusty in the corners, full of tattered furniture and mismatched cats. The paint was peeling on the cupboards, and the mess of plants and clock parts was just that, a mess, not some cozy hallmark of the home they'd built. How tawdry this all must look to Sybil's rich-girl eyes. How ordinary, unremarkable, and sad it must seem after the grand ballrooms and palaces she'd been in. Queen Mab's palace had been the first Esme had ever walked in, and she'd be very happy spending the rest of her life far away from such places.

But would Sybil feel the same way? Now that she had seen the glittering world of Fae, how could she ever go back to wanting a snug, quiet life with Esme?

Dreams for their future crumbled like the leftover scone on the table that Oliver was currently attacking.

Esme's voice came out rough, heavy with tears she wasn't going to shed. She'd been alone before. She would be fine. If the future was just her and her cats, that would be fine as well. "We can talk about who's going into Fae soon. For now, let's go to the Absinthe Underground."

Then, turning away from her friend, Esme buttoned her coat over her Fae dress, hoping to hide her breaking heart underneath.

PART FOUR

A Reckoning

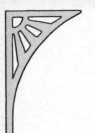

CHAPTER TWENTY-THREE
Sybil

A s they walked toward the Absinthe Underground, Sybil's thoughts churned. She knew she'd been awful to Esme, but she didn't have the time or the space to process what was happening. All she could see when she closed her eyes was Lucien being thrown to the ground, curled in on himself to protect his body from the Nightshades' blows. Why had Esme pulled Sybil through the door? Yes, she was right that Sybil could've been captured and that the guards or who knew what else could've come through the open door, but that felt like a risk worth taking to save her brother.

If those guards had really forgotten Lucien in that cell, now they certainly would remember him. What would happen to him? Could Sybil really save him if she went back into Fae? What was she, one half-Fae girl, going to do against the might of Queen Mab and her soldiers?

Sybil was still reeling from actually finding Lucien, and now she'd lost him again. As soon as they gave these jewels to Maeve and collected their earnings, she would head back into Fae. She wouldn't return until she'd rescued Lucien.

She shifted her hand into her coat pocket, making sure the gems were still there. They were, tucked safe and secure into the little bag. Before they'd left the apartment, Sybil had opened it, peeking inside. Now that they were out of Fae, the bag no longer looked like it was full of pebbles. Ropes of pearls, the great Moonshadow tiara, and all the other jewels glistened inside, though their size and weight were still magically contained in the small bag.

Esme walked beside Sybil, her coat collar drawn up, her steps sure. It was dark out but warmer than it had been for the past few days. A salt-laced breeze blew off the sea, and the sky above the city was cloudless and dotted with stars. A full moon painted the boulevards silver. People thronged the streets, despite the late hour, and the markets and bars hummed with life.

There was so much happening in Severon tonight, and Sybil didn't care. She just wanted to rescue Lucien.

Sybil glanced over at Esme, only to find her staring back. They both quickly looked away. The spot on Sybil's cheek where Esme had kissed her burned in her memory, like Esme had marked it.

Sybil had been wanting to kiss her friend for months, and now that it had happened, even in the smallest way, she wasn't able to return the affection because all of her was worried about Lucien.

They reached the Absinthe Underground, where a long line of waiting customers curled around the block. Music and laughter poured out of the club, and carriages and cabs lined up on the street, releasing scores of well-dressed people into the night. The gaslights flickered by the door, and there was an eager thrum in the air, as another night at the Absinthe tempted people through its doors.

"We're here to see Maeve," Sybil told the bouncer, flashing him Maeve's card again.

"Go on then," he said. "I recognize you from last time, and Maeve told us to keep an eye out for you both tonight."

Once again, the noise of the Absinthe Underground hit Sybil as soon as they passed from the foyer and coat check area through the bronze doors into the main dance hall. Tonight every glass in the room seemed to sparkle with green liquid, Fae and enchanting.

On the main stage, dancers kicked up their legs, revealing ruffles of petticoats; people whirled on the dance floor; blue cigarette smoke hung in the air; the band played on; and hundreds of voices laughed, toasted, talked, and clamored to be heard. Unlike the other times they'd been here, though, tonight Sybil was immune to the seductions of the noise and the drinks. She waved away a waiter who offered them glasses of absinthe.

Something about the room teeming with energy reminded Sybil of the garden party at Queen Mab's court. Maybe Sybil just had that party on her mind, but the texture of the air in the Absinthe Underground felt almost the same. Like too many otherworldly things were going on at once. Like the people in the Absinthe were Fae themselves, spiraling in a dance, fueled by enchantment and the green liquor everywhere.

Maeve waved at them from across the room. "Oh, my girls!" she said, as they approached. She looked radiant, her cheeks flushed and her red hair streaming down her back. She examined their dresses. "Are those spider silk?"

"Mine is," Esme replied dully. Sybil could hear hurt in her voice, but she couldn't do anything about it. Not now at least.

Maeve made a satisfied noise. "I know a Fae dress when I see it!" She paused, her eyes gleaming hungrily. Her voice lowered. "Does this mean you've done it? Have you gotten the crown jewels?"

Sybil nodded once, the gesture tight. "We have, but we need to get back into Fae. We have to—"

Maeve put a hand on her arm. "Not here, darling. Let's go somewhere more private."

She nodded toward her enormous opera box near the back of the club. Weaving through the crowd, Sybil and Esme followed Maeve through a small door in the wall and up a twisting stairway. At the top was a landing and a pair of double doors carved with elaborate flowers and artistic flourishes. Maeve flung the doors open, revealing a sprawling, decadent balcony. It was big enough to fit two couches, several chairs, and a low table. A bottle of absinthe and a tray of glasses sat on the table, next to a pair of candlesticks with tall green candles whose flames flickered. Gas lamps in ornate golden sconces cast a soft glow throughout the box, and the view of the club below was framed by sumptuous green curtains.

"I come up here to watch them dance," Maeve said, walking over to the marble balustrade at the front of the box and looking over the edge. "And to be seen, of course. Everyone wants to see the Green Faerie." Here she smiled, letting her glamour slip for one perilous moment, showing Sybil and Esme just how sharp her teeth really were.

Sybil was reminded of Queen Mab standing at the top of her palace steps, greeting her guests as they arrived for the Equinox ball.

What was happening in Fae? Was Queen Mab torturing Lucien at this very moment to find her jewels? Sybil dug her fingernails into the palm of her hand to quell her impatience. Soon enough. They'd be through this transaction with Maeve, and then Sybil could make a door into Fae. She'd do it in the middle of the club if she had to.

Maeve pulled at the satin ropes that held the curtains back, releasing them. They tumbled together, like a woman letting her long hair down from an elaborate bun.

"Now that we have some privacy, show me the jewels," Maeve said. "And please, drink, I insist."

She poured three glasses from the bottle of absinthe and passed them around. Sybil held hers gingerly, reluctant to drink it since she was planning on going back into Fae the minute this was done. She would need all her wits for that journey and whatever it brought. Maybe she could get Chloe to help her again—though why hadn't Chloe come with her in the first place? Why didn't she want Hyacinth to know she was mortal or that she was leaving? There were just too many questions and not enough time to answer them. Sybil exhaled, pulling herself back to the moment at hand.

Esme stepped on Sybil's toe. "Drink," she muttered, nodding toward Maeve, who was watching them expectantly.

Sybil sighed. Fine. One last drink, and then she would get this over with. She lifted her glass, forcing a smile, as Maeve clinked her glass against theirs.

"To many more successful jobs," Maeve said, drinking deeply.

"Wait," Sybil said. "We agreed to the one job—"

"Just an expression," Maeve said, her voice tight. "We can talk future jobs after we complete this one. Now drink it all."

Sybil did, dumping the entire glass of absinthe down her throat in one long gulp. It burned as it always did, but this time, it sat differently. It didn't fog her head in the same way. It was almost as if her time in Fae had left her a little bit immune to Maeve's enchantments.

Maeve reached her hand out for the leather bag.

Sybil wanted to tell her of hardships they'd faced getting the gems and how they'd lost Lucien while doing so, but she just took the enchanted bag from her pocket and put it on the table in front of Maeve. Sybil rested a hand over it. "Before you take the jewels, we want our money."

Maeve paused, her hand hovering over Sybil's. Menace flashed across her face, there and gone again, almost too quickly to be marked.

"Of course," she murmured. "You want what's been promised to you."

"And we want to free you from whatever's trapping you here," Esme piped in. "Isn't that right?"

Sybil looked over at her friend, trying to place what she was saying. In the whirlwind of getting the jewels and escaping Fae, Sybil had almost forgotten about that part of things.

Maeve made a dismissive gesture, her eyes not leaving the leather bag. "You truly will be freeing me when you give me these jewels. I don't know how to thank you, but this should be enough for your trouble."

She pulled a roll of banknotes from her pocket and tossed it to Sybil. Catching it, Sybil was surprised by its weight. They would indeed be set for a very long time. She slipped the money into her coat pocket.

"Now," Maeve said, jerking the leather bag from under Sybil's hand. "Give me what's mine." As she opened the bag, a loud satisfied gasp left Maeve's lips. "Oh, girls." Her voice was nearly reverent. "You've done very well indeed."

Black pearls clicked together as Maeve looped a rope of them around her neck. She clasped a diamond and amethyst bracelet around her wrist. The air in the opera box seemed to tremble as she did so.

Sybil clenched her glass. Was the absinthe making the world around Maeve shimmer? Across from Sybil, Maeve exclaimed over Queen Mab's jewelry as she decked her fingers in silver rings, each with enormous stones. She secured a black opal choker around her neck and fastened rows of emerald, diamond, and pearl bracelets up her wrists, and then she picked up the most magnificent piece of all, a tall silver crown covered in moonstones and black pearls and draped with chains that glowed with dark beauty. Maeve's eyes reflected the gems, glowing nearly silver themselves.

Sybil darted her gaze to Esme, who watched Maeve's every move as if she were studying a clock. Sybil knew that look. There was a puzzle here, and Esme wanted answers to it. "So, with this jewelry, you'll have enough to free yourself and keep the club open?" Esme asked.

"Oh, I have enough indeed," Maeve replied, her voice ragged with some emotion that Sybil couldn't name. "You've made me a queen, girls, thank you." Slowly, Maeve moved the crown toward her head. Again the air around her gleamed, as if it were slick with oil or crackling with lightning.

And then Maeve placed Queen Mab's crown on her head, making the candlelight flicker as the world fragmented before Sybil's eyes.

Chapter Twenty-Four
Esme

E sme's jaw dropped as the air around Maeve seemed to crystalize, freezing her for a moment in a great wave of silver. Maeve glowed, reflecting the light from the jewels, and then she spun around, a dark prism, turning in the moonlight.

"What's happening to her?" Sybil said, gripping Esme's forearm.

Esme was so grateful for the touch, as their mutual disbelief smoothed the bite of their argument earlier. "I have no idea," Esme managed.

Maeve held her hands out in front of her, examining the jewels, and turning her hands this way and that, as if she were seeing them for the first time.

"Maybe she's being freed from what's holding her here?" Sybil suggested.

Was Maeve really being held here by someone? Or was that as much a lie as Lucien claimed? Was she really the exiled daughter of Queen Mab?

Before Esme could say anything to Sybil, there was a blur of movement. Maeve's human facade ripped away, the glamour shredding. Her wings popped out from her dress, spreading wide and diaphanous, filling the opera box.

Esme had the small, silly thought that Maeve's wings were like dragonfly wings, but then she was pulled away by how Maeve was laughing. It was a cackle, rich and satisfied, like a villain out of a novel. Her eyes gleamed in the candlelight, and she looked so immensely pleased with herself, Esme wasn't sure what to do.

"Are you going to crush those jewels to make more absinthe?" Sybil called out to Maeve. She gripped the key around her neck with one hand and Esme's fingers with the other. "Wasn't that the plan?"

A great surge of admiration for Sybil's bravery went through Esme. Something was happening to Maeve, and here Sybil was, reminding her of why they'd stolen the gems in the first place.

Maeve turned toward Sybil, her glamour slotting back into place with a quick wave of her hand. All at once, she was again the familiar, lovely red-haired human woman they'd first met. Queen Mab's jewels were draped over her slim wrists and neck, but they'd stopped glowing.

"Oh, my sweet ones," Maeve said, in a voice like honeyed acid. "I *could* crush these gems to make more absinthe, but why would I do that? These are the most powerful gems in the Moonshadow Kingdom."

Sybil persisted, dropping the key and crossing her arms. "Yes, but we stole them for you so you could make more absinthe. We went through a lot of trouble and danger, and we met Lucien—"

Maeve held up a hand. Sybil opened and closed her mouth, but no sound came out. Had Maeve stolen Sybil's words? Esme looked frantically at her friend.

"Don't mention that man's name to me," Maeve said. "He has abandoned me."

"He hasn't!" Esme blurted. "He got locked up in Queen Mab's dungeon and couldn't get home."

This information caused Maeve to raise one perfectly formed eyebrow, and then she laughed, a high, breezy sound. "Never mind that, and never mind him. I don't need him as a thief any longer. I have you two."

Esme looked at Sybil, who was still desperately mouthing words, but no sound came out. How had Maeve taken Sybil's voice?

"He said you were in love!" Esme called out. "That he missed you and wanted to find a way back home."

Maeve shrugged again. "That sounds like something he'd say. We were business partners. If Lucien thought something else, well, then that was his fault, not mine."

Sybil's voice burst out, the spell lifting all at once. "What did you do to me?" Her voice was ragged, wheezing through each word.

Maeve met her gaze, a dangerous gleam in her eyes. "Careful, little one. Don't ask too many questions, or I'll take your voice for longer than a few seconds. Now that I have Queen Mab's jewels, a great ocean of magic has opened before me. Let me show you."

She spread her hands wide, and pink cherry blossoms rained upon them, soft and delicate. They landed on Esme's hands and her cheeks and snagged in Sybil's hair.

"An ocean of magic?" Sybil asked. "What do you need that for?"

Maeve brought her hands together in a soft clap, and the petals stopped raining, leaving only a carpet of blossoms at their feet. With another flick of her wrist, the candle flames danced upward, abandoning their wicks to bob around Maeve, casting shadows along her cheekbones.

"What can't I use it for! These jewels are everything." Maeve caught one of the flames and twirled it around her finger. "Now, bow, girls, to the new Moonshadow Queen."

She gestured again, and Esme felt invisible hands forcing her to sink into a low bow. Struggling against Maeve's magic, Esme twisted, feeling like she was in the grip of the Nightshade guards again, but it was no use. In seconds, both she and Sybil were on their knees, their heads lowered to Maeve.

"Let us go," Sybil ground out between her clenched teeth.

To Esme it sounded like every word had been ripped out of her. Both Esme and Sybil struggled more violently.

"Oh, fine," Maeve said. She waved another hand casually, and the invisible hands holding Esme and Sybil released them. Esme tumbled forward, falling on her face in the carpet. She scrambled to her feet.

Sybil stood as well, staring in horror at Maeve. "What is she going to do with the jewels?"

Esme didn't know, but they had to get out of that opera box and the Absinthe Underground. She'd like to never see Maeve again and maybe flee Severon, if possible.

But almost as if she were reading Esme's mind, Maeve moved lightning fast and blocked the double doors leading out of the box. "It's not time to go yet, lovelies," Maeve said. "Sit down, let's drink, and I'll tell you a story."

Esme wanted to fight, but before she could take a step, Sybil surged ahead, rushing for the door. Instantly, she was thrown backward, as if she'd hit an invisible wall. She toppled into Esme with a cry.

"I said, *please sit down*," Maeve repeated, her voice blistering. "Pour yourself another drink."

Esme and Sybil huddled on the couches. Maeve poured them glasses of absinthe. The crown jewels glittered with her every movement.

Maeve sat across from them, as she'd done a few times before. "Drink, and let me tell you about Queen Mab, the Most Gracious Moonshadow Queen, as they call her."

"Because you're Queen Mab's daughter, aren't you?" Esme spit out. It was so clear to her now, she couldn't believe she'd missed it before.

"What are you talking about?" Sybil asked, turning to Esme with a surprised expression.

"Lucien told me. Before you got there. . . ."

"Why didn't you say anything?"

Esme shrugged, wishing she had. "You stormed over here as soon as we got back! There wasn't time. And we were fighting. . . ."

Maeve snapped her fingers. "I'll tell my own tale, thank you. Yes, I'm Queen Mab's daughter. Her fourth of seven, and the cleverest one of the bunch, not that my mother could ever see it." Bitterness laced each word.

Sybil rolled her eyes beside Esme. "We've all got family problems, but what does that have to do with us?"

Maeve slammed her glass on the table. "When my mother exiled me to the woods, telling me to never come back—"

"What did you do to get exiled?" Esme interrupted, unable to help her curiosity. Lucien hadn't told her this part, and she felt like she could almost see how everything fit together, but this was the missing piece.

"It doesn't matter! It was a silly thing, a schoolgirl's trick to get noticed by her powerful mother, but Queen Mab was furious. She never could keep her temper, and so she banished me to live with an old forest crone for a hundred years, until everyone in the kingdom forgot Queen Mab even had a fourth daughter."

"We met one of your sisters," Esme said. "Princess Hyacinth."

Maeve scoffed. "Hyacinth. A baby and a traitor. She always was more interested in serving our mother than being a good sister. Do you know not one of my sisters tried to find me in my exile? None of them visited me. None of them brought me my favorite foods or sent letters."

A pang of sympathy went through Esme. Maybe there was still a way to connect with Maeve.

"That must have been awful and lonely," Esme said. "I also know what it is to be alone. . . ."

"What about the forest crone?" Sybil ventured. "You weren't *all* alone, right?"

Maeve scowled. "That old witch perished shortly after I got there. . . ."

Esme and Sybil exchanged a glance. Something about the way Maeve said *perished* made it sound like it was from very unnatural causes indeed.

Maeve continued. "And yes, I was *all* alone until Lucien arrived, opening a door into my cottage yard and appearing out of nowhere."

"And he brought you back here, and you started the Absinthe Underground," Sybil said irritably. "Yes, yes, we know. Can you let us go now, since you've told us your tragic backstory already?"

Maeve glowered at Sybil. Esme gripped her friend's hand, imploring her with the touch to stop baiting the already-furious Fae princess in front of them.

"You have no idea what I've lived through! But now that I have Queen Mab's jewels, I can make her pay! All her power will be mine!" Maeve gripped her glass of absinthe so tightly, the glass shattered, sending shards of crystal flying.

What was she going to do with that power? Who was going to be hurt by Maeve's ascension? How could she possibly make Queen Mab pay for anything? Esme didn't know, and she certainly didn't want to find out.

"Great," Sybil deadpanned, standing. "You have the jewels, and you've left my brother in your mother's prison. Now you can swan around the Absinthe Underground, playing dress-up in her jewelry and pretending you're a powerful Fae. Sounds like a lovely life. Can we go now, please?"

Maeve twisted one of the rings on her index finger. "Oh, but I am a powerful Fae. The most powerful. Whoever has these jewels is the Queen of the Moonshadow Kingdom."

"Well, you have them, so why don't you just go back there?" Esme said. That would solve so many problems all at once. Maybe they could even ask Maeve to free Lucien for them.

As if she were reading Esme's mind, Sybil raised her key. "I can open a door for you right now. Then you can leave us alone, and I can go get my brother while you take over your mother's palace or do whatever you want to so badly."

Maeve darted forward, wrenching the key from around Sybil's neck. Sybil fought off her grip, but Maeve pulled hard, the weight of her new magic behind the gesture. Sybil cried out as the chain holding the key snapped.

"Give that back!" Sybil shouted.

Maeve dangled the key in her hand. "I can't have you opening up any doors to Fae without my permission now, can I?"

"I won't, I promise," Sybil said, pleading. Tears stood in her eyes, and Esme knew she was thinking about Lucien and how she'd never be able to rescue him if Maeve kept the key.

"I don't believe you," Maeve said. "Besides, I'm never going back to Fae. I have all the power of the Moonshadow Kingdom here, and I don't have to deal with my mother." She gestured toward the velvet curtains that blocked what was happening in the opera box from the rest of the club. "I have a new kingdom, in this world. Perhaps I'll call it the Absinthe Empire."

Something in Maeve had broken—like a clock that couldn't be fixed—and she was going to destroy them all now that she had the crown jewels. And it would be Esme and Sybil's fault since they'd retrieved them in the first place.

"Humans aren't going to serve you, no matter how much power you have," Esme blurted.

Maeve's smile reminded Esme of a predator. "I've already got half this city eating from my hand. What do you think this club is all about? With every glass of absinthe they consume, every time they view my image and celebrate it in song or art, they're serving me. I can rule this entire city through this club. Having my mother's jewels just gives me the ability to spread my influence wider."

It was a vile plan, but one with such an obvious flaw in it, Esme almost laughed. "Don't Fae jewels and other items lose their power over time?" she said. "Isn't that what you told us? By that logic, won't Queen Mab's jewels soon just be pretty baubles to wear or display in a museum?"

Maeve examined her rings, then caught Esme's eye and held it. "Of course, that's how it usually works. But not these jewels. These are no common trinkets. These are the crown jewels, the source of power for the Moonshadow Kingdom. Why do you think I needed these specifically? They'll keep their power here forever."

"How do you know that?" Esme asked.

Maeve shrugged. "Something my mother told me when I was a child, as I watched her take them out of her vault one Equinox before a ball."

Esme glanced at Sybil. Her tongue was between her teeth, and a keen glint lit her eye. It was the look that said she was about to do something very, very unwise. Esme reached for her friend, hoping to catch her, but Sybil was faster. She surged forward, her poster-stealing knife in hand as she grasped for her key.

She missed, and in the space between blinks, Maeve wrenched Sybil's head backward by her hair. She twisted the knife away from Sybil.

"Oh, my sweet girl," Maeve purred. "You should know better than to attack me." She pushed the knife into Sybil's throat, pressing so hard, blood beaded beneath it.

Esme couldn't help herself—she screamed.

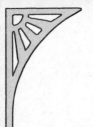

CHAPTER TWENTY-FIVE
Sybil

Maeve's knife dug into Sybil's throat, cold metal biting against her skin. Her other hand gripped Sybil's key, clutching it tightly. Sybil squirmed under the blade, wriggling away as much as she could.

"What are you doing?" Esme demanded. "Maeve! Let her go! You can't kill her!"

"I can and I will."

Holding her neck as still as possible, Sybil brought the heel of her shoe down hard on Maeve's toes. Maeve yelped, relaxing her grip on the knife, just for a second.

That bought Sybil enough time to scramble out of Maeve's grasp. Esme shoved Maeve backward, hard, into one of the heavy green curtains. Tripping over the curtains, Maeve flung her hands out to catch herself. The knife and Sybil's key fell to the floor as she did so.

Sybil stumbled into Esme's arms. "I have to get the key!"

"No! Don't! Sybil!" Esme yelled behind her.

Sybil heard her but didn't stop. It didn't matter that Maeve was getting up from where she'd fallen. It didn't matter that she and Maeve both dove for the key at the same time. It didn't matter that Maeve had the knife in hand again. Sybil needed that key to save Lucien. She was going to get it or die trying.

Landing hard on her stomach, Sybil wrapped her fingers around the key seconds before Maeve's hand landed on top of hers. The key's teeth dug into Sybil's palms, and then a pain—severe and sudden—lanced through her left side.

A great animalistic howl ripped out of Sybil. Still clutching the key, she looked down. Her own knife was buried beneath her ribs, all the way up to the hilt. Blood leaked out from the wound in a slow, steady flow. Sybil's head spun as she put her hand over the blood, as if to stanch it.

Shakily, Sybil got to her feet. She took one step backward, then another, before landing in a heap on the closest sofa. The motion sent more pain rolling through her. Who knew that getting stabbed would hurt so much? That was a senseless thought. But still. Getting stabbed hurt so much.

Esme rushed to Sybil's side, falling to her knees, her hands wrapping around Sybil's. Blood leaked over her fingers.

Sybil gripped the handle of the knife. Everything hurt, and some part of her was sure that if she could just get the knife out of her body, it would feel better. "I can pull it out, Ez."

"Don't you dare," Esme said.

Maeve poured Sybil a glass of absinthe. "Drink this, lovely. It'll help with the pain."

Sybil wanted to reject the drink, but her head was already spinning. Dulling the pain didn't sound like a bad idea. With shaking fingers, she took the glass from Maeve. She tipped it back in one long gulp, letting it burn down her throat. She closed her eyes, as the alcohol and the pain warred within her. Maybe as she died, she'd see a vision of her mother and brother, laughing with her in a Fae garden. Maybe in another life, she and Esme would be together, and they'd finally, finally kiss. Maybe—

"Help us, Maeve," Esme pleaded. "Save her. Stop this, please."

Her fingers dug into Sybil's shoulder, the grip so intense, it forced Sybil's eyes open. Beside her, tears ran down Esme's cheeks. Affection, tied tightly with grief over the life together they were losing, made Sybil ache. It wasn't until that exact moment that she realized how much she loved Esme.

"I know you want power," Esme continued, her eyes on Maeve. "And that you've been hurt by your mother—"

"You know nothing about that," Maeve snapped.

"I do," Esme said softly. She bit her lip for a moment. "I know all about having a mother you can't please. One who's too glittering and far away your whole life. Your mother sent you away, but mine drank herself away, which left me abandoned and alone, just like you."

An ache of pain went through Sybil. Poor Esme, who'd been lonely and living with loss for so very long. Sybil leaned her head against Esme's shoulder. Esme brushed a piece of Sybil's hair back.

"You're nothing," Maeve sneered. She shifted her shoulders back, making her bearing regal. "I'm a Fae queen, and you're a dirt-poor girl who knows nothing of power."

Sybil watched as Maeve's words hit Esme, each one a dart.

"You're *not* nothing," Sybil rasped out. She clung to Esme's hand. "You're my best friend. My everything. . . ."

Esme turned to Sybil with her eyes wide. Tears still clung to her cheeks, but in her gaze was hope, sorrow, and love. So much love.

For a moment, Sybil truly thought Esme was going to kiss her, right there, as she bled out on a couch while a homicidal Faerie gloated over them.

Sybil clung to Esme's hand, waiting for the blows that would stop their hearts. Instead, right as the clocks struck midnight, there was a tremendous crashing sound, as if a gas line had exploded within the Absinthe Underground. A familiar voice rumbled behind them, making Sybil's breath catch in her throat.

"How about you and I have a long chat, Maeve," said the person. "It's been so long, after all. I'm sure we have lots to catch up on."

Lucien.

Lucien was here. Now. Somehow. With her side throbbing, Sybil turned her head as her brother strode into the opera box, a sword in one hand and his key to Fae in the other. He winked at Sybil as he walked past, moving toward Maeve with deadly purpose.

Sybil had never been happier to see her brother in her life.

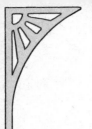

CHAPTER TWENTY-SIX

Esme

Esme *nearly fainted with relief as Lucien walked into the opera box.* He winked at Sybil, then Esme, but then his eyes landed on the knife in Sybil's side. His mouth pressed into a thin angry line as he turned to Maeve.

"What have you done to my sister?" he asked, his voice full of barely contained fury.

Maeve sneered at Lucien's tangled beard and filthy appearance. "Nearly killed her since you weren't available to murder. And you're not going to stop me."

Lucien moved forward so fast, Esme almost missed him. In a moment, he was at Maeve's side, turning her around so she faced the rest of the club. He pulled back the curtains, and Maeve screeched in rage.

"Help me up," Sybil gasped beside Esme. "I want to see."

Gently, Esme helped Sybil stand. There were still alarming amounts of blood on Sybil's dress, but the flow seemed to have slowed a bit. Perhaps Maeve had missed anything too vital. Together, Esme and Sybil stumbled toward the opera-box railing, standing beside Lucien and Maeve.

"Oh, Lucien, well done," Sybil said, her voice laced with pain but full of amusement. "You brought reinforcements."

"I did indeed," he said cheerfully.

Esme blinked, trying to make sense of what she was seeing.

There, striding through the center of the club, was an enormous sapphire-scaled dragon. Its legs were thick as tree trunks, its claws like swords. As it walked, it tossed its head, gnashing its long teeth. But the dragon wasn't what sent an icicle of fear through Esme. It was Queen Mab, terrible and lovely, sitting astride the dragon, her long blue hair still woven with gems. Queen Mab held a sword in one hand and her silver-and-midnight-blue dress caught the flickering gaslights in the club, a dark star burning with fury.

On the floor of the Absinthe Underground, people screamed and raced toward the door. A few of them tried to pet the dragon, like it might be a vison caused by the absinthe, but they were pulled away by frantic hands or shoved aside by the dragon's stride.

Just beyond the dragon, where the great bronze doors of the club used to be, there was now an enormous hole. Each step the dragon took rattled the walls of the mansion that held the Absinthe Underground, and glasses and bottles tumbled from shelves. Chandeliers swung recklessly as the dragon roared.

"Sorry about your door," Lucien said, his grip on Maeve's arm tight. "But the dragon needed a bit more space."

Maeve shoved Lucien away with preternatural strength. "You brought my *mother*?" she shrieked.

"She insisted on coming," Lucien said, his voice full of wry amusement. "She's so eager for a reunion."

Maeve roared, but Queen Mab's dragon thundered louder. Unfurling wings that spanned nearly the entirety of the club and flapping them, the dragon soared upward. A hot breeze lifted Esme's hair as the dragon rose, until it was hovering right beside Maeve's opera box.

Queen Mab glared at her daughter, her expression calculating. Not wanting to be recognized by the queen, Esme took a step backward, pulling Sybil with her.

"Daughter," Queen Mab said, her voice as vast and cold as the space between the stars. "You've been taking things that don't belong to you."

Maeve smirked. "Hello, *Mother*," she spat out the last word like a curse. "Technically, these two girls took the jewels, not me."

For one terrible moment, Queen Mab's eyes turned to Esme, then Sybil. Esme felt that look pierce her, an arrow of scorn. Queen Mab raised a hand, touching the rowan flower in her hair. "I've met them," she said. "And I owe them a boon, if I recall correctly."

Esme swallowed hard. Fae had to keep their promises according to stories, but that didn't mean it would turn out as she expected. Using the rules of Fae logic, Queen Mab might consider cutting off their hands or enchanting them to sleep for a hundred years a boon.

Lucien moved to Esme's side. "Take my sister and get out of here," he whispered to her, "before this gets nasty."

Esme wanted to move, but her feet were frozen in place. "Where can we go?" Esme said, desperate. "Sybil can barely walk."

"Anywhere," Lucien said, putting himself in front of Sybil and Esme. "Just as long as it's away from here."

Esme moved over to Sybil, gently hoisting an arm under her shoulder. Even with the care Esme took, Sybil groaned and clutched her side. "I can't move, Ez. It hurts too much."

"We have to. Now!" Esme said, hating the way Sybil winced with each step.

They started toward the back of the opera box, the double doors getting closer. Even if they made it, it was still so far to go down the stairs and exit the club. And then what? How could Esme possibly get Sybil to the hospital before she bled out?

"Stop!" Maeve shouted, holding up a hand. "If you think I'm letting you two leave, you're wrong." She straightened her enormous crown. "And, Mother, you're too late. I'm the Moonshadow Queen now, and you're nothing, just as you always told me I was."

Esme paused, holding Sybil close, unable to resist looking over her shoulder.

"You'll never be the Moonshadow Queen," Queen Mab growled. "You don't have the faintest idea of what that would take."

"I do!" Maeve shouted, sounding like a petulant child. "I have the crown jewels! Already, I feel the magic pulsing through me, hungry and measureless. My kingdom will thrive while yours falls away into dust."

Queen Mab drew her sword and laughed. The sound was one Esme knew she'd hear in her nightmares, if she lived long enough to have nightmares.

Swinging her leg over her dragon's back, Queen Mab jumped from it to the opera box. "I will *remind* you of the power I hold, daughter of mine." She turned to Maeve with a wicked gleam. "You've stolen my jewels, but I hope you've mastered your magic well enough to protect them."

Queen Mab whispered a word, and her sword flamed silver, the magic around it making the air shiver. Maeve raised her hands, gathering magic to her and swaying with power. When she spoke a word, a chandelier hanging from the Absinthe Underground's ceiling snapped, hurtling toward Queen Mab. With a shout, Lucien pulled Esme and Sybil to the ground, covering them with his body as the chandelier smashed into the wall where Queen Mab had been standing. Her dragon roared, sending fire toward Maeve. She darted out of the way just as the fire leaped onto the opera box's green curtains.

Queen Mab swung her sword, charging forward with deadly intent, while Maeve conjured a magic shield. The two Faeries shouted at each other in a language of their own, each word punctuated by terrible blows.

Esme couldn't look away.

"We have to get out of here," Sybil rasped, as she rolled onto her back. Lucien got to his feet, putting his sister's arm around his shoulders. "And, Lucien, we have to open a door to get them back to their world, before they destroy the entire city."

Esme glanced around, looking through the flames for an exit. The smashed chandelier now stood between them and the opera-box doors, blocking the way. Pieces of the ceiling fell around them as the battle between Maeve and Queen Mab raged, plaster and stone tumbling to the floor.

Esme searched for an exit, more desperate now. Flames licked at the curtains, eating them up. The fire caught in a pool of spilled absinthe, flaring high and green as it lapped up the magical drink.

"We're going to die here," Esme whispered, the realization hitting her all at once.

"We're not," Sybil said. She had a fierce look in her eyes. "I have a plan!"

Oh, how Esme loved her in that moment.

"There's no way out!" Esme couldn't keep the terror and heartache out of her voice. "The door is blocked. The box is on fire, and the Absinthe Underground is falling to pieces."

"I know what to do," Sybil insisted. "Can you get me to the edge of the box, Lucien?"

Still holding her wounded side, Sybil limped toward the edge of the balcony. The enormous dragon had perched there, its claws curled around the marble railing, watching Maeve and Queen Mab fight.

And then Sybil hummed a melodic snatch of a song, one that wrapped around them, despite the wild destruction raging. The dragon blinked once, considering, and it bowed its head.

"Come on," Sybil said, waving one arm weakly toward the dragon. "I found our ride out of here."

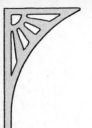

CHAPTER TWENTY-SEVEN
Sybil

Relief filled Sybil as Queen Mab's dragon allowed them to climb on its enormous back. Her plan shouldn't have worked. She had no business asking a royal dragon for a ride, but maybe it recognized Sybil's Fae blood or the song Chloe had taught Sybil.

Whatever it was didn't matter. Fire ate into the opera box behind them, and more flames licked up the walls of the club, turning it into an inferno. Queen Mab and Maeve had moved their fight from the opera box to the air above the dance hall. Now their wings unfurled, Maeve's glamour gone, they darted through the air, flying through silver hoops, sending jets of magic at each other, and making bottles of spirits smash into the club's walls. Although Maeve still had all the Moonshadow jewels on, she was clearly no match for Queen Mab, who was relentless in the way she used magic to cage Maeve.

"Hold on!" Sybil called out, as Esme and Lucien settled onto the dragon's back behind her.

"Take us down, please, near the front door," Sybil whispered to the dragon. Her side ached as she did so. Perhaps, she didn't have much life left to expend, but at least she could use what she had left to save her friend and her brother.

Esme's hands came around Sybil's sides, resting lightly below where the knife was. Sybil closed her eyes, leaning backward into her best friend.

"Esme—" Sybil started to say, but then the dragon leaped upward, unfurling its wings. Sybil's words were pulled from her mouth, and she gripped the reins of the beast. In one fluid motion, it drifted through the broken bronze doors of the club and landed in the enormous foyer. Its claws gouged lines in the marble as it walked to the front door of the Absinthe Underground.

"Shhh," Esme said, resting a hand Sybil's hair. "We'll have lots of time to talk later."

"But we won't. What if I—"

"We will," Esme said firmly, as if that were the end of that. As if she could actually fix all this. As if Sybil's wound, and the shattered nightclub, and the two furious royal Fae still fighting in it were all as rational and fixable as a clock with a rusty gear.

Fine. Maybe it was worth believing the world was ordered, even when it seemed utterly tumultuous. Sybil liked the thought of knowing Esme had been right about it all, all along.

"We will," Sybil repeated.

Lucien and Esme slid off the dragon's back, and then Lucien caught Sybil as she slipped from it. Her legs cramped, and another great rip of pain tore into her.

"Lucien—I—"

Her words were interrupted by Queen Mab, who now strolled into the vestibule, pulling Maeve by the hair. Maeve struggled against the magical silver ropes her mother had bound her in. The queen wrenched each of the crown jewels from Maeve's body, settling them on herself.

"Give those back, Mother!" Maeve screeched. "They're mine! I opened the vault!"

"As I recall, your thieves opened my vault, not you."

Queen Mab threw Maeve to the ground, where she landed in a heap in front of the dragon. The beast roared, sending a jet of flame curling into the painted green faerie on the wall. Maeve's image crackled and bubbled. A long sob tore from Maeve's throat.

"How did you take the jewels, Mother?" Maeve howled, touching her empty fingers, the top of her head, and the hollows of her neck where the crown jewels had just been. "You shouldn't have been able to do that!"

"There's so much more to this Moonshadow magic than you could ever know, Daughter," Queen Mab purred, like a tiger playing with its food. She adjusted one of the bracelets on her arm. "I let you spend all your energy fighting me, and then it was an easy thing to capture you. I ensnared you like I'd catch a baby dragon. Let this be a lesson to you: do not test me." She turned to Lucien. "Send me home, to my palace, now. I have an Equinox ball to attend, and I tire of this world."

He looked at Sybil. "I'll do it," she said, stumbling over to the door. "I'm already bleeding anyway."

He cast her a crooked grin, but his eyes were sad. Breathing shakily, Sybil painted the keyhole of the Absinthe Underground with her blood and then whispered her mother's words.

"A willow, a word, a slip into the night. Your blood is a map to find your way home, little sprite. . . ."

She turned the doorknob, and it opened, revealing deep darkness and the portico of Queen Mab's palace. The moon sat low in the sky, and a group of the Nightshades waited in front of the door.

Queen Mab jerked Maeve to her feet, thrusting her toward the door. "Time to go home, my dearest daughter."

"No!" Maeve yelled. "Don't let her take me! Lucien! If you ever bore me any love, please! Help me. Esme! Sybil! I'm sorry. Please, don't let her take me! She's going to kill me."

The smallest pang of sympathy went through Sybil, surprising her.

Queen Mab stopped at Maeve's words. "Oh no, Daughter. You're too low to kill. Allow me to assure you that no one will hear about this exploit of yours, nor your time in this world and your little games at this club. You'll be even more forgotten and less than nothing than you ever were."

Maeve shouted a string of curses, but Queen Mab shoved her through the door, into the waiting arms of the Nightshades. Queen Mab's dragon went through next, making itself small enough somehow to get through the doors.

Queen Mab bowed to them. "Don't let me ever catch you in my palace again," she said looking between Sybil and Esme.

"I promise." Sybil nodded weakly, knowing there was something else she should ask or say, but through her pain, she couldn't think of what it was. She leaned against the doorframe, her blood leaving a trail along it.

Queen Mab started to step through the door, but Esme rushed forward, grabbing her arm.

"Please, Your Majesty," Esme pleaded. "Our boon. The one you promised for the gift of the rowan flowers. I'm asking for it now: let Sybil live, please."

Oh, Esme. Brave, beautiful Esme. Sybil could've wept at her best friend's bravery, but instead she clutched her side.

Queen Mab glanced down, looking at Esme's hand on her sleeve like it was a crawling thing. Then she glanced into Fae, where the sound of music and a party floated out of the Moonshadow palace.

"Very well," she said, shrugging. "I don't have time to linger here. Take your boon." She plucked the rowan flower from her hair and pressed it to the wound in Sybil's torso.

The knife still in her side clattered onto the floor, as the rowan flower seeped into the gash. A flash of coolness filled Sybil, and her breath hitched. Suddenly, it was much easier to draw breath.

"Remember, don't let me catch you in my palace again," Queen Mab said, as she stepped through the door before closing it behind her.

A vision of Chloe, stuck in Fae, flashed through Sybil's mind, but then she collapsed, sinking to the floor.

Esme rushed over, holding Sybil's hand, smoothing her hair back. "Did it work? The bleeding has stopped, but—"

"I love you," Sybil interrupted, barely managing the words.

Esme's eyes widened for a moment, and then her face wavered above Sybil. In the distance, Sybil heard Lucien call out her name, but then Sybil let the darkness take her.

PART FIVE

Beginnings and Endings

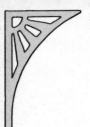

CHAPTER TWENTY-EIGHT
Esme

Sybil shouldn't have survived the stab wound to her side. Esme knew that. She'd read about such injuries in the medical textbook Lucien had loaned her from his library. She'd also been poring over Lucien's books about Fae, frantic for any knowledge of Fae boons, as she tried to discern if Queen Mab had tricked her.

She was still no closer to answers.

All she knew was that, somehow, Sybil wasn't dead. She was asleep on her couch in the clock tower apartment. She was still breathing. She just wasn't awake.

She tossed and turned sometimes, crying, whimpering, muttering words, but not waking up. Esme watched, concerned, puttering, trying to read or put a clock back together, but really unable to do much other than worry.

Lucien came by daily—now bathed, shaved, and dressed in expensive-looking clean clothes—bringing groceries and meals.

He spent hours with Esme, telling her about his adventures in Fae. Esme had decided she liked him quite a bit, but she wasn't sure how his being around would change their lives if Sybil ever woke up.

When Sybil woke up.

Yes, it was *when* not *if.* Esme had to believe that was true.

More days passed. A week. Two.

Lucien told her how the Absinthe Underground had been shut up after Maeve disappeared. It was rumored the club was cursed, and what was left of it after the fire had been thoroughly looted. The great carved doors stood open, and birds nested in the sign. The patrons, dancers, and drinkers had moved on to other clubs, and the Absinthe Underground faded into legend. It was now a memory, a fever dream for the city of Severon. Though Maeve's image still looked out from posters hung all over, immortalized by artists.

Spring fully arrived, and Lucien brought flowers for their table. Esme repotted all her mint plants, and finally leaving Sybil alone for the first time since they'd got home, she went downstairs to pay their rent for the next month from the money Maeve had given them.

She was just coming back upstairs from paying the landlady when the door to their apartment opened.

"Esme?" Sybil said, looking confused as she peered into the hallway. Her cheeks were flushed and her hair wild from sleeping for so long. But she was there, up and walking, and Esme cried out in joy to see her.

✦✦ *Sybil* ✦✦

Sybil's heart soared as Esme flung herself into her arms. Despite Esme's height, she curled around Sybil, burying her face in the gap between Sybil's shoulder and collarbones.

"I thought I lost you." Esme's voice was a ragged, broken thing. "You've been asleep for so long."

"How long?" Hot tears rolled along Sybil's skin. Whether they were hers or Esme's, Sybil didn't know.

"Weeks."

Weeks? How had she been asleep for weeks? Not that it really mattered. All that was important was she was here, now.

Sybil pulled Esme's body against her own. As Esme sobbed, Sybil stroked her hair, making soothing noises. Her body ached, but her side didn't hurt, and her mind was clear. She was wearing clean clothes, which meant someone, Esme certainly, had been taking care of her. Sybil was mildly embarrassed at the thought of what that might've entailed, but she pushed the feeling down, embracing instead the giddy relief of being at home with Esme.

"Are you sure you're really here?" Esme lightly touched Sybil's shoulder, her jawline, her cheek. She was so achingly lovely in that moment. Sybil wished for a paint brush and a canvas, to capture the fragile hope and desperate joy on Esme's face.

Sybil swallowed hard. "I'm really here. You could never lose me. I'll always find my way back to you, Ez."

"You're wrong if you think I'm ever letting you go again." Eyes blazing, Esme moved her hand from Sybil's cheek to the nape of her neck. What a thing it was to have a girl like Esme look at her like that.

Sybil rested her hand on Esme's waist and stepped closer. The crisp scent of mint leaves and dusty old books filled Sybil's nose, smelling of home and Esme. "Ez—I . . ."

Sybil trailed off, not sure if she could reveal her secret heart, even after all they'd been through. She had wanted to cross this line between them—the boundary between friends and so much more—many times, but fear always held her back. Fear of loss, rejection, or ruining the life they already had.

"Yes?" Esme said, her eyes not leaving Sybil's.

Sybil inhaled sharply, drawing up all her courage. This was more terrifying than facing dragons or power-hungry green faeries, but she had to do it. She had to leap. "I'm sorry," she breathed.

Esme brushed a piece of hair behind Sybil's ears. "You don't have to apologize for anything." Her voice was so soft, so tender. It offered everything Sybil wanted, but Esme didn't understand, she couldn't.

Sybil caught Esme's hand, twining their fingers together. "But I do! I have so much to apologize for! I'm sorry I didn't tell you I grew up rich or that I didn't write my father to help us. And I'm sorry I didn't tell you my mother was Fae like Maeve, or Queen Mab."

"I doubt your mother was anything like the two of them." Esme lifted one eyebrow quizzically, like she was studying a clock problem or reading a newspaper article that she didn't agree with.

Tension lifted, ever so slightly from Sybil's heart. "That's true. She preferred dancing barefoot under the stars to conquest or dragons, but I'm half Fae . . . not that I really know what it means."

Esme considered Sybil, her eyebrows coming together, all seriousness. "I know," Esme said gently. "Lucien already told me about your mother."

"That rat!"

Esme laughed. "Don't be angry with him. When you wouldn't wake up, we tried everything to cure you, including perusing a handful of books about Fae illnesses and medicines Lucien discovered in the Great Library. He confessed you were both half Fae—though I'd already suspected it. How else would you be able to open a door between worlds or convince Queen Mab's dragon to let you ride it?"

A small, rueful laugh left Sybil's lips. "That was handy, certainly, but I'm sorry you had to hear it from Lucien. I wanted to tell you."

"You've hardly been in a position to tell me anything. The most you've said for weeks is snoring. . . ."

"Esme! Take this seriously. You know what I mean."

"No, Sybil, *you* listen. Please. I know what you mean, but I also know it doesn't matter at all. I don't care where you come from or who your mother was. I mean, yes, you probably should've told me, but I know why you didn't. And, yes, I'm objectively curious about what it means to be half Fae and we really should discuss Lucien's theory about your grandfather crafting Queen Mab's jewels—"

"That's a good theory."

"Isn't it? And, I'd love to know what other abilities you might have. . . ."

Sybil absolutely wanted to know too. "Perhaps we can discover those someday, if we open a door into a different realm."

"Or go back to help Chloe escape."

"Exactly. But, Ez . . ."

"Yes?"

"That's not all I need you to know."

Esme leaned in, so their foreheads were touching. Sybil closed her eyes, breathing in the smell of Esme one more time before she crossed the final gulf between them.

"What else?"

"I . . . I need you to know that I've wanted to kiss you since the first moment I saw you. And that I still think about kissing you all the time. Every moment of the day."

There. The words were out at last. Esme could do with them what she would.

Esme's eyes widened for a moment, and then she laughed. It was a clear, giddy laugh.

Oh no. No, no, no.

Sybil shrunk into herself.

Laughing wasn't good. No one wanted to offer the fragileness of their heart and get laughed at.

Don't cry.

A flush of shame colored Sybil's cheeks. "I'm sorry. I shouldn't have said that. It's just— Forget it. We can just be—"

Esme gripped Sybil's hand, pulling her close. Sybil's heart started sprinting again at the touch.

"We can be what?" Esme asked softly, leaning in so her lips were beside Sybil's ear.

"Friends?" Sybil said in a small voice.

Esme's mouth grazed ever so lightly over Sybil's earlobe. Sybil thought she might pass out. It was the most singularly intimate thing anyone had ever done to her. "And what if I don't want to be just friends?"

Somehow, Sybil found her voice. "Oh, what would you like to be then?" she managed, as Esme's lips trailed lightly down her neck. She leaned her head back as Esme kissed a line to the hollow between her collarbones.

"Lovers? Life partners? Something that is large and lasting and just us against the world."

"Yes," Sybil exhaled. "Yes to it all. Always."

Esme stopped kissing Sybil and looked up. Sybil held her gaze for only a moment before they hurtled into each other's arms like waves breaking on the beach.

Their first kiss was tender, ravenous, and aching all at once. Sybil was breathless from it, and her lips moved over Esme's as their bodies molded together. She tasted like mint, as Sybil had always imagined. As Sybil took a step backward, Esme followed. Together, they slammed into the hallway wall, their lips pressed together. Esme kissed Sybil like she was essential. Like she was air and water, like Esme had been missing both for too long.

In her seventeen years, Sybil had kissed people of all genders, but no one made her blood dance like this. No one made her yearn in this way. No one felt like home so entirely.

Their kiss was a delicious storm of a thing. Hands, lips, mouths entwined as Sybil tried to tell Esme every small and every vast thing she hadn't been able to say over the past year.

I need you. You're everything to me.

"Why haven't we done this sooner?" Sybil asked when they finally separated.

"I wanted to," Esme confessed breathlessly. "Believe me, I did. But I was too scared of losing you or being just one more dalliance."

"Are you scared anymore?"

Esme shook her head. "You're here now. My fear is gone."

Sybil's fear was gone too. On the other side of that fear was freedom. The boundless giddy freedom she'd longed for her entire life. Sybil still felt like she was dreaming. Maybe it'd all been a dream, and she'd wake up, convinced she'd been to Fae, ridden a dragon, and then kissed the girl she loved. "Are you sure this is real?"

"Entirely," Esme said, leaning in for another kiss. She held Sybil's bottom lip between her teeth for a quick moment, and Sybil threaded her hands into Esme's hair.

Esme took Sybil's hand, leading her back into the apartment. "Come with me. I'll show you how real this is."

Heart still galloping along in her chest, Sybil followed Esme into the apartment, shutting the door softly behind her.

+ + *Esme* + +

Many hours later, Esme woke up. Sybil slept with her back to Esme on the couch, snoring softly. A rush of tenderness filled Esme, and she adjusted the blanket and curled around Sybil, fitting their bodies together like two gears meant to work in sync.

"Hi," Sybil said sleepily, stirring awake just as Esme started to drift off again. She rolled over and propped herself up on one elbow.

Esme felt suddenly shy, though it was Sybil, her best friend. But becoming lovers had changed things.

"Hi," Esme whispered, brushing a curl off Sybil's forehead.

A long awkward silence stretched between them, and then they both laughed. Esme knew with that laugh, they'd be okay. They'd figure out what this thing between them was soon enough, but for now, Esme was fine to kiss Sybil and save talking and sharing more of her feelings for later.

When they finally got up and dressed, they settled onto the couch, mugs of tea and pastries that Lucien had brought by yesterday in hand. Outside, the gaslights of Severon were on, as another exciting night took the city in its grasp. The clock tower struck ten, shaking the flowers on the table and the pictures on the wall. Jolie slept on the couch next to Esme, and Oliver played with a piece of paper, chasing it all around the floor. Lucien had taken Jean-Francois and Estella to look after while Esme took care of Sybil, but that had been weeks ago. Esme had a feeling those cats were living at Lucien's house permanently now.

"What do you want to do tonight?" Esme asked, looking at Sybil. "Perhaps find an adventure somewhere in the city?"

Sybil took a long sip of her tea and gripped the key around her neck. "You know," she said, looking around their apartment. A smile flitted across her lips. "I think I've had enough adventure at least for a little while. Can we stay in tonight?"

Esme raised her teacup and clicked it against Sybil's. "I'd like nothing better."

And so that was exactly what they did. Though Esme thought maybe, on a different night, or maybe many years from now, she might ask Sybil to open a door to Fae again—far away from Queen Mab's palace, of course—so they could explore somewhere new and Esme could finally get some of her many questions about how it all worked answered.

But that was for a different time, a lifetime from now perhaps.

Tonight, was for being at home, with her cats, her clocks, and the girl she loved most. Even if she knew that there were many more adventures waiting for them. Someday.

Author's Note

The Absinthe Underground has been living in my head for a long time, but it took me more than a decade to chase the story down. The first glimmer came to me back in 2012, when I went to an exhibit at the Milwaukee Art Museum called "Posters of Paris." This exhibit was a lively celebration of fin de siècle or Belle Époque Paris (~1890–1910, though historians argue stridently about these exact dates), and the galleries were bursting with colorful posters from Toulouse-Lautrec, Mucha, and many other artists. I adore these posters—my teenage bedroom, college dorm rooms, and first apartments were all covered in them—and this exhibit captured my imagination on every level. I wondered: What would it be like to have lived during this wild, wonderful time? What artists, writers, and thinkers might I have run into in the decadent night clubs of 1890s Paris? What would it have been like to spend a night drinking absinthe?

With these questions in mind, I wandered the exhibit, but it was on a tiny, plain-looking card that I found a story. This card explained (to roughly paraphrase) that gangs of poster thieves stole these exuberant posters, ripping them down from the street to sell to collectors. With those sentences, I had a vision of two thieves, cutting a poster down from a busy street, and then disappearing into the night. This image was burned into my brain—who were these thieves? Where were they going? What happened to them after the theft?—but, you can hardly build a book from just that.

It wasn't until 2022, when I was looking at Toulouse-Lautrec's painting, "At the Moulin Rouge" (google it, it's lovely), that my eyes snagged, as always, on the green-faced woman in the lower right corner. Staring at her, I had the thought, "What if this was a portrait of a real green faerie, trapped in our world and captured in her true form by Toulouse?" With that flash of inspiration, I knew how to tie my poster thieves book to absinthe and the world of Fae. Although *The Absinthe Underground* is entirely fantastical, here are a few real-world things I included in it:

✦✦ *The Posters, Thieves, and Poster Dealers* ✦✦

In *The Absinthe Underground*, I mention posters by Toulouse and Mucha, though neither of them created posters like the one I depict (the famous "Le Chat Noir" poster I describe in the book, for example, is by Théophile Alexandre Steinlen) and many other artists were making posters at this time. These prints were hung around Paris (at first above public urinals, believe it or not, and then eventually on the cylindrical Morris columns that are so iconic, and also on the sides of buildings and in other places). Crowds would gather to see new posters go up each week, and from there it was a short leap to thieves stealing them (there was even a famous anarchist who published a guide on how to get the posters down) and collectors buying them.

✦✦ *The Night Clubs* ✦✦

Belle Époque Paris was full of wild night clubs, from well-known cabarets like the Moulin Rouge to other more macabre places that had coffins as drinking tables, catacomb-like Gothic vibes, and ghostly, hellish themes. The Absinthe Underground club is an amalgamation of these sorts of spaces, and these clubs were definitely places of freedom, art, decadence, delight, and danger; and, they were also spots where conventional social rules and roles were challenged.

✦✦ *Absinthe* ✦✦

Absinthe was and still is known as "the green faerie," and many historical figures drank absinthe in copious quantities—including Van Gogh, Wilde, Manet, Rimbaud, Verlaine, Baudelaire, Hemingway, and many others. Degas, Manet, and Picasso all painted versions of absinthe drinkers, each work of art showing some of the wear and tear an absinthe-heavy lifestyle can have on people. Absinthe is credited by some artists of this time as a muse, but it's also famously the ruin of many others. Absinthe itself gets a bad rap, though it is not toxic on its own. However, in the quantities many people drank it during this time, it proved very dangerous indeed. By 1915, absinthe was banned in many European countries and the US (though you can now buy it in most places).

✦✦ *Queer Culture in 1890s Paris* ✦✦

There are many wonderful articles and books about queer culture during this time period, and the appearance of things like lesbian bars in 1890s Paris offered spaces for queer people to thrive. One thing I wanted to do in *The Absinthe Underground* is show that queer people have always existed in history, and I drew much inspiration from Toulouse-Lautrec's drawings, sketches, and paintings of everyday life for queer people. Images like his "At the Moulin-Rouges, Two Women Waltzing" and his "Le Lit" and bed series inspired many of the scenes and moments between Sybil and Esme in *The Absinthe Underground*. It is my hope that in their story and through their deep love for each other, I've crafted a reflection of many of the relationships that existed so long ago, even if these stories were not always allowed to be part of mainstream narratives.

ACKNOWLEDGMENTS

I always read the Acknowledgements in a book first because I'm perpetually curious about how a spark of an idea becomes the book you hold in your hands. I told you a bit about the intellectual, artistic, and aesthetic bones of *The Absinthe Underground* in my author's note, but now let's talk about how it really got made.

I sold this book on proposal in January 2022. A few months prior to that, I had experienced the most devastating loss a parent can face, and at the time of proposing this story, I was a heartbroken mess. Luckily, despite my emotional state, my editor and agent loved the idea, and so I threw myself into writing this book. What emerged was a very strange, very sad novel that was not at all like the heisty, romantic, magical story I had proposed (in fact, in that first version, Maeve had her own super emo POV and Sybil and Esme were in Fae for about 20 pages). And so, my editor and her editorial assistant sent me a brilliant edit letter and we had a long revision strategy call. After that call, I rewrote this book entirely. And then I got more notes and rewrote it again. And then a little bit more. And then still more.

Which is to say, Sybil and Esme would've never made it to the Absinthe Underground or into Fae without the help of a lot of people.

First, thank you to my agent, Kate Testerman. Thank you for your endless optimism, for having my back for all these many books and projects, and for always going with me on every bookish adventure. I so appreciate you.

Thank you to Ashley Hearn, my incredible editor. I am not exaggerating when I say I owe my writing career to you, and cheers to our fourth book together. Thank you for all the big love for this story from day one and for all your story structure and character brilliance.

Thank you to Zoie Janelle for your editorial insight. You were such a huge part of helping Esme and Sybil find their way into Fae, and thank you for both the amazing suggestions and the incredible note-taking/outline from our call. A special thanks to Noelle Park, as well, for your careful notes!

Thank you to the wonderful Peachtree marketing and publicity team, including Sara DiSalvo, Mary Joyce Perry, Elyse Vincenty, Kayla Phillips and Alison Tarnofsky. Thank you to Farah Gehy who has worked so tirelessly to sell foreign rights for my books. Thank you to book designer Lily Steele for making this book such an aesthetic treat. And, thank you to artist Andie Lugtu for taking my awful, awkward cover sketch and giving me a gorgeous dream of a cover that captures my vision for this book exactly.

Thank you to the book boxes who picked up *The Vermilion Emporium* and to all my foreign editors and readers who have been such fans of my fantasy novels. You have all helped get my books to readers across the world, which is truly a gift. Thank you also to Jeremy Carlisle Parker for the beautiful audiobook narration for both *The Vermilion Emporium* and *The Absinthe Underground*. You have brought these stories to life in ways I could've only dreamed.

Thank you to the amazing librarians, booksellers, readers, bookstagrammers, and booktokers who have been excited about *The Absinthe Underground* and *The Vermilion Emporium*. Specifically, huge thanks to Meghan Nigh, Katy Schroeder, Mike Lasagna, Rogier Caprino, Meg Hood, Chloe M., my street team, and so many more of you who have sent me messages, made videos about my books, shared them with your friends, and been here from the early days to support my stories. Thank you also to Jaria Rambaran and Vicky Chen for such incredible art for my books.

Thank you to my dear author friends, including Megan England, Becca Podos, Lizzy Mason, Jen Ferguson, Noelle Salazar, Roselle Lim, Rosiee Thor, Tess Sharpe, Joan He, Grace Li, Becca Mix, Sarah Underwood, Cindy Baldwin, Brigid Kemmerer, Allison Saft, Molly Owen, the PW15 group, and all the other friends whose names I'm surely forgetting here but who have been a part of my writing journey since the very beginning. I'm so grateful to you all.

Thank you to my dear friends, Ashleigh Bunn and Cheryl Clearwater, for taking such good care of us in these impossible times. Thank you also to my family, especially my sisters Kim and Renee, my brother Mark and his husband Nick, and my parents. Thank you also to my Grandma R., who passed while I was writing this book, but who loved us all so well for so many years.

And thank you to my great loves, Adam, Liam, and Marcy. Liam, I miss you and I love you always. Adam and Marcy: Wherever you both are, that's home. I love you both so very much. (Also, Marcy, thanks for all the cat suggestions/names for Esme's cats and for your amazing cat artwork, but no, we're still not getting seven cats. ☺)

ABOUT THE AUTHOR

JAMIE PACTON is an award-winning author, who writes swoony, funny, magical books across genres and age categories. When she's not writing, she's teaching college English, obsessively reading obscure history, hiking, baking, or playing video games. Her books include *The Vermilion Emporium*, *Lucky Girl*, and *The Life and (Medieval) Times of Kit Sweetly*.

Find her at *JamiePacton.com* or on Instagram and TikTok @JamiePacton.